Summer's Lie Summer's Lie

A NOVEL BY *Alan Boatman*

HARPER & ROW, PUBLISHERS

FIRST EDITION

LIBRARY OF CONGRESS CATALOG CARD NUMBER: 76-95992

For Dad and for Dale,
 who shared a darkness with me;
And for Ruth,
 who brought the light

Thou hast made me, and shall Thy work decay?
Repair me now, for now mine end doth haste;
I run to death, and death meets me as fast,
And all my pleasures are like yesterday.

         —JOHN DONNE

CONTENTS

SUMMER'S LIE

1.   He drove into Greenville with the sun climbing over his left shoulder and burning his eyes through the rear-view mirror while he shivered and heard howling in his ears. This time of morning, even in August, the sun was more white than yellow, more light than heat, as the blade of air cutting into his face from the slitted side vent proved. Later on the day would be hot enough, when the sun climbed higher in its slice of sky and settled in for itself; it would make up then for the struggle to overcome the chilled morning air that never turned warm without having to, and it would burn then with light *and* heat, and everyone would broil the rest of the day for having had the privilege of being cold in the morning.

Or maybe it was just that he was moving. He shivered from the air that was hitting him, though he was wearing a jacket over his short-sleeved shirt and arms deep-tanned from three months of outdoor work. The light hurt his eyes and made him squint. He scrunched down in his seat a little, but refused to close the window or touch the rear-view mirror. If he did that he would have to adjust it again; instead he took the green sunglasses out of his shirt pocket, where he had put them half an hour ago. When he took them off he had made up his mind, because of what had happened, not to put them on again until he got to Greenville, and he had turned on the radio with its brass noise, and exposed his face to the slice of cold air from the side vent. But the sun had not been quite so bright then, and he had not had it in his unprotected eyes for half an hour, so he put them on now and rubbed his eyes under the glasses. He was still sleepy, but not dulled into hypnosis the way he had been before, or thought he had been. The shocked awakeness of the adrenaline was still enough with him, and the cold air alone could keep him awake, and there was the radio, and the sun. He knew he did not need to worry now as he sat awake and cold in the big sun-colored Ford that was moving him west at fifty miles per hour.

He passed a sign that said:

GREENVILLE 2

and looked at his watch. It was five minutes to eight, so it looked as if he was going to be there on time. When it had happened about twenty miles back, just on the other side of Carson City, he had decided to stop at Carson City and have some coffee and maybe breakfast, but there had not been time enough. He had to be in Greenville at eight to meet Steve and the rest of the crew and get the maps and head out to work. So he had gone on through Carson City with its one open restaurant, where the highway becomes for a moment the town's one main street and then highway again, had kept on for another eight miles, and now he was slowing for the long right curve that led to the small town of Greenville. The sun was still bright, not burning now, through his green polarized glasses, and it moved slowly around out of his eyes as he took the curve, like a splotch on the surface of the mirror. He glanced into the mirror as it went and said quietly, over the soft-rumbling engine, as if someone were with him,

"Well, you stayed awake. Wide awake for twenty whole miles."

He had almost died half an hour ago, on the two-lane highway between Middleton and Carson City, passing through yellow and green land in a yellow machine, like a thresher on a path already cleared that was the highway, that went on westward through grain for a good many miles beyond the point he had almost stopped traveling it. It had shaken him badly, and at best he would not get over it for a while; the reaction was over but the secondary effects would start soon and last long. It had almost capped the summer for him with all that was happening—it had almost capped everything for him and been the final step, the closing of that final door, and he was afraid. Because: he had allowed himself to be lulled, to not think about what was happening except on certain occasions. He had thought about it, had tried to avoid thinking of it—and then this weekend he had thought about it and today allowed himself to be lulled again. And so it seemed he had not seen it, and he thought: *No; you never can be careful enough.* He had not been careful enough, and as a result of that it had almost all ended back there on the road between Middleton and Carson City.

There were three direct causes, he thought, deciding to dispense for the moment with all possible indirect causes, since he was moving slowly now through the bend and onto the straight again where the cornfields and wheat fell back away from the road and the town in the long, flat farming country. First, he had stayed up late talking to Sam again, over at Sam's house, drinking Sam's beer and sitting outside with the mosquitoes on Sam's back porch with the night mumbling to itself around them in voices muted and calm as their own, mosquito hums in the darkness around and within them. They had not stayed up as late as on Saturday night, when they had gone out to the Winchester Lounge and listened to their friend Huston play the trumpet and got pretty high and, looking back, quite close to the truth. But late.

After leaving Sam with his books and his way of life that Sam had almost learned to like, he claimed, though they both knew better, he had gone home and climbed into bed in the room he no longer shared with his brother Matthew, and lain awake thinking about Susan, who was off living with her parents in Seattle for the summer and would not be back to the university until September—which was not so very far off now, with most of it all behind, but was still far enough. That and what he and Sam had talked about two nights in a row now stayed in his mind, mixing up and keeping him awake, he who had trouble sleeping anyway this summer, combining with the beer and the heat to toss him all night in a myriad of psychedelic visions and rolling dream worries that allowed him a semblance of sleep, but little rest.

Then he had gotten up at five, shaking nervously in the shock of the alarm that always irritated him—especially if he could not stop it within two seconds, which he had not—not particularly sleepy but with a slight bone ache of tiredness that he knew would hit him later in the day: the tight feeling in the stomach and groin that announced Not Enough Sleep as if he did not know it. He fumbled with his clothes in the room where his brother slept in the other bed, breathing in the dark and knocked out, sleeping as only Matt could sleep, close to death—he standing naked in the pale light that seeped through the window with the now chilled air, standing on the warm rug and it too dark yet even for shadows, and slipping into his clothes while Matthew breathed.

And then, half into his clothes, he stopped and looked at the other bed, the single Hollywood bed with its clean sheets and blankets and moon-white bedspread and cool smooth pillow.

He sat down again on the side of his own bed and looked across a space of years to the place where his brother was not now, at the hollow he filled sometimes with a fantasy of presence, a sound of breathing once heard and there always though gone for a year and a half. Did the room breathe, remembering, and the darkness pulse to a giving and taking of air?

He got up and finished dressing, remembering where Matt was. He wondered what Matt was doing right now. Sleeping, probably. Sleeping, he hoped.

When he opened the bedroom door to step out, he could hear Matt roll over, hear him say softly, *You leaving, Aaron?*

He answered, did not answer, without turning, *Yes. Sorry I woke you up.* This in the quiet low voice the morning gives, and darkness.

Take it easy on those poles. Take it easy all over.

Sure. See you—next week.

So long. Matthew, two years younger, somewhere a world away yet here too, lay watching his big brother and both of them feeling the strange far-closeness of being awake together when all else slept, as Aaron hesitated in the doorway, and Matt did not roll over and go back to sleep until the door closed softly.

2.   His suitcase and shaving kit were packed and waiting in the hall where he had left them the night before. He took the shaving kit into the bathroom and used it to clean up with, looking in the mirror at his straw-stiffened brown hair blonded now by the sun, his tired face very dark, and when he was through he repacked the kit, and carried it all outside without eating breakfast. This early in the morning he never

was hungry, and if he timed it right he could make Greenville and be able to have breakfast with the crew before work, when it would be better.

It was chilly outside and starting to lighten all over the sky. He loaded his things into the trunk of the Ford, which looked white instead of yellow in the early light, and got his jacket out of the front seat and put it on. He could not see his breath in the air, but it was brisk.

He got in and checked his boots and mosquito spray and his clipboard and state map, the mileage sheet he was required to keep, and the expense account booklet for his meals that the company paid for. His portable typewriter was in the back on the floor, for poems if he got the time and letters he would write to Susan, since his handwriting was so bad now and too slow for the time he was able to devote to letter writing. There were several books he was reading.

Then he sat in the car, rubbing his hands together and feeling the usual awareness, the uniqueness of early morning in summer, the suffused light paling out all the colors into pastels and the stars still visible though the moon had long ago, early in the night, fled away down the sky: the stars numerous and bright, paling slowly with the rest as he watched and beginning to blink out like stage lights after a performance. The quiet always amazed him. It was that short space of time—he had hit it exactly—when the insects have stopped singing and gone off through the silver-dewed grass to wherever those things go, to do whatever it is they have to do, and the birds not quite awake yet, but only an occasional *tweep* to let the world know someone is keeping an eye on things. All else silence with no cars yet and no neighbors up or lights on save for night lights coloring squares through bathroom windows, on the ground around which the grass is darker, and the chill air like a threat it never can make good this time of year, but makes anyway each morning, hopefully. All of it fresher and sweeter smelling than it would be for the rest of the day.

And he was beginning another week—his thirteenth week of doing this, leaving home in the night of Monday mornings—and he wondered what would happen this week, and in this new section of the state. So much that was new had happened this summer, the past half year, the past two years. Then he thought: *God, what does it matter? I'm too far into all this to be able to make any kind of choice or preference or do anything except go along with it and try to make it mean something.*

Qué será, and *selah.*

He started the engine and was immediately warmer, hearing the power and feeling it of three hundred fifty-two cubic inches, and he backed out and glanced once at the house and pulled away.

If he had calculated right (he had not: that was the third reason, with the staying up late and the not resting when he slept, for what had happened, and for his resigning himself to no breakfast) he could make Greenville in an hour and a half. It was five-thirty when he left; that would allow him an hour or so for breakfast, and probably the crew would not pull out until eight-thirty anyway, what with handing out maps and getting everyone oriented, not to mention finding the motel and signing in, if they did it this morning rather than tonight. None of them had worked in Greenville before; Aaron had never been there; it was far west in the center of the state. He had only been west when they worked out of Muskegon and Grand Haven for a month (*there* was a drive) and he did not know the center of the state at all. He felt sure he could find it all right.

By the time he got out of town and onto the highway the morning had turned from its faded blue to a steel gray that drifted up from the roadside with the dew, all the way up to the lightening sky. His engine finally warm, he flipped the heater switch and the fan pumped its artificial heat into the car as the sun began to come up. Aaron stopped for gas at the edge of town, used the rest room, splashed water on his face, bought a candy bar and watched the young wrinkle-eyed night man, who had not yet been relieved.

"Up early, ain't you?" The man rolled the handle of the gas pump, shoving the curved snout deep into the car's insides.

"Got a long way to go. Just starting my day," said Aaron, yawning.

"Huh. I'm about finished with mine. Lousy way to live, working nights."

"Yeah. I used to make tappet sockets all night. One summer of that was enough for me."

"It ain't the best hours there is. If I wasn't going to college I wouldn't put up with it." He leaned against the side of the car, watching for his relief, though the pump had switched off. He sighed, pulled the nozzle out and hung it on the side of the pump. "Three dollars even."

"What are you studying?" said Aaron, paying him.

"Electrical engineering. Why?"

"Just wondered. You know how far it is to Greenville?"

"Greenville. Is that south?"

"West. About the middle of the state."

"I dunno where it is. I got a map inside—"

"No," said Aaron, "skip it. It doesn't matter. Take it easy."

"Always. See you."

He pulled out onto highway 47, an old, narrow two-lane road that cuts through flat and quite bare country more typical of Illinois or northern Indiana than of Michigan, fields on both sides and occasional farmhouses and barns, but not many hills or anything green. He followed the road south to Saint Charles, a tired town that Aaron liked, and on through to the junction with highway 57, just north of Oakley, west of Chesaning. He turned west onto 57 and immediately began to pick up straggling trucks and tractors and occasional farmers' cars that slowed him down. Highway 57 is two lanes also, but prettier; the land begins to roll as it moves west, and passing becomes more difficult, more risky.

Somewhere between Fenmore and Ashley, Aaron became aware of the morose feeling that had been intermittently with him, the small, crabbed, yet enveloping irritated sadness as he thought about the last two nights and where things were going in spite of Sam and the talk, in spite of anything he seemed able to do about it. The still fresh memory of Saugatuck, fogged as it was, twisted in him like a knife blade, tied up with the whole thing about Susan, all really a part of the same thing, he suspected: and yet he was helpless. He slid into the mood again as before, surrounded by it, and he did not even notice that he was losing time behind the slower cars, was not aware of passing through Ashley, though he woke up somewhat at the crossing with highway 27, where he was forced to stop and look for cars. Then Pompeii was lost to him, and Middleton.

East of Carson City he got behind two cars held up by a third, the one in front a ten-year-old pickup truck rattling along at fifty miles per hour with a farmer and a boy on the seat—though Aaron did not see this until he went around, and then it was only to glance at them and smile—cruising as if they had all day, and Aaron, his mind sitting on Sam's back porch in the night, petered along behind, not thinking until on a curve he was brought back and realized sleepily that the other cars were not passing the little truck. He yawned, as they moved up a hill with a field of alfalfa to the left, and he was watching the alfalfa and thinking sleepily of the times he had driven out to the junior college before he started at the university—and at the crest of the hill he pulled out and eased the accelerator down, coming out and around and down at a tractor-trailer semitruck that was whining up the hill at him.

Aaron started to forget the details as they happened, and later, sitting in the restaurant in Greenville, he would think he had been more sleepy than he was, and he would think about judging distances and split-second decisions: but in spite of everything he would add and take away, the incident would remain vague for him, and he never would be certain he was remembering it right.

As the truck sped its tonnage at him, Aaron was thinking of several things: of a game that Steve, his crew chief, had told him about, and of the green alfalfa that still was in the corner of his eye on the road that was much like that that goes to the junior college—and somewhere in the back of his mind was Sam and the night, and Susan off in Seattle, and always the other thing.

Passing the blue pickup, Aaron turned his head and smiled at the old man and the boy and then, looking ahead at the truck that was meeting him, he realized that the heavy semi would not at all be able to maneuver, because of its size and weight, and besides there was the line of cars and the other people involved. So Aaron turned the wheel a little to the right and pulled into the right lane as the truck, braking hard and blasting its air horn, thundered past him and over the hill.

He kept the accelerator down until he had lost sight of the other cars, shocked wide awake now and approaching Carson City. Then he pulled off onto a side road and stopped and got out of the car, sitting down on the grassy bank beside a ditch and only now beginning to shake. He sat there for several minutes not thinking at all until he had almost forgotten that anything had happened, and then he said, testing himself and wanting to hear his voice, "God, that was a close one." His voice was normal, sounding the words as if the sentence were ordinary and alluded to nothing real, so he stood up and got back into the car.

Although he was no longer sleepy, he took his sunglasses off and turned on the radio loud and cracked the side vent, convinced now without even thinking about it that he had been very sleepy and that he should stop in Carson City and eat something and drink some coffee, and he thought he would do that.

But when he got to Carson City there was not time enough, so he kept going and drove on into Greenville.

3.   He looked for the little green sports car owned and operated, with something more than occasionally approaching abandon, by Steven Garrett, his crew chief, who had pledged solemnly on a fresh unopened bottle of Southern Comfort to meet everyone "in Greenville" on Monday morning at eight o'clock. He had not said where, figuring Greenville to be a small enough place that they could find each other, even allowing for the Monday-morning syndrome that sometimes made it a bit hard for them to recognize one another. Usually, when starting a new section based in a new town, they would meet in the parking lot of whichever motel Steve had scouted out for them in advance, but Steve had had other things on his mind and body this time, besides the general deterioration of sense of duty to job and employer that had settled upon all of them when they learned they were to be moved out of the Grand Haven area, away from the things that were there (even Aaron regretting it genuinely, who had not made much use of them), and had not had a chance to scout the area in advance or find any motels. So he had sent the crew off on Friday evening with the promise that on Monday he would meet them all "in Greenville" and lead them to the best motel in town, which he would take care of finding and arranging for over the weekend. So all they had to do was be here and

find each other and wait for Steve, who would find them. Nobody ever found Steve unless he wanted them to, which he generally did not, except for Paul Maloney, who usually did not need to find him because he was with him.

Aaron turned right at Lafayette Street and made a slow cruise through the heart of town. He did not see anyone he knew, and when he began to enter a residential district he turned around in a driveway and started back. He had not seen any motels, and, having driven all the way through town again without seeing anyone or any cars he recognized, he decided to go on out a little way on that end to see if possibly there was a motel on the street, where they might be. Normally it would have irritated him a little to be the first one here, he being one of the only ones on the crew who usually tried to arrive on time, but he did not think about it at all today, merely wondered where everyone was.

He was making his third circuit through town when he noticed, out of the corner of his eye, someone waving as he passed a street. He looked, saw the black Chevrolet first and then Vanneman hooked onto the end of the arm with which he was flailing the air. Aaron waved, drove on down a block, turned left, went one block, turned left, went one block, turned left, and pulled over to the curb in front of City Hall, behind the dirty black car with California license plates, on the curbside fender of which sat Philip Vanneman, New Yorker-turned-Californian, now in residence at the University of Michigan, staying over this summer between terms. He was idly swinging his tan Bermudaed legs, bouncing his tennis shoe heels off the tire.

"Hey! Aaron, boy!" Exuberance. Vanneman reeked of it to the point where, for the first two minutes he had known him, Aaron had not guessed he was a lazy itinerant student, not particularly interested in this job, therefore in perpetual danger of being canned.

"Phil, baby," he said from habit, getting out of the car, not feeling any of the greeting, certainly not any joy at seeing Vanneman, who was no special friend of his, but saying it anyway because of what had happened in Grand Haven a few nights ago.

It made Vanneman happy. When Vanneman was happy it always took the form of gross, sardonic verbosity.

"I'm glad *somebody* could make it, fella," he said in his cynical New York voice that the beaches had not cured. "I was beginning to think I'd have to go out and check ten or twelve mapfuls of poles all by myself today." Fat chance. Vanneman was lucky to bring in the minimum count. It was only because he had developed a tough skin on the edges of his teeth that he managed to keep a tenuous bite on his job.

"Seen anybody else?"

"Hell, no; those boys know old Steve isn't likely to be heah until ten o'clock on Monday morning after being moved away from Muskegon, and then taking a run down to Saugatuck. I'm the only one who has enough appreciation for his job—nay, *love*, real honest-to-God *love* for his job—to even show up on time on a Monday morning in a foreign city." He grinned. "You're even late, Aaron, boy. It's ten after eight."

"I didn't see you here when I drove by a few minutes ago."

"Looking for you guys, of course. Driving around this burg trying to find the Holiday Inn."

"And where is it?"

"Just where you think. So I decided to park it heah and let you guys do the looking. Find me, for a change. By God, *I* was heah."

"Just out of curiosity," said Aaron, leaning back against Vanneman's car, not really curious, looking around at the town with other things on his mind, "what *are* you doing

here?" Phil Vanneman was always the last to show up anywhere, if he showed up.

"I just told you. Are you deaf? Anyway," his grin deepen-
ing, lower jaw dropping like a barracuda's, "I drove down
from Bly Lake. It was a shorter drive than I thought." He
turned to gaze back through the window into his car, and
looked almost sad. "These damned maps you have in this
state would confuse anybody. Heah I am, *early*, for God's
sake, and nobody else even heah."

Aaron almost said *I'm heah*, but said instead, "You'd get
lost in a motel room." Everyone on the crew knew that
Vanneman could not read a map unless he had drawn it himself and sometimes not then.

"Oh, I don't know about that. I've known a few guhls who
thought—"

"There's Rod." A blue Buick went past, turned around,
parked across the street.

"Yeh. Hey, *Rod*, baby!"

The tall man who got out of the car smiled tiredly and
shuffled across the street, dark even without the tan, well-
built but slim, quiet but a mover. Aaron liked him but did not
know him well, had never worked with him, and because
Rod Sievers roomed with Vanneman in the motels Aaron had
not been around him as much as he had the others. He had
been curious about Rod for a long time and would have liked
to know him better. But that always made him think of Steve
and how things could backfire, so he never pushed himself.

"Gentlemen," said Rod.

"Hi."

"I'm glad you could make it, son." Vanneman clapped his
roommate on the shoulder. "I'm sincerely glad and happy that
you decided to show up this morning and help hoof it
through the fields of golden grain with the rest of us poor
boys who don't have Buicks to drive—"

"What the hell is *he* doing here?" Rod grinned at Aaron.

"Teaching me how to read a state map."

"I can imagine it."

"Oh," said Vanneman wistfully, "to think I could have slept in a whole hour longer . . ."

"What'd you do, get the distance wrong again?"

"Yeh. I allowed two and a half hours and it only took me an hour. I've had breakfast twice and everything."

"Two and a half *hours?* Where the hell did you come from? New York?"

"Bly Lake. It looked farther on that lousy map. And the roads—"

"What were you doing up at Bly Lake?"

Vanneman grinned; Rod had asked the magic question. "Fella, let me *tell* you . . ."

Aaron yawned and rubbed sleep out of his eyes. Vanneman would be turned on now until the rest of the crew came in. Bly Lake was up north, a weekend gathering place for college students, and he would now descend into the grisly details of his conquest of whatever he had conquered up there, and he probably had conquered something. He was not bad looking, big and tanned and horny. He was reasonably honest, within limits.

Aaron was not in a mood to listen to him, though, and when he saw George Dooley's Volkswagen go by, he decided it was time to get some breakfast. He had seen a restaurant on his first drive through.

"If Steve and Paul ever get here, I'll be in that restaurant around the corner."

"Hey, try the muffins, fella. They're great."

He got around the corner before George Dooley arrived. Vanneman's talk *and* Dooley would have been too much to take this early in the morning. Dooley was from Saginaw, like Aaron.

Dooley was his roommate. Dooley was his nemesis.
He needed some breakfast.

4.　　　Typical small-town restaurant at eight-thirty in the
morning: counter and stools on the right as he comes in,
booths on the left. Toward the back, several rows of tables
set up to make a more genteel dining area, shut off now by a
rope and a CLOSED sign. Between the back booth and the
roped-off area, a jukebox against the wall with its garish
colors and cheap gilt, not playing now. The tile floor not
particularly clean. Kitchen on the other side of the wall behind the long counter, with boxes of rolls and glass jars of
doughnuts sitting on one end of its red Formica surface. They
reminded Aaron of a song his father had sung to him when
he was small:

> Says he: there's a hole in the nickel, clear through;
> Says I: there's a hole in the doughnut too.

A couple of girls were working behind the counter, one of
them good looking, one ugly. The ugly one came over after
Aaron had hung up his jacket and slid into a booth. He
ordered sausage and eggs, muffins and coffee and a doughnut,
then watched the good-looking one for a while, but after Ann
and after Saugatuck even that bothered him. (So Steve had
gone to Saugatuck again, and probably Paul Maloney with
him. Maybe Rod. He wondered why Vanneman had not
gone there too, instead of north. Aaron shook his head.)
He looked at his hands and gripped them into fists to
see the muscles rise between the thumbs and forefingers,
thinking of those hands on the wheel of his Ford and marvel-
ing at how they had so dexterously, in doing only what they
had been trained to do at the slightest quick signal from his

brain, how they had so easily and unconcernedly saved his
life an hour ago. They had moved that Ford back into the
right lane like Phil Hill in the days when he drove for Ferrari,
or Dan Gurney on a wildly closing in street at Monte Carlo,
with the sea coming at him just over the edge of that cliff
there. With a flick of the wrists just–like–*that*, and you
live. . . .

The hands had done their job–done it well, as they sometimes did not, driving or drinking or trying to make love.
The hands had done their job but the head almost had not,
and what a strange thing that was, such a very strange
situation for him to find himself in, where the mind thinks
for one second and makes a decision that will kill you, and
then corrects it–allows the body itself, the hands, to correct
it–before it leads you all to hell for its rashness.

Two men came in and ordered breakfast, then one of them
got up and walked back to the jukebox. He studied the listing
of tunes for a long minute, dropped in a quarter and began
to tap on the keys. By the time he started back to his friend
a metallic twang of guitars filled the restaurant, and two
singers let out joyously with a song Aaron had heard a number of times over the summer, one that he could not help
liking. He listened through the first verse, not quite making
out some of the words in the country-grown style, in and out
of the guitars.

It was an inane song, an absurd, ridiculous, hick song–
maybe all of that, yes. But it had a nice rhythm and a tune
that he liked and whenever he heard it he always listened because he liked it in spite of its inanity, perhaps because of it,
like a homely old dawg that could endear itself to you by not
doing anything except hang around until he became part of
your surroundings. This song was like that for him, had become a part of his summer simply by being there, popular at
the right time, although there was a bit more to it than that.

He had first heard this song before the summer had started, once when he had come home from the university—or had it been even farther back, in the autumn before the term had begun, while he was living at home? It had become difficult to remember things that happened before the university, before this job and before Susan. In one way it had become difficult, while in other ways it had become too easy. He thought about it and decided that that was it. It had been autumn; his mother had been dead for a year; the three of them—Dad, Matt and himself—had begun to pull out of the nightmare unreality of her death, the inevitable drifting apart of the three, after a period of closeness based upon despair that each would repress to an extent as soon as possible, although that would not be for a while yet even for Aaron, who had considered himself somehow tougher than Dad, who, after all, had lost a wife, and Matt, who had lost a mother while he still needed one. Aaron, on the other hand, was at the brink of stepping off into the hot life stream of the university and being more than ever before on his own in the world; had been expecting it, anticipating eagerly. On the edge of a new life anyway, he felt it would be less hard for him to pick up the shattered pieces of his existence than it would be for Matthew and for Dad.

So Matt and Aaron had been sitting in the lot of the McDonald hamburger place at the corner of State and Center Roads, with the sun down, no longer shining on the curving gold arch that rose over them against a smoky autumn sky with stars and rather large moon, crisp bite in the air though not yet troublesome since it was only September and even in this state autumn lasted until November, and sweet all the way, before finally tightening down the screws and setting in with a softly increasing coldness that would stop a heart, and long-lasting. But that was not yet.

Matt was home again for a while, and they had been sitting there finishing up hamburgers and dragging out the chopped ice and root beer, talking of inconsequential things and feeling closer to each other in more than one way than they had felt for a while since they had ended their folk-singing team, the overcompensation having begun as soon as each realized his life was going to continue on for a measure of time after all, that there was some respite from pain. After being close they had fallen apart, and now they were slowly drawing back together until neither would quite see where the split had been, as if that were only an imagined thing and not something that had happened.

They finished their root beers and their talk for the most part, and Matt dumped the containers and hamburger wrappings and red-and-white-striped french fry bags into the waste box, standing outlined in his green jacket against the blue-white fluorescence misting coolly out from the glass-fronted pavilion where boys sold hamburgers, Aaron looking at him outlined there and suddenly thinking: *Is that my brother? Is that boy-man the one, the same one?* Then Matt got back in the car and they pulled out into Center Road and waited at the light to turn left onto State Road and home. The song had begun playing on the radio then and Aaron, just catching the chorus, laughed and said, "Are they kidding?"

Matt, who kept up, had heard the song before. "It's all right. Listen to the guitars just before the end."

They listened to the guitars doing things they could not do, and Aaron had conceded a bit to pleasure over taste as they blasted down the white wide cool street together.

The last verse went by his ears and into them without registering the words coherently. He had ad-libbed a last verse

tune once before and now he imagined they were
singing his words, although he forgot his own last
fore they were finished:

> It's good to see you, good to see you're really
>   looking well;
> In spite of all the sorrow, you are always
>   looking swell;
> You've got yourself a vict'ry in a race you've
>   never run;
> It's good to see you, good to see you,
>   (da, da, da, da, dah.)

And then the guitar part he liked, and the song was done,
and with it the scene and the memory that lived in him each
time he heard the song and at no other—the long cool evening
fading with the others, the month fading with the months
gone, the months come and gone since, falling away so he
could not keep up even in his head.

Something else came on, and something after that, but he
was not listening, and when the girl brought his breakfast
he was sitting with his arms folded on the table, looking at
the corner of the booth with a slightly angry expression on
his face so that the girl said, "Excuse me. . . ."

Coming down that hill he had had a good long-distance view
of the highway and had seen the truck coming and had, in the
second of decisionmaking, estimated the speed of the truck
and the speed of his own car and that of the pickup leading
the line he was about to pass. He had not consciously thought
about it all as he did it. It was the type of mental calculation
that comes by instinct to anyone who drives a great deal, a
reaction as automatic as reflexes. Usually you could do it
well enough to tell whether or not you would succeed in a
maneuver like passing. It was not that difficult and if you
allowed a margin for safety you always made it. If you did

not leave a margin and had calculated well, you made it anyway. Otherwise you didn't make it, and there was a good chance that you died. He had calculated perfectly and had almost died, and the question that was bothering him right now was why he had almost died and also why he had not.

He ate his breakfast slowly, watching the colored lights on the jukebox but not hearing the music any more, or the talk that went on around him.

He had seen a man die once, a suicide, and murder four others in the act, though no one but him ever knew it was that: murder and suicide.

He had been driving out to school one morning in April, a warm, sunny morning, warm earlier than usual, during his freshman year at the junior college. The traffic was bad, as it always was bad morning and evening on that road, and he was moving at fifty miles per hour behind a line of cars, and a man came up behind him in another Ford, an old black one, came up on him slowly, not really in a hurry, and plodded along behind for a while until they got to one of the few straight sections of that road. And then the man pulled out from behind Aaron and slowly moved up even with him, and Aaron thought: *You're nuts to try to pass this line on this road, especially in that old car, and if you don't get moving—* Then a car was coming from the other direction and Aaron waited for the man to drop back behind him into line, but the man did not move at all except to stay even with him, and Aaron turned to look at him to see what he was going to do, and the man had looked very calm, a calm face and large eyes, and wearing (this was like a photograph in his brain) a tan sweater over a black-and-white checked shirt. In the two seconds that Aaron looked at him, both of them moving much slower than they really were, past a field of green alfalfa, the man had looked at Aaron for a second and smiled, and then his mouth, which had been loose and soft looking, kind looking, had set into a line and his soft eyes looked strange, and Aaron knew right in that second what he was about to see. The man had looked at Aaron and smiled and then slowly as his face changed his car moved forward and he was passing the line of cars, many of which were already hitting their brakes to let him in, as Aaron began to pound on his horn. But the man did not fall for that, his mind was made up, and when he was within three cars of the head of the line, the oncoming driver saw him and turned to the right off the road—but not fast enough, and Aaron could hear the flat-sounding *cruuumph* clear back where he was standing on his brakes now, as the black Ford folded up tiredly and spun, what was left of it, to the left, striking broadside the car on its right, which had not been able to get clear, and flipping over off the road as the car on the right went off into a ditch and the car he had struck head-on sat quietly by the side of the road, dead.

In each of those two cars there had been two people, farmers in one, students in the other.

Everyone thought the man had been trying to pass, had miscalculated and died, except Aaron, who knew the man had not miscalculated at all.

> Says he: there's a hole in the nickel, clear through;
> Says I: there's a hole in the doughnut too.

The old song rattled around in his head as he looked at the doughnut that was all that was left of his breakfast except for the coffee, and then his eyes filled with tears. The music came through again, a wild and variable-pitched wailing, and someone in the restaurant laughed.

5.   It was already warm when he came outside; the sun was gearing up for business and beginning to put out with a

perversely admirable single-mindedness. The temperature had been steadily in the eighties for three weeks now, and it felt as though today would be no different.

When he rounded the corner, the whole crew was there, clustered around the little green Triumph in which sat, talking and gesturing, Steven Garrett. His skin was darkened by days working in the sun and other days on the beach at Grand Haven, and behind his prescription sunglasses his eyes seemed tired but not unhappy. As always, Steve looked like someone who had been hired from a casting agency to sit in the car, slightly larger than life: as unreal as a Warner Brothers movie. He had a company map spread out on his lap and the steering wheel.

"Glad you could make it," he said, glancing up as Aaron entered the group of young men and maps around the convertible in which Steve held court. Aaron said hello to Paul Maloney, who grinned around his cigarette, and nodded at Dooley. George still had a bruise on his jaw, but he nodded grudgingly. Steve added, "I hope you didn't cut your breakfast short."

"I was, apparently, here before you got up, *boss*."

Steve grinned. "Had a long drive to make—all the way from Saugatuck."

He waited for Aaron to react, but Aaron only looked at him, noticing that Steve really did have a natural leer in his smile, had taken on more and more the air of a young stud. *You bastard.*

"Let's travel," said Rod, bored with standing around. Rod never liked to waste time.

Steve had been sorting out the maps each man would use. He handed a roll to Dooley. "Here you go, George."

Dooley took the three section maps, each with a hundred or so power poles circled in ink along the country roads, many going through fields and farmers' back yards—a few, as Dooley would discover, set in woods and swampland.

"These don't look so bad."

"You deserve a break after Muskegon." Steve grinned. "They ought to keep you busy for a couple of days."

"Gee, yeah." Dooley caught Steve's grin then, and said unhappily, "Oh, no . . . I guess maybe even longer than *that*, huh?" But he was game, and smiled his buck teeth at Steve. "Can I have one of those county maps?"

Steve looked pained. "I could only get two from the Triple A; I need one and Paul's going to need the other one; he's got some rough country."

"*Two?*" whined Vanneman, sitting on the tree strip now with his broad back against Steve's car. "Why the hell only two? *I* need a map—"

"You couldn't use it if I gave you one, Phil, baby."

"Why only two?" said Rod.

"They're all out, because of the vacationers heading for the lakes."

"Did you tell them why we need them?"

"I told the lady we're taking a field survey on Consolidated Power poles and that we don't know the county. It didn't matter; they were out of maps."

"Yeah, but—" said Vanneman.

"She said they'll have some more in a few days. Don't worry about it."

"But *I* don't know this state!"

"I'll show you on my map how to get to your area. Okay? Think you'll be all right then with the section maps, *fella?* Your sections are side by side, anyway."

"Screw." Vanneman, thinking of his latest miscalculation, looked as though he were going to cry.

"Let's move," said Rod.

Dooley had already gone. Steve gave each of them a set of maps drawn up by the Consolidated Power Company and turned over to the crews—mostly college students—who had been hired to do the field and leg work on the project.

When Rod had pulled out, Steve tapped the steering wheel and said, "Hey, I saw Marie the other night."

"Yeah, I know," said Aaron. "You fellows went back to Saugatuck."

"Just Rod and me."

"I figured you'd seen her. Want to give me my maps?"

"We had a good time," said Steve. "She's a pretty nice girl."

"For a whore. She's a little college whore, is what she is."

"Yeah, well, maybe. But what has that got to do with it, Augustine? That didn't seem to bother Mister Pure last Thursday. She was wondering where you were, kiddo. It was all I could do to keep her mind off you."

"Just like Ann, huh, Steve?"

Steve locked eyes with him a moment, then looked away. "Low blow," he said. "I told you I was sorry about that whole thing."

Paul picked up a roll of maps and tossed away his cigarette. "I hope you boys aren't going to start in—" he began, then coughed once and doubled over, leaning back against the side of the car and sitting down on the grass at the curb. He coughed until he choked, and Aaron stood watching as Steve got out of the car and knelt beside him, putting a hand on his shoulder.

"You all right, fella?"

Paul nodded, gasping. "I'm—okay." He got up with Steve helping and took the roll of maps. "I'll see you guys," he said, and crossed the street to his car.

Steve watched him and leaned on the fender of the Triumph. "I don't like that. He did that the other night too."

"I know," said Aaron.

Steve's eyes came back to him and he said, "What's the matter with you? Are you mad about Marie?"

"No. It's okay about Marie. You can have Marie, and my compliments."

"Then what's the matter? Why do you look so— What's wrong?"

"Never mind. Just give me the maps and let me get going. Give me the damned *maps*."

Steve handed him a roll of maps and said slowly, "These are all off highway fifty-seven. Just follow it through town and on out. Did you get the motel? It's the Sunset." Steve told him how to find it. "The rooms are all reserved. You'll have a single." His grin came back. "I guess you're tired of being in with George. Only the doubles have air-conditioning, though. Would you rather—"

"It's all right. He's a little mad at me still." He waited a moment and said, "Dooley drives me nuts."

"I figured. See you at the motel at five; we'll check in."

That first day Aaron's poles were in square-cornered farmland sections with easy-to-find roads that crossed each other. Yet the country was so rough that he was hard pushed all day, climbing embankments, working through thickets between the roads and the fields, constantly leaving his car to head off on foot following lines of poles set at right angles to the road.

By five o'clock he had checked only a hundred and twenty-five poles. He pulled into the motel drive at five-thirty, having worked fifteen minutes overtime to make a good showing. Covered with sand and sweat, he filled out the register form and unloaded his things into the room, then took a long shower and stretched out on the bed in his underwear, exhausted. The room was shabby compared to the plush motel in Muskegon, though it was the best Greenville had. Even with all the windows open it was stifling without air-conditioning, and Aaron regretted he had not given in and taken a double with Dooley. He wondered how Dooley felt. But it did not matter; he was sick of Dooley—sicker of him than of the heat.

After a while he dragged himself up and dressed and went outside. Steve and Paul were gone; everyone was gone, even Dooley. Aaron drove downtown for supper, saw a couple of the guys, but ate by himself. When he got back he undressed and fell onto the bed with his stomach full but not satisfied. He thought of the books and the typewriter he had left in the car; he really should write to Susan. But he was too sad and too tired. He lay on the bedspread in the hot night, with a breeze beginning to come through the window, the darkness very close around him like a hot wet blanket in which he was being quietly strangled.

1.   It had not started in Greenville in August, but in Ann Arbor in January. Some of it, at least a good part of it, had started then, although some other part of it, of the larger thing, went even further back.

On April 28, a Thursday, Aaron drove south from Saginaw to the little town that houses the University of Michigan. The weather had been nice for a week, but today it had rained and now it was cloudy and windy and cold, and the picnic that he and Susan had planned was certainly not going to take place. Classes had been over for a week; Aaron had gone home but Susan was to be in Ann Arbor until the weekend and then, having sent her things ahead, would begin the drive to Seattle.

Aaron had called her in the morning, with rain misting down outside the window, blowing like a filmy sheeted egg white into the trees and hanging there, dripping.

"Susan?"

"Hello," she said glumly.

"Looks like no picnic."

"Yes, isn't it terrible? This is the *third* time it's happened to us, do you know that? the *third* time. Our plans don't ever seem to work out." There was a slight petulance in her voice, a rising inflection on the word "ever" that made it sound like an accusation, as if she were blaming him for everything. She wasn't; it was a characteristic of Susan's. She liked plans to work, and if they did not it was perhaps on the order of a personal affront.

"I guess they don't," said Aaron, feeling acquiescent, a necessary virtue when dealing with Susan at such times. There was a pause and he added, "Well? Shall I come down anyway?"

Another pause, and she said, "Are you kidding? Of *course* come. If you *want* to."

Aaron felt his patience bleeding away, the slow irritating helplessness of a breakdown in communications. He wished he could hang up and start over. "Of course I want to see you."

"Well, good. We can play Scrabble or something," and this was said in a tone of genuine sorrow and he realized that it was not only he who had been counting on this picnic, this last day together.

"Sounds great," he said sadly.

The edge came back. "Well, if you don't *want* to—"

"No, hey, wait; let me finish. I was about to say that I'd rather play Scrabble with you than go on a picnic with anyone else."

Another pause, and her voice changed again. "You can be awfully sweet sometimes."

"I know," he said, winding it up on a false good note. "See you around noon."

Now the rain had stopped and the sky was rolling like something out of baroque art, with the sun spraying through the gray masses intermittently, the wind blowing harder and everything in shaky, spasmodic motion. U.S. 23 goes from Saginaw to Ann Arbor like an undulating ribbon four lanes wide and split down the middle. Aaron could make the trip in a little over an hour by speeding. He was speeding because he had not seen Susan for a week, and already the feeling of desolation that he was afraid would plague him when he was away from her was beginning to show signs of itself. This would be the last time he saw her all summer, and he did not feel much like playing Scrabble.

He had met Susan at a war protest meeting in the Fish Bowl, a glassed-in crossway between two buildings that got a lot of student traffic. He was not there to oppose the war: he had not thought much about the war one way or the other except to hope that it ended soon. He had missed the famous teach-in at the university the year before, being still at the junior college, and since his arrival he had not paid much attention to any activities at all. The only reason he stopped was because he could not get through the crowd. He was on his lunch break.

So he stood on the fringe waiting for the hallway to open up as people came and went, used to these mass meetings, not particularly interested, listening vaguely to an SDS man haranguing about war crimes and public apathy. Finally he was able to get as far as one of the stone benches, just as someone was leaving. He sat down beside a pretty girl he had seen before who seemed to be half listening and half reading something by Bertrand Russell.

"What's it about?" said Aaron.

She looked at him inquiringly. "The book?"

"The meeting," he said, nodding at the platform where the man had his microphone in a stranglehold. It occurred to Aaron that he could find out simply by listening to the speech, and he thought a glimmer of the same notion crossed the girl's face, but she said, "SDS is protesting the war."

"Oh. He really works at it, doesn't he?"

She looked at the man and laughed a rather humorless laugh.

"Yes. I don't care for that one; sometimes I think SDS specializes in evangelism. I'm in sympathy with them, though," she said, and looked at Aaron.

"I don't know. I don't really have an opinion."

"That must be nice." She kept looking at him, as if questioning whether he might not be of some worth in spite of himself. She was pretty in a way hard to define; despite a loose mouth and large eyes, there was a definite faint chilling quality about her face—possibly the way she changed expressions before she spoke, as if deciding ahead of time which look best fitted what she was about to say. And after saying it, the speculative glance—how would he take it? how respond? It reminded Aaron of something Sam had said: "Talking to a college girl today is like talking to a census-taker." But Aaron had not met any girls he liked much as yet, and Susan's self-assurance charmed him.

She cocked her head a little and said something that was lost in a great clang of electric guitars as The Blue Vultures decried America's lack of conscience and, inadvertently, taste.

"What?" said Aaron.

"I said weren't you in a *class* of mine?"

"I think so."

"*Ideologies.* Communism, fascism, democracy?" she said as if offering them sliced on a plate.

"Yes."

"Your name is Aaron Young."

"Yes."

"I'm Susan Rayder. You used to sit in the back row and take notes and scowl a lot."

"Right. Hi." Aaron laughed as they shook hands formally, and she gave him a half-quizzical smile.

Susan, it turned out, was from Seattle, and her father was a banker. "I'm trying to make up for it," she said seriously.

"What in the world are you doing at Michigan?"

"Studying what I want. I went through forty catalogs before choosing. My parents wanted me to be a Bennington Bitch. But I like this town and I like the School of Social Work. I wanted to make up my own mind, get away from home and be independent."

"Well, you certainly got away from home."

"I'm independent too. Where are you from?"

"Saginaw; about ninety miles northeast of here."

"Theodore Roethke's home town."

"How did you know?"

"I told you, I'm from *Seattle*. He lived there about fifteen years—"

"Right, right; I must be dopey today," he said, looking at the very slight crinkle in her nose that came, apparently, with her impatience.

"Are you an English major or a philosophy major?"

Aaron laughed. "English. Does it show?"

"*One* of them does, but I couldn't decide. What does your father do? Are you going to be a poet?"

He waited a moment, grinning at her serious face until she broke into a smile that startled him in its innocence, as if there was a totally different side about her that he was right at this moment seeing his first glimpse of. Right at this moment, too, determining unconsciously to see more of—it *was* this side, wasn't it, that attracted him?

"My father is retired," he said. "He builds furniture and boats. I think really that's what I'd do if I had—whatever it is, whatever it takes. I guess I haven't got his hands. I'll probably teach."

Aaron looked at the snow whipping up in the wind outside, wondering why a person should feel embarrassed about confessing that he wrote poetry. Not about writing it, but about telling someone. Because it was impractical, he supposed. You could not make money at it. It galled him because he did not particularly care for practical things.

"Look," he said, "I have to get back to my apartment for lunch. Maybe if you aren't busy some night, we could go out."

She gave him one more appraising glance and said suspiciously, "I'd like that."

Driving home through the snow he felt the elation that comes at the beginning with a new girl, a more than usual amount of it this time. Later, in his Shakespeare class, unable to concentrate on the lecture, he began to scribble in his notebook:

> Her eyes are mostly brown, but a strange shade,
> a combination of brown and red the color of
> Carolina earth—the color, almost, of one kind
> of flint; but, if the hardness is there, surely
> her lips will be soft.

Like a damned teen-age girl, he thought disgustedly. But he did not tear out the page, and he would still have it later when there was no use for it any more.

2.   After he first met Susan, before he had gone out with her, he went home for a weekend and said to Sam, "I've met the first girl I've ever seen that I think I could fall in love with."

Sam was cautious. "That sounds good—I think. What's so special about her?"

"Well, I'm not sure," said Aaron.

He went to bed more than one night thinking about it and not sure, yet it did not seem odd to him that he expected to be sure even this early. He wanted to know and thought he should know; he understood himself at this point just well enough to believe he could rationalize it out until he saw it.

Well, she was dark, had long dark hair and skin a shade darker than most and that was nice. That was a beginning.

And she was slender with fine slim legs and arms and a small waist and small shapely firm-looking young breasts, and he compared her, in describing her to Sam and others, to the actress Susan Kohner, and to Susan Strasberg (how perfect that their names were the same!), and later, after he and Susan had gone to see *David and Lisa,* he compared her to Janet Margolin, who had played Lisa.

In fact, Susan did not look much like any of the three, save that she had dark hair, but she was pretty as they were beautiful and in her own way she equaled them for Aaron and was more besides.

And there was her self-assurance, her ability to frankly evaluate people and surroundings; Aaron felt often later that, when talking with someone, Susan was mentally lifting that person up like an objet d'art and *handling* him—turning him this way and that in front of a good light, fondling, testing— and if her silent fingers did not like the texture or the firmness, it was like squeezing an overripe melon, and the distaste showed in her face if you knew where to look. This fascinated and repelled Aaron, more the former, for reasons not clear to him except that she functioned, she got along, and this was a positive thing and attracted him even in fright.

And finally, though he was not at first conscious of it, Susan resembled Aaron's mother—very slightly, and only at times, but it was there and after a while he saw it and later it made him think of Randall Jarrell's poem called "Woman" and what every man is after:

> But then, a woman never is a man's type.
> Possessed by that prehistoric unforgettable
> Other One, who never again is equaled

By anyone, he searches for his ideal,
The Good Whore who reminds him of his mother.

But he did not think of that for a long time, and then only in a bad mood when they had been apart.

Their first date was an evening for setting tones, coloring the backdrop, establishing lines and types of lines that would connect them later when they became more honest with themselves and each other. It was the kind of hodgepodge typical of first dates and yet it was not simply a first date and not simply typical. And it stayed with them later.

He had driven past her house earlier in the day so he would know where it was, and that night it was not as cold as it had been, and he felt an adolescent excitement as he parked around the corner across from where she lived. He had almost forgotten his wallet, but had not, thanks to Elliot, his roommate, who had reminded him as he was going out the door. Now he walked up the steps of the big old house with the porch light on and clanked a brass knocker. An inner door opened and a girl's face peered out, matched by another peeking over the balcony of the stairway just inside. The girl on the balcony gazed at him critically for a moment, decided he was not hers, and went back inside her own room, as the downstairs girl, who was not Susan, opened the door for him and he said, "Is this where Susan lives?"

"Yes, come in," said the girl, a big chesty Amazon with long hair, wearing a chemise. "Are you Aaron? I'm Janice."

"Hi."

She took him through a short hall past the stairway and into a living room, closing the door behind them.

"Want to take your coat off? She'll be right here, have a seat."

"Okay. Thank you."

Janice disappeared into the kitchen. From another room he heard Susan's voice: "Is that Aaron?"

"Yes," he said.

"Be right there."

He took off his topcoat, to discover himself in his shirt sleeves. A lead weight dropped into his stomach and he thought: *God, you've forgotten your jacket. . . .* Then he noticed that it was there, inside the topcoat; he had slipped them both off at the same time. *Idiot.* He glanced around to see if anyone had seen him. He put his jacket back on and thought: *Take it easy. You'd think you'd never had a date before.*

He sat down in a big easy chair and the bottom dropped out of it and then caught, leaving him a few inches from the floor and feeling increasingly uncomfortable. At this point another girl came out of a room. "Hi!"

"Hello," he said, working to get up.

"Why in the world are you sitting *there?*" said the girl, a short-nosed blonde with long hair worn up.

"Oh. Well, I thought it was a chair. What is it really?" he said, finally making it to his feet as she watched him curiously. "Pop art?"

She laughed. "It might as well be. It needs the bottom fixed."

"Oh—it does? Are you another roommate?"

"Yes. I'm Lorraine. Are you Aaron?"

"Uh—yes, I am. Aaron Young."

"Hi. Sue will be right out."

"I know."

"Excuse me. Why don't you sit over there?" She pointed to the sofa, and vanished through a doorway.

Before he had a chance to sit down Susan came out, dark-haired, brown-eyed, wearing something wonderful that was dark gray and that a long time later she would tell him was called a jumper—which seemed an ideal name to him. She was wearing black tights.

In the moment of heightened nervousness before she came
out, Aaron had been trying to remember what she looked like.
It had always been a condition of his, and irritated him about
himself, that even (or especially) with people he liked at the
first meeting, their names or faces fled his sad attempts at
recall so that when he saw them again or heard their names,
it was like a delightful but embarrassing reintroduction. He
had seen Susan a little over a week ago, and it was the same.

Now she was there, slender and dark and animated. "Hello!
What's it doing out?"

"Hi," he said, looking at her and feeling it all tumble back
into place like a reversed home movie of a child's crumbling
blocks. "It isn't doing anything."

"No snow? No rain?" She said this with a wide-eyed
innocence that was a full coin turn from the way she had been
in the Fish Bowl, except for that one brief moment when
she had smiled at him and become a different person—become
this person, the one before him now, all the sharpness gone,
no noticeable guard up, no obvious defenses.

"It's nice out. It's mild."

"Oh, wonderful. I could picture a freezing rain!"

"Yes," he laughed.

She had her coat, and Aaron helped her into it and she
called out, "We're going!"

Two voices answered from somewhere in the apartment,
"Good-bye!" "Have fun!"

Then they were out into it and she said, "Oh! It *is* nice!"
and he took her hand.

She was such a very pretty girl, and Aaron was acutely
conscious of her physical nearness as she slid over to the center
in his Ford, and he thought: *You've just gone too long without a date, chum*—which was not actually so; it had been a
month or six weeks, part of that taken up by the Christmas
vacation, and Aaron had done much longer stints of dateless-

ness and not incurred any terribly sharp hunger beyond what he considered the normal, nothing impossible to cope with.

But this was not a completely physical thing. This was what he had told Sam about: the intense awareness of a great possibility here, a wonderful and frightening sense of potential unlike anything he had felt for a long time (he did not like to think how long that had been, how far back it went and how it had ended), and as they talked on the way to the show, moving through the deceptively mild February night, he felt a tingling excitement for the very fact of life itself—the first such feeling, though he did not think of it, since his mother's death and the estrangement from his brother, the collapse of something he had worked very hard on and pinned a great deal of himself on. It was a kind of renewal, and it caused in him a feeling almost of gratitude, gave him a feeling of great promise.

The movie that night was a modern sex comedy and it was not a very good picture; neither of them enjoyed it much, but the effect of talking to each other, of moving side by side through the Saturday-night lighted streets of Ann Arbor with everyone out, the temperature more like October than February, glow-cheeked and scuffling along to queue up in front of the Campus Theater—the effect was so positive in every other way that both of them pretended at first that the picture was better than they really thought. Afterward they went out to eat and sat in a booth late drinking coffee, talking over and around and through each other, and Aaron was stunned into a mild state of shock at how well they did together, what a really fine couple they made and how much they both enjoyed the evening.

"This is the age when poets are eaten by bears."

"Well. But I mean, *poetry* . . ."

He had started in on his big topic, with Susan filling the conversational gaps until he saw that she really was interested, albeit in a rather unempathetic way (she felt that poetry was a genuinely good thing, a genuinely good irrelevant-to-the-times endeavor), and he carried himself away and told in tones of growing excitement of his desire to become a first-rate college-teaching poet, a Randall Jarrell, a Theodore Roethke, fine poets both and great teachers quite literally adulated by their students.

"Well, look," she said. "They were good, I know," and she paused and added politely, "but, I mean, wasn't Roethke insane? And the fact is, I haven't seen much Jarrell, if he was all that—"

"Oh, my God." Aaron, momentarily placing his head in his hands, nodded and pursed his lips.

"Well, hell," she said. "I mean—"

"Yeah, Roethke spent some time in a few institutions," said Aaron quietly, not looking at her and growing quite solemn rather suddenly. "He was about as crazy, I think, as anybody has to be to make it nowadays as a great poet. You know, on the day that Roethke died, in his own home town it was impossible to find one copy of any of his books in the stores."

"That's—that is sad."

"As for Jarrell, you'll start hearing about him soon now—now that he's dead, safe. He'll be showing up in the anthologies now, especially when a few more of his enemies—people he was honest about in his criticism—when they die off. My God."

Susan looked at him for a long moment and said, "That kind of thing—bothers you, doesn't it? It really does upset you."

He nodded. "It scares me too. I've always believed—I mean, I was *raised* to believe—there's some small amount of justice in this world, in this country. America. Even when you don't believe it any more, when you've learned, it still hurts and scares you to be reminded of it. Jarrell said somewhere: 'What mortals these fools be. . . .' Jesus, Jesus, it's true."

Susan did not quite give him a look. She mulled something over for half a minute and when he reached for his cup she said, "How were you raised? I mean, there's— I mean, are you religious?" She said this word with great care and respect.

He told her. He had been raised a fundamentalist in small Indiana towns, finally in Indianapolis, finally in the Saginaw Valley of Michigan, and they had cajoled and promised and threatened him right out of the church and into college, where he wavered now, according to mood, from an ethical Christianity to black nihilism, often both at once.

"Existentialist?"

"God, no. Not yet, anyway. I keep meeting people who eat up Camus and Sartre and spout them back at me in a kind of mulch—all these terribly sincere people haunting the bookstores, wanting to define themselves through conflict. Zealots, most of them; they remind me of Jehovah's Witnesses."

"I see." She sipped her coffee, watching him now with that other face, the one he had met first, tight and calm and half humorous all at once, and she said, "Where does all this leave you?"

He gave her a fake sneer and growled, "You might say I'm a Christian nihilist. A humanistic absolutist—an anthropological optimist." When they stopped laughing he fell down in his explanation of the terms, which seemed as unclear to himself as to her, and ended by saying, "My motto is: 'Heidegger was right!' "

She did give him a look. "But Heidegger—"

"I know," he said.

And he had forgotten what Heidegger was right about.

"It's funny," he said, "and sad, I guess—since my mother died two years ago I've been reacting to everything I ever believed in."

"Reacting?"

"Well—" He hesitated, looking at her face and away to

focus words on the thought. "You see, I came from a really marvelous family. I had a wonderful childhood. I guess I hadn't expected things ever to end. I hadn't ever been hit, and when I finally got it—"

"That's strange. That's very strange."

"Hm?"

"What you said about your family and your childhood—" She stopped with a perplexed little smile.

"What do you mean?" said Aaron, and her face seemed to him caught at that moment between personalities, in a state of perplexity so genuine that it took precedence over the girl-in-control, took precedence also over the one inside who sometimes forgot and showed herself, peeking out of the brown eyes. Now it was a caught look, a face in speculation but not consciously, not *considering* now but rather *wondering* with all that that implies.

"I don't know," she said. "It sounded so strange, the way you said it. As if you really—well, meant it, but not only that but something else too that I can't—can't say. . . ." She shook her head and smiled again. "I'm sorry; go ahead."

"Well, I've always been a brooder, I guess. But I think I was coming out of it nicely just before she died; things were straightening out; my brother and I were discovering a closeness we had lost somehow a long time before. . . . Anyway, that all went to hell when she just died like that, still young, such a good wife to my father and a good mother. We were a close family." (She cocked her head in a quick involuntary movement.) "I looked death in the face for the first time that fall, and for the next year. Then I came down here to the university and slowly forgot about it, got my mind off it and occupied with other things, although it took a while. And sometimes I wonder if I'm really over it yet. . . . Excuse me; I'm soliloquizing."

"What about your father?"

He brought his head up a little. "What. What?"

"You mentioned your mother and your brother. I wondered what effect this had on your relationship—"

"No, listen," he said. "Really, I'm dominating this whole conversation and it's time I shut up and found out about you. You aren't religious."

She considered, not this but something else. "Well, my parents think they are. They belong to a fashionable church, very sleek, run by people who are mostly too fat, and all of them like to talk at you. My parents like to talk at you."

"Are you not on good terms with them?"

"We have a good hate relationship."

"Oh . . ."

"No, wait," she added, drawing invisibly on the table top with her finger. "I don't hate them. They're just irrelevant. They just don't mean anything at all except to other irrelevant people—no, they don't even mean anything to them. They don't mean anything to anyone; I suppose if you look at it objectively, they might as well be dead."

Aaron said nothing for a moment until she looked up at him, and then he said, "Oh, you must be exaggerating just a little bit."

And she said, "No. If I were exaggerating just a little bit I wouldn't be here learning to do something and be something that is relevant. I wouldn't need to."

"Need to what?"

"Oh, well, I hate to say 'prove it.' Prove myself; make up for them—but I suppose that's what it is. I'll probably always be doing that, or trying to do it. Make up for those people and the ones like them. That's where all their money goes—to an ungrateful daughter who is out to bring them down. More or less."

Aaron looked at his coffee. "That's sad."

She nodded. "Mm. Well, my parents aren't really any

different from most of them, except maybe they have more money." She waited a moment and added, "You understand, of course," and she grinned maliciously, "that I am an existentialist. One of those terribly sincere zealots who haunt the bookstores with my—with my *mulch*."

He opened his mouth to show that he was biting his tongue, and she laughed. And he thought: *Susan is practical.*

Yes. Since beginning college the vague sharp uneasiness inside her had expanded into something fearsome, and she fought it with sociology and the new morals. But she seemed at the moment to think she was doing all right.

They got onto television and movies and comic books, with most of which Susan was surprisingly unfamiliar, and Aaron, who had devoured comic books as a boy, told her the plot of "Uncle Scrooge and the Horse-Radish," one of his favorite stories of Disney's recalcitrant old duck, dealing with piracies on the high sea, deep sea diving and untold fortunes hanging in the balance. He considered it all a kind of art. He told it like some ancient teller of tales, with a love in his voice and his eyes that surprised the girl and furthered the building of a long affection in her that would last even beyond the time when she realized they were not for each other, when comic books and horse-radish and Aaron were not enough for her and not the things she could value most. Aaron saw it in her as she talked of the ghetto problem and of ending the war, saw even this early that Susan was the kind of practical American woman for whom childish babbling dreams of love are not the answer. She knew, not what she wanted, but what she must have, what she dared not compromise in this day of iron wills and armored feelings, that fleeting unreachable misty nothingness that is the dream of the practical and is sometimes found and realized. But never for Susan. Aaron saw it even then; yet, in spite of it or because of it, and because there was a crack that allowed her to listen to him and care, he felt there was a chance.

The restaurant closed on them. He took her home and they sat in the car and talked. Aaron asked for another date and she said yes. He walked her to the door of the old house and kissed her good night under the porch light. Her lips were soft.

And knowing well now that something had started, not so much with her as within himself, he drove back to the apartment and went to bed, but not to sleep for some short while yet.

3.   On their second date they went to a coffeehouse and listened to folk music (Aaron feeling an urge to leap onto the stage and grab the guitar from the sickeningly sincere but voiceless one and deal out his own brand of music) and on their third, to see Olivier in *Othello;* on their fourth, to see Truffaut's *Jules and Jim.* There was a point somewhere at which they ran out of introductory small talk, the borderline between liking each other and trying to make good impressions, listening patiently for the other to stop talking so each could leap in with his own witticism or calculated-to-impress bit of wisdom or planned sensitivity—what is generally referred to as the snow-job stage—the line between that and really knowing, starting to know each other, to sit and talk with more than their careful governing heads. During this slightly uncomfortable and dangerous and exciting period, when everything hung in balance and a wrong move or word could end it all before the roots were down, Aaron was sharply aware of what could happen now. It could so easily be halted, because it had yet to really begin. The relationship was like clay in their hands, to be allowed to cool, or molded

into a thing each saw differently and only as desired. They watched each other warily. They shifted pieces on the boards within themselves before touching the reality, considering the risks, estimating possible losses, the result of losses—and committing themselves totally with sure caution to play it out to the end.

Aaron came over to read poetry to her, and later they talked while she fed him cookies and fruit and a tea she made that he liked. Susan had been reading Freud's *Interpretation of Dreams* for a course, and they talked about dreams, sitting in the small sun porch off the living room that the girls used as a combination library/sitting room/den. Susan leaned back, lost in a huge wicker chair she had found in some obscure Detroit furniture mart and tied to the roof of her Volkswagen like a sedan atop a baby elephant. Aaron sat across from her in an overstuffed chair, reading out of his book by the light of a lamp that stood behind, arching its neck over his shoulder as if to read with him. They shared a footstool. The light in the little room was yellow and cozy against the wind outside where it was still February.

"I've never dreamed much," said the girl, sipping tea and then hesitating with the porcelain cup held in front of her mouth so that Aaron could not see her speak but only hear. "Maybe that's the reason I'm so interested in things like this. The idea of going to bed every night looking forward to a kind of film strip of your own subconscious design *appeals* to me. I simply can't do it."

Aaron smiled. "I don't think it works quite that way. Everyone dreams. I imagine you don't particularly care to remember what you've dreamed, so you forget it."

"Why wouldn't I want to remember?" she said suspiciously.

"I mean that probably it isn't very important to you."

"It used to be. But that's true. Beyond a mild interest in

the erotic ones, I don't really care. I have other things to think about."

Aaron munched a cookie. "I think if I couldn't often remember what I dreamed about, I'd lose my mind trying to. Not that my dreams are especially pleasant."

Susan tilted her head so that half her face was in shadow. She sipped her tea again, watching him out of eyes that seemed at the moment very liquid and shining in that light, and yet the edge came into them almost immediately and she was working, she was after something, she was holding him down on a slide with something sharp in her other hand, her soft small subtle hand.

"What do you dream?" she said.

"I really couldn't tell you."

"Are they so erotic?"

He laughed. "Sometimes. No, I'm only kidding. As a matter of fact, if you're really interested, I have a recurring dream that's been with me for a couple of years or more. It comes along every few weeks, like a grubby old friend."

"What is it?" she said softly.

He laughed. "You sound as if you're trying to analyze me!"

"I am. I analyze everyone. What is it?"

"Well—" He dropped his eyes, realized that he wanted to tell it, and surprised himself by beginning. "It's one of those staircase deals. What does Freud say about staircases?"

"I don't remember."

"It usually takes place in a school or somewhere; I'm either struggling to open a locker or trying to get to class on time. With the locker business, I'm never able to get it open—I've forgotten the combination, or maybe I don't know which locker is mine. Either way, I fight the damned thing, spinning the dial, trying to get it open. Then, if I finally do get it open, it's filled with old things I'd forgotten about—as if I hadn't opened the door for years: old tennis shoes and books and papers and stale lunches in paper bags, a lot of junk like that. I grab something and run for my class, because I'm late.

"This part is always the same. I'm late for class and I have to hurry; I *have* to get there. Except I can't hurry, because I'm weighted down, as if my arms and legs are hollow and filled with lead. It exhausts me to move at all. And the room—this is funny—I never know which room I'm supposed to be in. This being late and not knowing where to go—it ties me all up in knots.

"Then I go up the stairway. The place is always built on three levels, and of course I'm on the lowest. So I start climbing, and I get up to the second floor all right, but that isn't the one. I have to go on up—I belong up there. This is where I begin to sweat. The stairway to the third floor never has any railings. I start going up, and I can see down on both sides of me, a fall of hundreds of feet, and I can't keep my balance. I can't take another step or I'll lose my balance and go over, and I can't turn around because it's so far down. I stand there, trying to decide, to go one way or the other, but I can't. I'll fall if I try. So I stand there. I just stand there."

He looked at the book of poems in his lap, tapping his finger on the cover. "It's weird."

She did not say anything so he said, "Well? What do you think? Doctor?"

She smiled. "I think it's very interesting. Do you wake up screaming, or anything like that?"

He laughed. "No. Actually I've gotten so used to the thing that if a month goes by and I don't have it, I start wondering what's wrong with me."

"Do you ever fall? Off the stairway?"

He was looking at the book. "Hm? Nope. No—I never do fall off; I'm too cautious for that, I guess. I've never had any of those dreams of falling, that I can remember. Unless I've repressed them."

"So that's all, then."

"Yes. Except—"

"Except what?"

"Well, I used to wake up, not screaming, or anything. After my mother died, you know. For a long time after that I would wake up in the night and suddenly realize I was going to die. You know how that is, when you really realize it—it seems like the strangest thing in the world, and something has to be wrong, because it shouldn't *be* that way. I used to lie there in a cold sweat, really terrified, thinking about it. But all that is natural, I think, and it sort of wore off. You know." He looked at her inquiringly.

She nodded. "Yes." They looked at each other for a moment. "Read me some more poetry," said Susan.

So he read Yeats to her, and she seemed slightly bewildered yet pleased at the young man who read so honestly his love of words, opening himself by what he loved as well as what he feared, reading another man's words as if they were his own. And they worked on Susan in a way she could not have known they would, for there *was* a girl there, inside the sociological armor, a girl vulnerable surely to beauty if presented well and by a right person. So that the hardness with which she had cataloged his dream and himself drained out of her when she was not looking, and what was left had been worked over by Yeats and by Aaron, and she said quite honestly when he stopped, "It's beautiful. You're going to have to be my own personal poetry consultant, you know. I've read so little poetry and now I'm finding out what's there, and I've missed so much. And the way you *read* it—"

Without thinking, then, Aaron put the book down beside his chair and reached across to take her hand. He was on his knees a second later and he pulled her slowly out of the wicker chair to the floor and kissed her as she leaned back against the footstool. It slid away and they were lying outside the pool of light, breathing quickly and moving their hands over each other.

After a while when they relaxed he said, "I'm crazy about you. I'm beginning to feel I should run like hell, or something." He stopped, mulling over the thought, not quite sure what he meant. He gave up and said, "What do you think?"

There was a pause, a somnolent vibration, the slight whistling of air pushed out by the register beside a bookcase, fluttering pages of a magazine, and the wind outside, and Susan said, "Do you mean, seriously?"

She said this in a tone he had not heard her use before, a barely detectable rise in inflection, a minuscule sharpening that sent a shock through him as he realized he had broken through something that mattered, that something was about to come through this opening he had made so offhandedly, almost humorously, and he thought for a wild second: *Wait, wait, you've misunderstood, you've missed the trace in my voice (it* was *there, wasn't it?); I'm not ready for this yet, not yet—*

And in his moment of unsettledness, of seism almost, he said, unthinking, "Well—yes . . ." and looked at the pearl ring on her hand as she paused again.

"Then I think," she said, in a voice so different from any she had used with him until five seconds ago, a voice he would learn to read more from the tone than from what it said, "I think we should just go along, and not push it or anything, and see what happens."

But *"that is not it at all;/That is not what I meant, at all,"* he would have thought if he had had the time, for he suddenly found himself slipping, all unintentionally, across the line he had drawn, the line *they* had drawn—and he did not know that he was ready for it yet, though she, apparently, had assumed he was ready, or was ready herself.

While he was trying to form an answer out of the incoherence in his mind, she went ahead:

"Because there really isn't very much time before the end of the term, and it just wouldn't be wise to push ourselves into something that might cause a great deal of pain later on. . . ."

"I guess so," said Aaron, not at all sure what he guessed, not sure what she was saying, but fascinated, mesmerized by her voice.

She was not looking at him, had pulled herself to a sitting position with her back to him, and now she leaned back in his arms. "You see, this is exactly what happened to me before, this same kind of thing. I know what can happen. I was very close to someone and it took a long time to finally realize we just weren't right for each other, it would never work out—and it's awfully hard, you see. Everything is so difficult, so unsure. I haven't had enough experience, and things like love . . ."

He thought later that he might well have had her right then, had he been more sure of himself, had he been less honest or more experienced, had he simply taken her and insisted. But he was not thinking of this at the time—he was thinking of what she was saying—and when he realized she was finished, waiting for him to move or speak, he caught one of his whirling thoughts and spoke honestly, like a character from a film. "I don't know," he said. "I've never been in love with anyone. I don't know anything about love."

Then there was a long silence as both of them thought of things that had been in the back of Aaron's mind, perhaps, but which he had never even begun to think about as ideas, had certainly not meant to call forth, and certainly not now. The girl had perplexed him, quite simply, and he thought: *Who is she trying to convince?* Was she telling him, taking the opportunity afforded her by choosing to misinterpret his question, that they must not figure on anything lasting coming of this budding about-to-bloom relationship? or was she saying only that they must go slowly and allow things to develop naturally without haste—implying thereby that a strong chance existed of something rather important emerging finally; or was she telling *herself* one of these, and if so, which, and if not, just what exactly was she saying and to whom and for what reason; upon what prompting had she decided to break the bonds of this surface friendship and in effect commit both of them to keeping a wary eye out for—now—*expected developments?*

So the serious note had ended the evening, and he got into his cold car, knocking snow from his shoes and thinking of the various possibilities now open for speculation. It seemed at first that she had meant to say she wanted no emotional involvements. She had obviously been hurt before that way. So he contemplated for a moment the possibility of a physical relationship: if nothing else there could at least be the gained experience of that, and he wondered at his sudden feeling of unsettledness and realized with a little shock that he *wanted* an emotional involvement with Susan, even more than a physical involvement. He did not at that point, moving through the cold night, realize why.

Nor did he then think of what she had said about her former affair. It did not matter enough to him to be thought about, although a few years before it would have been so painful to his fundamentalist self that he would not have been able to face it. He had learned, at least with his head, that there was more to reckon with than this.

When it did occur to him, later that night, he smiled and thought: *I'm probably wrong anyway. I'm probably speculating too wildly and reading in things that simply aren't there.* He had a habit of talking to himself in his father's voice, and he thought: *Hang on, Aaron, boy; hang on and we'll see what happens. You can't be sure.*

But he had already begun to know Susan, and he did not believe himself.

4.   At one point, later, Aaron said to Sam, "I think I'm going to marry that girl." He was kidding, but only half. Aaron had never learned to move around, select girls like junk in a souvenir shop, shuffle them like cards. Only on rare occasions did he feel a desire to do so, and even then he was never without the knowledge that it was beyond him—the leering thoughts would have been ludicrous actions, committed by someone other than himself.

When he was a boy his father had told him once: "When I first met your mother, I knew she was the girl for me," and Aaron's mother said: "He told me, before we had even got to know each other, that he was going to marry me. I told him he was not, but he did."

And in Aaron, in that tumble world that had yet to be washed down with salt-water reality, the kick-in-the-teeth of experience, Aaron with his strong sense of "family," his need to have someone, some *one* for himself, to duplicate as soon and as completely as possible the thing his parents had had, the existence they had made for themselves and for him and for Matthew through absolute love, total commitment: in Aaron this was the drive, the core of heat that went deeper than he suspected in himself.

So there was Susan, and it must be Susan, would be Susan. He did not really know of the decision, but his ganglia did, his skin knew of it; all his actions, unconscious, reaching electric fingers to the surface, moved him toward it. When finally he realized, much later, that it might be nice to work out thus—the logical extension of what he had already made known to

himself—it was only the formal statement, the written order
sent down from committee to the pseudo chief, the helpless,
sad and ineffectual figurehead. Aaron had never, really, had
a chance.

She took him around Ann Arbor like a dog on a leash,
while he wagged his tail. Places he had not been aware existed
were her stamping ground, and he would pilot her Volkswagen with Susan navigating, a three-month rally driving
and walking around and through the university buildings, the
town, the countryside. They planned picnics in April that
failed because of rain, Ann Arbor sopping and steaming and
foggy and cold. They pushed through the museums with an
attention to detail matched only by that of the curators. They
burrowed like badgers through the warrenlike esophagus of
the graduate library, a claustrophobe's nightmare, chugging
up and down the stacks in the one tiny half-working long-
outdated elevator—getting stuck between floors once for ten
minutes—following the yellow painted guidelines that wound
snakelike around the floor, in and out of the books.

"Do you know what bothers me most about you?"

"No," he said. "Should I care?"

They were sitting in the coffeeshop of the student union
on an afternoon in early April, and as usual it was raining
outside. Between their coffee cups Susan had deposited an
admirable collection of psychology and sociology texts, magazine articles culled from the School of Social Work Library,
charts, graphs and trend sheets, and, in some remarkable
process known only to her, achievable only by Susan or someone like her, she was correlating all of it into one master
notebook, crimping the bizarre information onto the lines in
her tight scrawly hand with an incredibly fine-pointed, black-
inked Osmiroid fountain pen.

She held the pen slanted into the air with her wrist cocked, head cocked, eyes bright and hard "like monumental marble," as someone almost said, and looked at him over her mound of information.

"You should care, yes indeed. I've been thinking about you for a long time—"

"Flattery will get you anything."

"—and I've about figured out what your problem is." Her look now was halfway between thoughtful and smug.

"I wasn't aware that I have any problems," said Aaron, putting his Bic ballpoint down on his own notebook and folding his hands politely.

She smirked a little. "Oh, yes. That's what threw me off about you for a long time. You *seem* so damned normal and healthy. But I've got it now."

"Well, as they say in the comic books, don't give it to *me*."

"Are you afraid to find out what's the matter with you?" she said, grinning. "Are you afraid it might be terminal?"

"I'm sure it is. If it interests you, I'm sure it must be." She surprised him by sticking her tongue out—and then her face became all business again. "All right," he said. "Lay it on me."

"It was what you said one night—what you've said several times, as a matter of fact. About your family."

"What could I have said about—"

"You kept on," she said. "You always keep on about what a great childhood you had, what a good family you came from and how close you all were. It was pretty obvious the first time, but I guess I didn't really catch it."

"What the hell," he said, sitting back in the booth, unfolding his hands. "Catch what?"

"That you were making it that way. I mean, *nobody* ever had a family like the one you're always talking about. They don't exist any more. It's like a Victorian convention, the togetherness bit."

"You're wrong," said Aaron.

"What I don't see is why you keep insisting on it," she said thoughtfully. "Why it's so important to you to make it that way, a way it couldn't have been."

"You're wrong," he said.

"The Western family unit is not only on the way out, it's practically *gone* among upper-middle-income Americans. What I can't decide is whether to envy you or feel sorry for your insistence that—"

"Is *that* what you're doing?" he said. "Is that what you're reading about?"

"Partly. I'm doing a paper on it, yes, but that has nothing to do with you. You're like a very special case, and you interest me—"

"Thanks."

"Come on, now. McLuhan says—"

"Screw McLuhan."

"What are you getting upset about?"

"I'm not upset," he said. "But this—cynicism of yours eventually gets to me. You don't know anything about my family, and yet you can sit there and analyze me into one of your graphs. People don't like to have that done to them— and I especially don't like to have it done to me, and especially by you."

"I'm just telling you about your hangup," she said, smiling with a kind of fierce conviction that made her face tight and hard, her eyes bright.

"You're telling me about *somebody's* hangup."

She said quietly, still smiling, "What do you mean by that?"

They looked at each other for a moment.

"Nothing," he said. "I'm sorry."

But he had said it, and it started her, so he had to sit and let her talk. "I think you should know something, friend." She moved around some in the booth, not looking at him now, fingering her cup. "I like you, but you can be pretty damned maddening sometimes. The difference between you and me is simply that I have no illusions. I know what my family are and I wouldn't give two cents for the lot of them. I don't feel any guilt about that—my only guilt comes from knowing they have all that money and damned little conscience to go with it."

"Social conscience, you mean."

"Don't be so smug. I don't have to convince myself they're anything better than what they are, a half-educated banker and his socialite wife. If I do anything at all it will be the first step the Rayders have ever taken to look and act outside their own interests. My childhood was the same blah mash everyone else's was. But I don't *need* to make it any better than that."

"Good for you," said Aaron.

"Well, why can't *you* see that, then? Why do you have to insist on this Glorious Family bit?"

"Because we loved each other," he said. "I had a great childhood."

"Oh, God." She put her chin in her hand and glared at him as one would a particularly doltish and stubborn child.

"Sorry about that," he said.

"Grumph," she said, or something similar. "What were you writing?"

"Poem," said Aaron. "Want to see?"

She took the notebook and read it over several times:

> By the cream light of the white moon
> I will lie down in a field
> Of anemones with you, blue
> And fragrant in the mumbling night
> Near and under the bird trees.
>
> I will hold you as I grasp my sore
> And unsure, addled life, whisper

To you the things I never know
But love, and you will call me darling,
Stroking my hair in the darkness.

"Like it?"

She looked at him hard, but her face had softened somewhat around the eyes with resignation. Some part of Susan must have been aware of the difference, the turn of the wheel that separated them, and questioning which was best. Aware of it, though, she could never surrender, it being far too late for her.

"Third-rate imitation Roethke," she said. "But not bad." She opened a stick of chewing gum.

"High praise from a social worker."

"From the world of the relevant."

"I think," he said, "you should show more respect for us poets. It might keep something from happening to you."

She threw her gum wrapper at him and said, "*I'm* not afraid of you."

"Maybe you should be," he said.

"Why? What would you do to me?"

"Well–" He thought a moment. "I might kiss you until your socks roll up and down."

"Pooh," she said. "Talk is cheap."

He yawned and stretched, looking at the steady fall of rain outside the window. "Yes," he said. "It certainly is."

They moved, then, through a world of their own devising, Susan carefully and consciously, weighing each step, allowing for her moments of emotion, planning them sometimes, and always overseeing with her head. The times she was uninhibited, gay, joyful were times of controlled gaiety, allowed joyfulness, and always she retained the fascinating and, to Aaron, horrible facility for turning things off like the twist of a faucet. Susan's heart seemed, at times, only a mild stimulant–all the rest was will. There remained a suspicion on her part toward him, a basic accepted condition of their relationship, that she distrusted him slightly for being unable to see that his family life could not have been as good as he thought it had been. As a matter of fact, his inability to see it irritated her no end.

But Aaron's wild erratic heart pumped him into delirium, drowned his caution, numbed his brain, floated him bargelike down the river. He was beginning to see now, vaguely, that his attraction to Susan had elements of danger in it: her practicality bordered at times on the inhuman—she could go for hours with such a lack of warmth that he would find himself unable to believe her, wondering what could possibly mold a girl like Susan into what she obviously was, yet drawn to her perhaps because of that. The worst was when he found himself slipping into a barely conscious, almost unconscious accustomedness to her awful self-sufficiency—so that it almost, if he was not careful, became less than awful, almost natural. Yet she remained a vague and alien form of security; she got by, and this attracted him more than he knew.

They went out one night to a bookstore to sell some used textbooks of Susan's that she did not want to keep, books required for a course that had not interested her much, and that, being Susan, she could neither want nor need. It had turned cold again, as it does in Michigan, where there is no real spring, and Susan was bundled up in a sensible winter coat, an expensive camel hair with a wide fur collar that she pulled up around her ears against the wind and the spitting snow. Aaron was cold even in his heavy jacket, and, forced to park three blocks away, they hurried in the windy dark with their books, around the corner, across the street, and into the warm deep paper-smelling shop.

He was in a mood of some kind or other, and unable to put his finger on it. Final exams accounted for much of it, he suspected, but there was more than that, more than the exams in his hanging-fire unsettledness. He had a feeling of vagueness, a reaching for something that being with Susan intensified, that being in the bookstore intensified, and he moped around with his hands in his jacket pockets while Susan engaged in a five-minute negotiation on the amount of purchasing credit to be allowed her for the books she was selling. He felt like griping, but to whom and about what he could not have said.

They frittered away time in the bookstore and Aaron found something that interested him. But Susan had drifted away on her own (a habit she had that irritated him at the best of times, and doubly so now; he wanted to be *with* her, for them to be *together*) and he looked for her through the shelves and finally saw her, talking to a young man who was quite nice looking, and both of them smiling.

He was so surprised when the feeling moved into his chest that at first he did not recognize it, though in part it was simply an intensification of what had been there. But there was something else too, and when he did recognize it he almost smiled. He had not thought he could be so childish, and now the persistence of it made him slightly angry with himself, as if something in himself were betraying him. He had been sure that he was above middle-class morality, fundamentalist-ingrained dogma. To discover that what he thought did not jibe with what he felt was a humorous but irritating shock. So he stood there watching them talk and trying to decide without thinking about it what to do. And without thinking about it he did decide, but by the time he had rounded the stack of books and snaked in and out of several browsers, preparatory to cutting in on the conversation, the young man had flipped up the collar of his gray topcoat, put on a pair of black gloves, laughed a good-bye to Susan and trudged out into the night. And then Aaron arrived.

"There you are," she said,

"Here I am." He waited.

"Well, I'm ready to go if you are. I have to buy this." She held up a newly published paperback copy of *Magister Ludi*.

"Friend of yours?" said Aaron.

"Hm?" she said, moving ahead of him to the counter. "I'd like this." She gave the book to the graduate student running the cash register, a sterile intense sort by his look, probably in English.

"Ah, um—have you read Hesse?" said the man, hesitating politely.

Susan, pulling the credit slip out of her pocket, hesitated with him, or rather against him. "I've read *Steppenwolf*."

"Oh, yes. Actually, I doubt— Have you read anything else? *Siddhartha?*"

"No," said Susan, with only the beginning of an edge in her voice. "Why?"

He didn't take the hint. "Well, this one is rather difficult. I think it would be easier for you if you got *Siddhartha* out of the way first—"

Susan had a way of growing slightly taller in moments like this. She did so, presented her credit slip and said in a voice only slightly colder than the wind outside, "I *think* I am capable of choosing my own reading matter, thank you."

"Um," said the man. "Oh, yes. And thank *you*."

When they left the bookstore Aaron did not take her hand or talk to her, and she realized immediately that something was wrong.

"What's the matter?" she said into her collar.

"Nothing."

The wind cut them into pieces incapable of speech and she waited until they were in the car and moving toward home.

"The *nerve* of him! 'I think it would be easier for you if you got *Siddhartha* out of the way first.'"

Aaron could not help laughing, but the laugh trailed off into a humorless smile. She watched him for a while and seemed to be considering, and apparently she decided to let it ride. For a while, then, there was a break in their carefully built rapport, while Susan ignored it and acted as if nothing was the matter.

This made him feel worse; such consideration was unlike Susan, and it *was* his fault. He was being a heel. It was evident that he should either drag it out into the open or straighten up.

"Who was that guy?" he said.

She looked at him. "Who?"

"That *guy*."

"*What* 'guy'?" She thought a moment. "In the bookstore, you mean? The one I was talking to?"

"Oh, boy. Yes," he said with exaggerated patience. "The one you were talking to in the bookstore."

She watched his face without answering, and then started to laugh.

"What," said Aaron, "is so damned funny?"

She choked a little.

"What're you *laughing* about?"

"So that's it!"

"What? *What?* damn it!"

"That's why you're so out of it. You're jealous!" She laughed again, a rather healthy and deep and human laugh that he might have approved of, had it not been directed at him.

Instead of answering, he sat there, brooding, his spirit seeping down into a moldering cross between despair and crabbiness. It seemed to him that it was getting colder and colder outside.

She watched him with what he considered satanic amusement; she outwaited him.

"I'm not either jealous," he said grumpily. There was a longish pause. "You just seemed to be having such a good time with that son of a—"

"He's Janice's lover," she said. "They're crazy about each other and they're going to get married this summer. That's who he was."

"Oh . . ."

"I mean, in case you were interested."

He looked at her quickly, then back over the wheel. "You've got canary feathers all around your mouth."

"Meow." And she added innocently, "It's just that I never knew you *cared*."

Well, hell, he thought later, after the prolonged good night, the air clear again, the night a little sharper to his eyes—*hell, he* could *have been one of* her *old lovers, the one she was so involved with.*

While he was kissing her she had started to laugh again, so that he was kissing only teeth.

Well, hell. Maybe he was overdoing it; maybe he was getting too involved too quickly. She had considered his jealousy hilarious.

And he was not now totally unaware of the ludicrous quality in their relationship; a perceptive, objective part of him knew that in all likelihood they were not right for each other. Susan, he knew, was a product of the fast sixties, a result of the somnolent fifties, a professional catcher in the rye—all of the practical, glib and desperately *dedicated* things that Aaron was not, or liked—tried—needed to believe he was not. Susan, for her part, was not warm, was not, at times, even believable as a person, and very likely, he knew, they could not really make it together.

Yet even as he knew this, even as he almost-but-not-quite reached the point of wondering why he clung to her (why, also, she bothered with *him*), even now he was pushing it all away, folding it up, tucking in the corners, hiding it behind the sense of relief he felt that his jealousy had not been justified, had been—if the intensity of the good night was a gauge (after she stopped laughing and hurried—again uncharacteristically—to soothe his injured pride)—had been even silly, jealousy a fault unworthy of him, its direction toward her an unfair one.

So he knew but did not know, refused or failed to see at this point, for reasons not only unclear to him but unthought of—and thus continued to let himself in for things he had also not thought of.

And very shortly after that the term ended.

5.   By the time Aaron reached Ann Arbor the rain had stopped; the sharp wind tore the sky into shards blasted with an incandescence that came and went like flickering arc light. He stopped at Angell Hall to pick up a paper out of the box of one of his instructors, alone in the huge dark echoing long-halled building, his footsteps clicking away from him and coming back past the milk glass office doors, a shadowy loneliness around him so that even the wind and glaring hot spurts of random sunlight were welcome as he trotted down the wide steps and out to his car. He drove to Susan's. She was alone today, with her roommates out somewhere, and she had lost the sharpness from her voice. She kissed him and whispered, "I think our picnic plans are still ruined. I hoped it would clear up."

"That's all right," he said, holding her. "We can stay right here and make love."

He could not tell whether or not she went for that idea; she merely looked at him until he decided that he had been two-thirds kidding anyway; then she divided with him a bottle of blood-red strawberry diet cola, and they sat down to formulate plans for the afternoon. While they talked a stream of sunlight fell through the window onto them, with a thin content of dust motes slowly circling in it like mosquitoes.

"Looking nicer out," said Aaron.

"Why don't we go for a walk?"

"Why don't we?"

Susan put on a thin coat and they stepped outside.

"Which way shall we go?"

"This way," said Susan. "To the school."

It was an elementary school only a block from Susan's house. They locked arms against the spring wind and leaned into it toward the red brick building and around to the schoolyard, deserted now with all the children home on some kind of elementary school holiday, and the wind died a little and the light turned golden as autumn and fell through an immense green of new leaves surrounding the yard. There were several riding toys there for the children, small plastic animals set on springs that allowed them to wobble back and forth and at all angles like liberated hobbyhorses—a duck, an elephant and a turtle; painted in pastels with polka dots, they stood like lonely creatures escaped from a nursery, refugees from a poem by Eugene Field, patiently awaiting the next riders to stumble onto the green shaded yard and find them calm and ready.

Susan climbed onto the duck, straddling its yellow back and slipping her feet securely into the stirrups, as Aaron found himself drawn to the ancient green turtle standing sprung on his legs with a Chinese wisdom painted on his face in the form of a dull smile. The duck and the turtle carried their loads, careening back and forth in the sunlight and shadow, pelted by winds.

In a moment Aaron stopped, caught by the vision of Susan

recklessly galloping, struck with a sense of the outrageousness of it, the kind of bizarre scene that stays imprinted on the mind for years, and he thought: *I will see us, if ever we are lost to each other, rocking in the wind of a schoolyard on the pastel steeds of children, riding hard and going nowhere on green and yellow dreams.*

Susan looked at him, cocked her sure and saucy head at him as if she knew his thoughts, and she curled a lip. "I wish I'd brought my camera, to get a picture of you on that. You look like early Walt Disney."

"Middle at least, I'd say."

She laughed. "Come on; I want to go back and get it. I want pictures of you in your second childhood."

"Nice of you to humor me, though. I'd almost think you *liked* that duck. I'll get my camera and we'll have a contest to see who can catch the other when his defenses are down. I'm sure you'll win."

She made a face at him, thinking he was kidding; she had missed the edge in his voice brought there by the fact that he knew she *would* win, would always win in a contest like that.

Susan agreed with him, said something that made both of them laugh, and they left the animals standing there under the trees together to wait for someone else; laughing, almost forgetting them.

They picked up Susan's camera and Aaron got his own out of the car, and they walked down to a drugstore and bought some film. "Why don't we take a ride?" She wound her arm into his and gave him a bump with her hip. "Out to where we were going to have our picnic."

"Good," said Aaron, and they drove out Main Street to Huron River Drive, which wound them slowly around and down until they crossed a bridge and came to the little park that is there with a stream cutting through it toward the river. The cement parking lot is at one edge of the park, and a little trail winds from there into the woods past barbecue pits and swings and slides and picnic tables to the stream. They walked down the trail, really a kind of dirt road, feeling both good and sad in the sharp day in the sunlight. They jumped onto the swings and took pictures of each other, pumping high up in the air racing for height, Susan soon losing. She watched as Aaron went on, up to where the swing would buck and the chains loosen their strain at the top of the arc, and he would be jerked and fall back spinning crazily like a spider at the end of a double strand of web in the breeze.

She allowed herself enough honesty, enough of the childlike quality that was really her, to call out, "You're amazing!" and he grinned down at her on the backswing.

"It just takes strength and timing and coordination and courage and a good sense of balance—"

"Such modesty ill becomes you!"

"I know it!" he called, sailing past.

They left the swings and the other toys to stand unused, the park almost empty on this cold April day, and wandered into the trees, over the mossy ground to the stream. They skipped stones into the water and did not talk.

But the air was too cold to stay out in and the sunlight was growing longer and brighter and lowering in the sky, shadowing the woods, so they walked back up the road toward the car. Aaron took his last picture of her standing in the middle of the road in the late sun with her hair blowing in the wind.

She looked pensive, and he wondered if possibly even Susan could be affected by a knowledge of the distance that would soon separate them. "What is it?" he said.

"I have to go to the john."

"Oh."

There was one nearby, one of those wooden buildings with MEN on one side and WOMEN on the other; they went into their respective doors and Aaron lingered for some time, standing in front of the clouded mirror in the unheated lavatory, his hands shoved into the pockets of his topcoat. He could see his breath, it was so cold, and he looked at the young man in the mirror and felt lonely, looked up through the open top at the spring-leaved trees of the park, thought of himself alone here in the building, this half of it, alone in the park, in Ann Arbor, alone.

The man in the mirror was young, pleasant in appearance, well-dressed, of medium height and complexion, eyes set only a little deep, no lines in the face, all pure and clean there, all potential, alone in the autumn-seeming spring. He wanted to ask himself something, could not remember the question, if he had ever known it, and so looked at the man in the mirror, hands in pockets, frosting his breath out so he could see it, see that it was there.

When he came out, Susan was sitting on a wooden bench along the wall of the building. She was not a large girl, a small one rather, sitting alone in her light spring coat and looking cold, looking as if she were cold without knowing it.

Aaron walked over to her, stood in front of her, waiting for her to rise, but she sat there and looked around at the park, finally looked up at him with something new in her face, new at least in its intensity, so that he sat down beside her and started to put his arm around her, and she started to cry.

It lasted only a moment, his arm around her and her dark head against his shoulder with the tears coming silently, and then she wiped them away and they were gone, and Aaron shocked, feeling foolish, looking into her face without a word. He had never believed that someone like Susan could cry, did not believe that modern American girls ever cried, unless they wanted something and did it for effect. But Susan had not cried for that and he knew it at once and said finally, "Hey . . ."

"I don't want to go back there and work in my father's

bank," she said, looking at her hands folded in her lap and saying it in a voice that confirmed, unconsciously, much that Aaron had felt for and about her.

"Then don't," he said.

She made a chortling sound and looked at him quickly, wiping her face with one hand. "That sounds funny, coming from you. I *promised*—I let myself be maneuvered into promising them I'd come back there for the summer; he's got this opening all ready for me and everything, good money, and goddammit, I need that. I hate, I *hate* to admit it, but I do."

"Why do you need it?" He watched her hands pulling at themselves in her lap.

"To get away from them once and for all. I'm really not as independent as I talk, not when it comes to the money, anyway. I don't want them paying my tuition next year—or paying anything else except for what I earn. I ought to be working in a ghetto this summer, in Detroit or somewhere. I can't afford it."

There was something else there but he did not quite see it yet. Instead he reflected on Susan and her mad-modern hang-up, and he felt genuine sympathy for her if not more than that.

"Is that why you were crying?"

"Yes," she said, getting up. "I'm a stupid baby. Let's go back to the car; I'm freezing."

But it did not seem to him that Susan would cry for that. Still, he had not thought anything could make her cry, so maybe it was as she said.

Then they sat in the car and necked ferociously for more than an hour and finally lay slumped in the seat, resting against each other as if their lives were there with them complete and fulfilled in each other.

"What are you thinking about?"

She was nestled against him, her hand against his chest with his arms around her, and she glanced up at him with a guilty smile and then looked away. "I was picturing you," she said, "walking up to a Dairy Queen place with several children around you, and buying them milk shakes."

"Hm," he said, startled again, a little. "What kind of picture does it make?"

"It looks pretty good, as a matter of fact; you giving them your fierce look, and letting them talk you into anything."

"Not me. I really am fierce."

"Maybe. It's an interesting thought, I guess."

"Novel, you mean?" He growled at her. She looked up and he kissed her. He thought the picture was rather nice himself.

Later he pulled his guitar out of the back seat and sang for her—he had brought it just for that. He had not played the guitar much since his mother had died and he and Matt had stopped playing together, busting up their team, breaking, almost, for a time, their own brotherhood as each pulled back into his own grief. But he liked to sing, he wanted to sing for Susan, so he had brought the guitar.

She had not heard him sing before, and seemed a little politely awed by this side of him; but she liked it. He sang folk songs that he remembered singing with Matt: "Fast Freight" and "Blow the Candle Out" and "South Wind" and others, and while he was singing the light paled out in the west and burned the horizon and was gone, and before either of them realized it darkness had come and they were completely alone in the park. When Aaron put down the guitar a long sound of insects filled the air and it was night.

Aaron looked at his watch. "Nine o'clock. I guess I lost track of the time. Shall we go somewhere and eat?"

Susan nodded. "I hate to leave. Oh, Aaron, I'm going to miss you."

"I know," he said, not even realizing the magnitude of this change in tone and statement from Susan, this same girl. He was thinking of his own feeling and he said, "Let's not think about that right now." He started the engine and they moved out of the darkness of the park. It was quite cold now;

Aaron turned on the heater and they did not talk much as they drove back into Ann Arbor with the purring fan warming out of them a chill they had not been conscious of before.

They ate at a restaurant he could not normally afford; still, though the food was good, neither of them wanted it much, and they talked over coffee of innocuous things and left, huddled together in the cold.

Finally they pulled into Susan's driveway and Aaron switched off the lights. They kissed in the darkness and could see each other dimly while they were close.

"Do you want to come in for a while?"

He looked at the light in the window. "Your roommates are back, aren't they?"

"I think so."

"Well," he said, "I guess we'd better just say good-bye here."

"What a word."

"It was nice, wasn't it?"

"Yes. It was."

"It was some day. I'm not going to forget it soon."

"Neither am I."

He kissed her again and ran his hand over her.

"Oh, Aaron . . ."

"This has to last me all summer," he said, misunderstanding. Then he felt her hand on his thigh.

"I'm going to miss you," she said for the second time that evening. "I wish I didn't have to go. I wish you could come with me."

"So do I," he said. "I wish I could." He thought perhaps he had a better idea now as to why she had been crying. He could not believe it, but there it was.

They listened to the muttering fan and grew sleepy and excited at the same time. Aaron unbuttoned her blouse, and after a while he dropped his hand to her knee and slid it up beneath her skirt. She took a breath and he stopped, afraid to go further. She kept her legs primly together and he thought, stroking her thigh: *You should have made love to her. You were so afraid of being rejected, of insulting her, of being turned down, you were so properly proper and conventional, and now it's too late and you love her but you've never made love to her. Now you'll have to wait all summer for that.*

He kissed her for a long time and she murmured a little, low in her throat, and both of them were breathing hard. "Aaron—" she whispered, breaking off.

Aaron stroked her long smooth legs and imagined what it would be like to make love to her. It seemed to him that she was in love with him too and he had simply cheated himself out of her by not trying. She had commented to him once, a long time ago, "You seem very moral," and he had taken it as a compliment. *What an idiot,* he thought, *what an inexperienced fool not even to* try. He had never made love to a girl and had not minded because he had never been in love with one either, and now he loved one and had been afraid to make love to her, afraid to try. Now he was losing the girl he loved for an entire summer without ever having loved her, and he thought: *I'm a sad son of a bitch. . . .*

The thought struck him then that somebody else had had her, though, and he felt the breaking inside himself that had come before. He pushed it away, pushed himself away too and said, "You know we're going to have to end this."

She looked at him. "End it?"

"It's getting late. I have a long way to go tonight."

"Oh." She laughed. "I—I thought you meant end it—permanently."

"No," he said, holding her close. "I'm afraid it's a little late for that, on my part."

"Me too, friend. God. I felt a shock go through me. . . ."

They laughed and kissed and then Aaron buttoned up her blouse. "Better get you all straightened out."

"It's so warm and nice here with you—I hate to go in."

"It's late."

"I suppose."

When he opened the car door a breeze hit them and the dome light blinded them both for an instant. It was like waking out of a dream, and Aaron thought: *Well, this is it. This is really it.* He walked her up to the door and they clung together under the porch light.

"Have a nice summer," she said.

"You too. It won't be very long."

"No."

"Will you write to me?"

"Of course. I'm not much of a writer, very undependable, but I will. And you'll write to me? And send me poetry?"

"Yes."

They stood close together. The trees made quiet sounds around them, still absorbing the rain that had fallen in the morning. There was nothing left to say.

"Good night. Drive carefully."

"Sure. So long, Susie."

They kissed once more and did not want to break. Then she went inside and closed the door. Aaron walked down the steps and across the lawn, colder now, looking up to where stars should have been, but there were none. The sky was tumbling and dark.

6. Shortly afterward, he wrote a letter:

DEAR SUSIEGIRL,

I'm sitting here on the couch in the basement with an electric heater at my feet and a cold heart, thinking of you. Corny? Maybe so, but you'll have to take it and me for what we're worth. In the background, if you listen closely, you may detect strains of Dukas's *The Sorcerer's Apprentice.* I've been reading some poetry too, but I started thinking about you and about the last time I saw you—last time for the summer, the whole summer —and I got all sad and lonesome, and I decided to write you a letter, and here it is.

I suppose you're working gaily at the bank, and have all but forgotten me by now. That's okay. This will serve as a reminder that you have Another Life in your background, with the university and Ann Arbor and me and a lot of places I wouldn't have wanted to go to with anyone else. But enough of this effusion; I think you get the picture.

I've got a job. My friend Sam (of whom you've heard) used to work for the Consolidated Power Company and knows people there. I applied and got hired. Apparently they haven't kept track of information stamped on their poles (date of installation, type, height, etc.) so this summer they're hiring crews to run an inventory in the field.

What it means is that I'll be moving around the state all summer with five or six other guys out of a force of several hundred. The company pays all expenses and we'll sleep in motels through the week and come home on weekends. The job itself involves a lot of walking through every kind of terrain—any place a pole can be put. It sounds healthy and is—I expect soon to begin to resemble a bronze god.

Later. I've had dinner and helped my father work on a coffee table. He has a lot of tools and is very good at building cabinets and tables and things; no boats just now. He's the kind of craftsman that borders on the artist, and I only wish I could work with words the way he works with wood. My uncle too. He and his family live with us, and my father and uncle make a good team.

This is lining up as an interesting summer, with the job and all, but it's already bad without you. The fact is, I'm looking at it more or less as a stretch of time to be put in and gotten over before I start to live again. It's good I think that the job will keep me busy and on the road all summer. I pulled out to the university a year after my mother died, and haven't really lived here since. This is no place for me to live now. After two years I can't yet allow myself to think about it much or I start feeling haunted and guilty and everything and I can't take that for long. Better not to be around here except for brief periods. My father and Matt have done remarkably well; I don't know how people adapt but it seems hard for me.

Well, enough of that cheerful subject. It's late and I have to get up early. We'll be here for a few more days and then we move; I don't know where yet. Write to me, and be happy.

Love, of sorts,

AARON

P.S.   Don't let that sign-off scare you; the word has many and varicolored meanings.

P.P.S.   Why must people always modify and soften or apologize for the things that mean most to them? Why can't we come to each other openly and without elaborate defenses, especially to those we care about?

Love, period

AARON

1.   He had never seen Owosso before, and it seemed to him, on that Monday morning as he drove through town and out to the motel, a very unpleasant place. Not, perhaps, as bad as Flint or Detroit, or sections of several other cities—but not as large, either. It was a rough-looking town, an old and beaten, mean-looking town, and for its size it got the award.

In the evening he sat on the side of his bed and waited while George Dooley got ready to go to dinner. The room was hot and wet; he had taken a shower after working all day, and then Dooley had taken a shower and opened the bathroom door afterward to let the steam out so he could see to shave. It had caused the whole room to cloud up, but it had not helped much in the bathroom. Dooley had finally taken his towel to the foggy, wet mirror, and now he swept the cloth down it periodically, leaving a clear swath through the beady film of moisture. Aaron had opened the window, and a breeze was slowly clearing and cooling the room.

Finally George was finished in the bathroom. He came out in his shorts, mumbling to himself, the wet towel over his shoulder, his hair damp and exploding from his head like a dark sunburst. He threw the towel down on a chair and started working himself into his clothes.

"Whew," he said, but not really to anyone. "It's like a Turkish bath in here."

"How you doing?" said Aaron, watching him from the bed by the window. Dooley had been at this for an hour. Everyone else had already gone to dinner.

"I'm gettin' there," said Dooley. He continued dressing and mumbling to himself: "Where's my socks?" (Down on the floor, peeking under his bed, crawling around to look under the chair in the corner; under the television table; finding them at last behind his suitcase, the clean rolled pair he had taken out and dropped there over an hour ago.) "Here they are. Damn."

He was a fascinating thing to listen to and especially to watch. Aaron leaned back on one elbow and looked at him. Dooley was constructed somewhat like a featherless stork, all ribs and knees. He was about five feet ten and incredibly scrawny, the half-starved runt of the litter, thought Aaron; skin stretched tight over some functional framework: an Erector set product. His thatch of straw hair looked darker now that it was wet, and he was too new to the job for the sun to have bleached it yet; it was brown and stiff and straight.

Dooley, his pants on now, swabbed his head—like a rifle cleaning rod with bristles on the end—through a T-shirt, stretched the tails down until the head came through with a muffled little *pop*, and began to comb his hair. It did not so much resist him as ignore him, and he patiently gave it twenty-five or thirty sweeps perfunctorily, expecting nothing and getting it. He had not put anything on his hair. Finally it gave a little yawn and began to droop in spots, hanging over his eyes and roostering out at the rear like something perched on his head. Satisfied, his humble demands met, mumbling and moueing approvingly, Dooley began to work on his shirt.

Aaron thought: *Oh, Lord, Lord, what have I got* here?

Of course, he was a math major.

With the sun almost gone, they drove into town in Aaron's car, having decided to alternate each night. They would both drive in the mornings, eating on the way out to work, and they would not be together for lunch because each of them was expected to find a place near his area at noon to save time and mileage. They would be working from the edge of Owosso to pretty far out, and the company paid for the driving.

Dooley was a third-year student at an engineering school north of Bay City. Loaded down with every math course he could handle, he did not know what he wanted to do.

"I like math and all," he said by way of explanation. "Fact is, I'm better at it than I am at other stuff—everything else kind of bores me. But I don't know yet what I want to go into yet."

"What does your father do?"

"My dad is a plumber in Saginaw. It's funny, you don't need any math to be a plumber, and I could get in. That's what *he* wants me to do. He makes a good living at it too. But I don't really want to be a plumber—we don't hit it off too awfully well, really. I don't think that's what I want to be, so I'm taking all this math because I like it and I want to use it to go into something else. Only I don't know what yet, see?"

"Sure," said Aaron.

Owosso was not bursting with choice places to eat. They finally found a truck stop, and with Dooley going on and on, they went in and ordered. None of the others was there, but Aaron thought they would all probably have gone back by now, or be hitting the bars as some of them liked to do. The place was almost empty, and while they waited for their meals

Aaron listened politely and fingered the jukebox extension in
their booth while Dooley talked about electrical engineering
and its advantages over aerospace, which was harder.

Aaron stopped listening eventually, fingering the jukebox
keys and feeling hungry and tired. This was the most stren-
uous job he had ever had and he was still new to it. It exhausted him every day in a pleasing physical way. He had
already begun to harden from all the walking and he was
starting to tan a little, although his nose was sunburned and
he still had to regulate his skin's exposure.

The food arrived and Dooley lapsed into a relative quiet.
Aaron brightened a little, but he had a feeling of emptiness
which he attributed to his being tired and hungry, away from
home now and far away from Susan.

He wondered what Susan was doing. It was eight o'clock;
that meant eleven in Seattle, he thought. (He was wrong, and
had it backward; it was *five* in Seattle. He would make the
same mistake again later on.) On Monday night she probably
had gone to bed or was not far from it—reading perhaps, or sewing. He looked at Dooley and wished Susan were there and
were his roommate instead of Dooley. Thoughts like that can
start you raving, he decided, feeling better simply from thinking of her, from knowing what she was probably doing, where
she probably was right this minute.

"What do you think of the crew?" he said without actually
thinking about it, interrupting Dooley and then coming awake
to his own question and realizing he had asked it.

George stopped with his mouth half open, immediately
forgot what he had been talking about, and thought it over,
looking at his plate, his fork motionless in his hand.

"That Vanneman kills me; God, but he's cool. I wish I was
a Californian. Me and a guy in high school used to plan every
summer to go out there, drive out there, you know? and live
on the beaches for a couple weeks and see the sports car races,

but we never did it. I wonder if all Californians are like Vanneman?"

"He's from New York, you know. He's only lived out there for three or four years, Paul says."

"I dunno," said Dooley. "Maybe it did it to him quick. Me and this guy were gonna go—"

"How about Rod?"

"Sievers? Oh—he's okay but, I don't know, there's something—like he isn't too awful friendly or talky or something, do you think?"

"I haven't talked to him. He's funny. I think he's okay."

"Maybe. And Paul's a nice guy. And Steve is too, I guess," he added after a moment, as if he'd just thought of it. "Only—"

"What?" said Aaron.

Dooley started tapping his fork on his plate, idly mixing in peas and mashed potatoes and gravy. "He's like— Steve is weird; he's like kind of a mixture. I don't know what he's like."

"Neither do I," said Aaron.

"I mean, him and Paul are great buddies and sometimes he's almost as friendly as Paul. But he's really not like that, because he can be wild like Vanneman—and this is kind of weird: sometimes he's like even stranger and quieter and scarier or something than even Rod Sievers. Almost as quiet as you." He looked at Aaron quickly. "I mean, really weird though, not like you, except I can't figure out what he's really like. I saw him around in Saginaw. I can't figure—whether he's wild like Vanneman or nice like Paul or all tied up with himself like Rod—or something else. I don't know what. What do you think?"

Aaron was slowly drinking his glass of lemonade with the last of the meal. He did not answer for a while, until the lemonade was gone; then he set the glass down carefully and said, "I think I'm going to like Steve a lot. But you're right. He's a weird one."

Dooley was about to answer when the waitress came and they ordered dessert. After that he had forgotten what he was going to say.

When they got back to the motel Aaron felt an exhaustion all through him, and knew there was no question of reading or writing tonight. It was after nine o'clock and he only wanted to sleep. He sat down on his bed and started to undress, and did not even know until he heard the rattle of canned laughter that Dooley had turned on the television set.

He stopped undressing and sat motionless with a sock in his hand and thought: *Yes, oh, Lord, yes—he* would be *a television watcher. What else?*

"George," he said, turning his head slowly to look at a picture of a girl riding a horse on the wall several inches above Dooley's head, "George, do you—watch TV much?"

"Hm?" said Dooley, who then laughed with the electronic audience at something happening to somebody somewhere far away in time, place and credibility.

"Do you watch much *television*, George?" said Aaron, a little louder.

"Sure," said Dooley. "Don't you?"

"Well, I read a lot—"

"What?"

"I said I *read a lot.*"

"Oh."

Aaron looked at the pattern on the bedspread and smiled a little, knowing that he and Dooley were the newest members of the crew and were not likely to be changed with anyone as roommates. A loud crash wiped away the smile.

He gritted his teeth and said, "George, it's pretty late, isn't it? We have to get up early, you know." Dooley did not answer. "George?"

"Huh?" Dooley was grinning his buck teeth at the screen.

"I said, haven't you got that turned up a little too *loud?*"

"Oh, sure; sorry, Aaron." Dooley turned it down a hair and sat back down. "That okay?"

"It's late . . ." said Aaron, pleading.

"This'll be over in half an hour," said Dooley. "I always watch this. Half an hour and I'll have to turn in. We gotta get up early."

"What?" said Aaron.

"I said we gotta get up *early!*"

Aaron said, "Sure," looked at the sock in his hand and wished it were a nylon stocking.

He undressed and got into bed, but he had always been a light sleeper, and, tired as he was, the light in the room and the maniacal jabber of the television set, coupled with Dooley's laughing, kept him awake. Dooley had an interesting and singular laugh; it would dribble along for a while like something halfhearted and insincere, building slowly:

Huh. Huh. Huh, huh—

then there would be a moment of silence and then the release, which was like something let out to keep from strangling:

Uh-hyuck!
Uh-hyuck, uh-*hyuck!*

Aaron almost laughed at the laugh, hating Dooley and wishing he would choke on it and die, and smiling in spite of himself. For half an hour he lay on the borderline of sleep, drifting in and being pulled back so that it seemed endless and cruel, a punishment out of Orwell: the light, the gibbering, the laugh, and he thought wildly with a half-awake mixture of bitterness and humor: *Not me, not me; do it to Susan!*

Do it to Susan (feeling vaguely sorry for Susan, but weak in spirit and justified by that weakness)—and then he fell asleep.

2.　　　　He woke up when Dooley turned off the television set and the lamp and went to bed.

He was no longer sleepy and he thought: *I will die and be a crabby old man in the morning,* but it did not help, and he lay there thinking about the crew.

It was in Saginaw in early May that Aaron, following Sam Lowry's advice, had put in his application for summer employment at Consolidated Power.

He wanted a job. He did not particularly care what sort of job it was so long as it kept him busy. His horror was of sitting idly around the house for four months thinking about Susan and filling out the days with the kind of made-up time consumers he had once been expert at creating. During high school he had had the usual odd collection of summer jobs— pushing an ice cream cart, bagging groceries—and the black summer before last he had worked nights in an automotive plant. And last summer—the worst, the very worst—he had done nothing. That was when he had learned to let the days pass without noticing.

Oh, yes, he *had* done things. He had played tennis with Sam three times a week, had spent evenings with Sam and other evenings in the upside-down apartment of Huston Reeve, who played trumpet at the Winchester Lounge. Nights when Huston was off they sat in the clutter listening to jazz and talking in the dark, switching on a lamp only to find the refrigerator and beer or Huston's cigarettes, brown harsh un-filtered cigarettes with which Huston was slowly killing himself because his third wife had left him, taking all the furniture except for two large cushioned chairs and the stereo Huston had built from components. The trumpet and the stereo, the beer and cigarettes, Aaron and Sam, seemed all that was left of Huston Reeve's life, and he was working on that by dragging the bitter smoke deep into his lungs, and every third cigarette he would cough for thirty seconds and then light another. It did not seem to hurt his playing, but Aaron was no expert.

Occasionally Huston would get high on something or other and tell them the story of his life, which both had heard. Huston had been born in Louisiana. He had run away from his father's cannery at the age of fourteen and gotten a job in a New Orleans brothel. Fortunately the place employed a band, and Huston, who had brought his third-hand trumpet with him, slowly learned the music and the life of the jazz musician. For the next twelve years he had played all over the South, making love to fifty women along the way, acquiring two wives and losing them, until he met Jennie in Indianapolis and made her the love of his life.

Sam had met Huston when he was in college in Indiana, became virtually a member of the family and had met his wife-to-be through Jennie. Aaron had never met Jennie, although he had known Sam's ex-wife. Jennie had left Huston just after Sam and his bride returned to Michigan, and Huston turned up on their doorstep one rainy night (this was *true*), thirty years old, lonely, drunk and crying—and moved in with them for three months. That was where Aaron had met him.

Huston moved to his own apartment with his meager belongings and began his final dissolution long before Sam's own divorce, and that summer the three of them—Sam, Huston and Aaron—leaned on each other like three musketeers with bent swords, playing jazz, listening to endless sections of

Sam's novel, which he had been writing for three years, and drinking beer. Each took comfort in the misery of the others.

For the rest, Aaron spent the days sleeping late, occasionally fiddling with his guitar, knocking a cotton golf ball around the back yard to perfect his drive so he could play golf with his father on weekends. He had other friends, high school friends with whom he no longer had anything in common, if indeed he ever had; he usually avoided them. Matt was gone, somewhere in Texas learning to kill, though he returned briefly once before leaving again. The summer slipped away like an interminable void and finally was gone, leaving little to remember.

So Aaron applied at Consolidated Power, not wanting a repetition of last year. A week later he was called into a room at the Holiday Inn and a man named Erikson outlined the job to him. Erikson, a short muscular balding man with the unmistakable outdoor look about him, like a professional geologist, was supervisor for the survey. He showed Aaron that what many people think are telephone poles really carry power lines.

"The company's records on the poles themselves are sketchy. Until this year it never mattered. Now, for tax purposes, we need to know certain information stamped on the poles, especially the date of installation. We have to check every pole of ours in the state this summer, so the office people can make up their charts and have them ready come tax time."

"Sounds like a healthy job. Woods?"

"Woods, thickets, swamps, wherever the right-of-way goes. Some of the lines were put in as far back as nineteen twenty; the country has grown up pretty thick around some of them. They all have to be checked."

Aaron did not get to work much in Saginaw. It rained

through most of May and the six crews pulled together for the area spent most of their time in a big room at the Holiday Inn, transposing information from completed maps onto data sheets—a job normally done by the office staff. The crews never worked outdoors in the rain and it gave Aaron a chance to meet some of the men and relax into the job.

Finally the rain stopped and, having broken in with a crew chief, Aaron got one week of checking poles in the suburbs, including some near his own back yard. They finished most of the county, divided into crews again, and were sent out to other areas. Aaron met his crew on Monday morning in Owosso.

Steve Garrett and Rod Sievers and Paul Maloney were there when he arrived, George Dooley came in, and eventually Phil Vanneman showed up, late. Most of them were acquainted. Steve and Paul were old friends and had been rooming together for a month. Dooley had signed on in Saginaw just after Aaron, and Rod and Vanneman had been on another crew before Rod was pulled into Saginaw. Vanneman had been working farther south.

The first person to shake hands with Aaron in that Monday-morning fogginess was Paul Maloney, a Michigan State dropout in forestry. He was stocky and fairly big, had large warm football hands (he had played second-string back) and a Kennedy mop of hair that hung over one eye like a sheepdog's above a wide smiling friendly mouth that always, rather incongruously, held a cigarette. His face seemed to Aaron incredibly *open*, and at first Aaron did not trust his impression, since few people who seem the way Paul seemed really turn out that way.

Aaron had hardly got out of the car before Paul stumped over, looking sleepy and old in the morning. "Glad to meet you. Didn't get a chance in Saginaw. Where you from? State?"

"University," said Aaron.

"Oh-oh." Paul grinned maliciously. "I see in the papers that Bump Elliot plans to field a team this year."

"And Duffy's worried?"

"He's not the type. Some of us old alumni are, though. You a football fan?"

"I can sort of take it or leave it. At Michigan it's easier to leave it."

Paul laughed. "Well, you had your Rose Bowl a little while back. You know these other guys?"

"I've seen—uh—Rod, isn't it? in Saginaw. Hello." Aaron shook hands with Rod, who nodded sociably and shook firmly, then sat down on the fender of his Buick, watching the mist in the fields across the road.

The other one had his head and arms lost under the hood of a green Triumph. Aaron could not see who it was and did not recognize the car.

"Hey." Paul banged a hand on the hood. "Stick your head up here and meet this Michigan boy."

Aaron recognized him when he looked up from between the open hood and the engine. He was dark-haired and wore a pair of prescription-lens sunglasses with wide brown frames. He looked at Aaron for a moment and said, "Hi. Steve Garrett. I saw you in Saginaw, but I don't—"

"Aaron Young."

"Sure. Welcome to our stellar crew." He looked at Aaron for another moment. "Excuse me for not shaking hands. Grease." He put his head down and then looked up again. "You know anything about sports cars?"

"No. What's the matter?"

"Just a split water hose and a little tapping sound I don't like." He stuck his head back into the engine. "The guy I bought this thing from in Flint last week assured me on his mother's honor it would buzz on and on like a sewing machine. It grieves me," he said seriously, "about that guy's mother and what she may be pulling on him."

Later Dooley came into the driveway in his red Volkswagen. Steve was out in the open by then, sitting on the closed hood of his car. "You and George'll be roommates," he said to Aaron. "I guess we might as well register and get our keys. Vanneman may have got lost."

The rooms were still occupied so they could not unload their gear. When Vanneman arrived they were checking over the maps Steve had given them, ready to move out. Vanneman crashed his Chevy into the driveway with a scattering of gravel, and climbed out with his surfer grin. "Am I late?"

"You're early," said Steve. "It isn't even quite lunchtime yet. Did you have trouble finding us?"

"I got on the wrong highway. So you're the boss," he said, looking around.

"That's right, fella. Brady has turned you over to me, and I am going to avenge him by working you to death."

"Well, I'm used to that." He noticed Rod and slapped him on the shoulder. "Hey, fella. You got your roommate back!"

"Boy, goddamn, I sure have . . ." said Rod fervently, looking at his shoes.

In bed, in the dark, Aaron decided that his crew seemed pretty good, as people went. Dooley was the kind who gave no false impressions—a few minutes of watching him move around, all bones and laughing that laugh, shuffling like a hairy ape, had marked him. Like Aaron's high school friends, he was simple and obvious: he was as he appeared.

Likewise Paul, who had convinced Aaron that he was indeed genuine. He said to you: *Here I am; you may not believe me, but here I really am.* And after wanting to believe for some time, you did so, glad to be able to believe.

Rod was a silent one, reticent, yet his handshake had been warm and Aaron thought he would like him.

Vanneman. Aaron did not think he was going to care much for Vanneman, with his peculiar New York/California blend of cool bluster and phoniness. Possibly he was a real clown and genuine, but these are rare, and Aaron did not as yet believe it.

And Steve—

In Saginaw, walking across the Holiday Inn terrace with a roll of maps under his arm to turn in at Erikson's room, Aaron had gone past an open door and heard the twanging of a guitar, a sound that always stopped him in his tracks, and he glanced in long enough to see a man sitting in a chair by the bed. He was clad in Levi's and a T-shirt, was barefoot, and wore a pair of brown horn-rimmed glasses with dark prescription sun lenses, although it was raining outside. Aaron had a quick favorable impression of him as he sat tight-lipped, eyes closed behind the glasses, flat-picking a blues tune Aaron had not heard before. Aaron had never played blues and he loved it, fascinated by the flat pick snapping across the strings and not missing any notes, and as he started on to turn in his maps the man glanced up for a moment and both of them nodded. He decided to come back.

But he stayed talking to Erikson too long, and when he passed on the way out the door was closed and the music had stopped; he could hear the shower running.

Lying in the night, hearing Dooley's snores like warthog grunts, he knew that he needed more friends: since the death in his family he had not tried hard to make any friends, could count on only Sam and Huston—his Texas Corporation, he wryly called them, though neither was from Texas—could count only them as close friends, and though they made up for much, he needed more than two friends, especially now without Susan, with the summer coming on and promising all sorts of things; he needed friends here, on this crew.

A breeze came through the window, carrying the high humming tire sound of a truck far down the highway, a sound he once, as a boy, had taken for that of a flying saucer, getting up and looking out his bedroom window at an August night, expecting something to land on the lawn, afraid and half hoping that it would. But it was only truck tires. The humming lasted a long time, and he heard it going away and away and thought of the journey that truck driver was making, wondering where the truck had come from and where it was going—and feeling suddenly certain it was bound all the way to Seattle, wishing then that he were on it, crouched behind boxes of freight on a pallet in the long dark trailer, moving through all the night on the humming tires and thinking: *Susie, baby, I'm coming. . . .*

3.   In the morning he was a crabby old man.

Dooley's alarm clock went off at an impossible hour. George had wound it up tight and set it on the other side of the room so he would be sure to get up to shut it off. Fortunately the bell was worn out and it gave off a wild clanking rattle like a miniature army tank.

Aaron buried himself under the covers, but George Dooley, true to himself, struggled out in his polka dot pajamas and got it just after it had run down. He came back and sat down on the side of the bed, and from beneath the covers Aaron heard him yawning and stretching and grumbling. Finally he twisted around and said sickly, "Hey. It's morning."

Aaron said, "Shut up or I'll kill you."

"Well. Good mornin' to *you* too, Sleeping Ugly."

He got up and stumbled into the bathroom.

Aaron peeked an eye at the window and noticed how dim everything was. He quietly announced every curse he knew and went back to sleep.

Dooley woke him up again when he came out.

It was cold outside, but by the time they finished breakfast in the same restaurant where they had eaten the night before, the sun was up bright and already beginning to dry away the dew, and felt good.

Rod and Phil showed up at breakfast, Rod folding himself into a booth behind Aaron's, and Vanneman yawning, bleary-eyed.

"God, what an hour."

"Morning," said Aaron. "You guys feel the way you look?"

"Coffee, coffee, coffee." Vanneman slumped into the booth with Rod and, yawning, grabbed a menu. He did not eat as if he was tired. Neither did the rest of them.

Steve and Paul failed to show up. Either they had eaten somewhere else or slept in: the privilege of the crew chief and his roommate. Steve had given out Triple A maps of Shia-wassee County and Consolidated section maps the day before. In these areas, from the edge of town out, there were generally from fifty to seventy-five poles marked in dots on each map, and the crew had four or five maps each—perhaps two days' work. As they finished maps and turned them in to Steve, he replaced them with fresh ones from the rolled and stapled batch he had gotten from Erikson, representing their total amount of work for the area.

The four of them came out of the restaurant at a few minutes after eight and stood by their cars looking at the morning.

"It'll be a nice day," said Aaron.

"I don't know, fella." Vanneman sniffed. "Smells like rain to me. . . ."

Rod had just got into his car. He opened the door again and stuck his head out.

"What did he say?"

Dooley laughed. "Says it's gonna *rain!*"

"You sure hope so, don't you, Phil, baby?"

"Hell, yeh—I could use a little more sleep."

Rod grinned sadly and started the engine. "Take it easy."

"See you," said Aaron, and made ready to pull out.

It did not rain that day or the next, and Aaron worked several miles out to the north of Owosso, discovering what the job could be like.

He began by checking several section maps side by side with the highway running like a snake down the middle of each map. He did not at all like working on the highway, where traffic loomed up whenever he slowed to pull onto the shoulder. He was checking poles on both sides, and this gave him the choice of doing one side and then turning around and coming back on the other—or crossing the highway twice every minute or so. He experimented with both, crossing the highway when traffic permitted it, using the other method when he had to. The latter cost him time and so was not preferable.

He had put the maps side by side and finished off the highway first to get it out of the way, and did so by Tuesday afternoon. The other poles were in lines running parallel to the roads, all nicely squared off and uncomplicated, easy to find and follow. Unfortunately, as soon as he got away from the highway, his real work began.

Experienced members of the survey crews (those who had signed on a few weeks earlier than Aaron) had worked out several procedures for checking poles in rural areas. The simplest and fastest was to work both sides of a road from the car, leaving the engine running while a man carried his map and clipboard out to the pole, checked off the date and whatever information might be there, and came back to drive on to the next. This worked when the poles ran parallel to the roads, were not too far back or separated by brush. Consolidated Power had, whenever possible, purchased its right-of-way as close to the road as it could, and generally a man, by working hard, could check enough poles in the morning to take a long lunch hour and a more subdued pace in the afternoon.

In much of the farm country, the right-of-way was set back at considerable distances from the road—going through the fields rather than along the shoulder and usual ditch there. This required, besides crossing the ditch, almost always having to climb a fence, then walk out some fifty yards to the pole—through corn or wheat or alfalfa—check the pole and return to the car.

In situations like this it was sometimes preferable to park the car at one end of a crossroad, enter the field and walk the whole line as far as the map went, staying in the fields and passing farmhouses from behind, after checking the pole and transformer that always serviced a house. Then the man could cross the road, if that side was on his map, and check the parallel line back to the car.

Aaron began a section just off the highway, where the line was some twenty yards out in furrowed fields, and no fencing along the road. He worked fast, bringing the car to a halt and hoofing it out across the field to the pole with his clipboard. The installation date and pole type were either stamped onto a brass ring nailed to the pole, or branded into the wood itself. The rings were usually easy to make out, but for most of the poles it was necessary to walk around and examine closely for traces of the brand, which might have worn away. If the date was not there, he had to estimate the installation date according to the nearest pole that did have a date.

At first most of Aaron's poles carried the brass rings and were still in remarkably good shape. As he worked away from the highway he got into increasingly rough land, with trees and brush between the roads and fields, and old wire fences that had to be climbed. Occasionally he was aware of being watched, as someone in a farmyard stopped to look at him vaulting the fences, trodding across the furrows and circling the poles. Usually, when he was seen to be checking the poles, he was again ignored, although occasionally someone would question him or engage him in a friendly harangue as to why and where a certain pole in the yard should be moved.

When the country got rougher, Aaron locked his car and left it on the shoulder, worked through head-high corn and walked two or three miles across the fields, from pole to pole with his clipboard under his arm, beneath the wires, upon which flocks of curious birds sat and watched him. The wires gave off a high singing sound that he had never been aware of before, and only now, away from all noise but the wind and the birds and his heavy shoes in the dirt, did he hear it plainly like whistling over his head.

The birds watched him, and he wondered how birds could sit up there on bare wires without being burned to a crisp. He knew little of how electricity actually works. Someone had told him it was because of their toes—that the toes of birds were armored or insulated in a way that protected them. Aaron did not think this sounded logical, and supposed instead that it was because the birds sat on the wires, free from grounding and thus safe. They would gather at the end of a field where he came in from the road, sitting in a noisy flock; and they would follow him down the line, changing positions on the wires to keep up with him.

Sometimes, far out in some field, away from roads or houses, he would call up to them or talk to himself or sing songs that came lonelier there than in a room with his guitar and friends to listen. It was a lonely job—he went all day and saw few people—and he felt strange and strangely satisfied to be there doing a crazy thing like checking poles that probably no one had ever done before this way, and wouldn't need to again—all alone with birds and corn or birds and beans or birds and wheat, where only farmers had been and they seldom alone or at least with a noisy tractor. He did not even think of carrying a portable radio, would not have considered taking one, and did not think why until later, although he could soon have figured it: he was doing a one-time thing; after this summer he would probably never do it again. The survey would be completed and maybe no one would ever do it again, in this state at least; he was out there in a place where he had never been much since his childhood, a city boy since then, and it was, quite simply, in spite of loneliness and the slightly ridiculous nature of the job, an experience.

He would hike three miles and emerge to find himself walking down some country gravel road to his car, wondering what he was doing, by God, *here*, and how he had got there. And with a slow look around at the impossible solitude and he the only live person for miles maybe, the question thrummed itself out to meaninglessness, because here he was— a few moments ago in a lecture at the university, or making out with Susan, and now *here*, and that was all. The feeling, the awareness of it, of himself alone in all this, and comfortable there, recurred to him again and again.

4.   One evening after dinner he took a completed map to Steve's room and saw that the door was open. He heard

the sound of guitars and looked in to see his crew chief in the repetition of a scene from the past.

Seated on a bed strewn with maps, a guitar case, clothes, an open suitcase, Steve banged a rhythmical folk-rock piece on his Martin guitar, and hummed with it. He was sitting without glasses, eyes closed, facing the space between the beds, oblivious of anything but the music. On the other bed, back against the headboard and knees up, Paul Maloney accompanied on a reddish-colored Gibson.

The music moved, and Aaron, unwilling to break in on it, stood just outside the doorway, listening. The guitars played with each other, splitting their sounds into the evening, and when the two had finished and paused, grinning, Aaron said, "You guys don't kid around at it, do you?"

Paul glanced up. "Howdy, Aaron. Come on in."

Steve turned his head, twisting around with the guitar on his knees to peer myopically at Aaron. "What say, Aaron? You like guitar?"

"Yeah, I do. I used to play some with my brother."

"Yeah?"

"Mostly folk style. I haven't done much for a year or so. You guys sound great. . . . Got a map for you."

Steve set the guitar down against the wall and grabbed his dark glasses. "Signed and dated; okay."

Aaron hesitated and Steve seemed to pause with him, as if for a moment each were debating some possible move. They did not quite look at each other. Paul lighted a fresh cigarette, watching them, and as Aaron turned toward the door Paul said it: "So you play guitar?"

Aaron stopped.

"Well—yes. I mean, I used to play some."

Steve, looking at the map in his hands, waited, waited, and seemed to decide. "Hey, you want to play something?" He said this quietly, paused, and turned resolutely to his suitcase.

"I have to fold these maps and put 'em away." He nodded at the guitar. "Go ahead if you want to."

Aaron looked at the Martin with its wide pick guard and chrome tuning pegs. It was a five-hundred-dollar instrument.

"Well—yeah, actually. Thanks."

He took the guitar up and sat on the end of Paul's bed, chording softly. He noticed again as he had a month ago, playing for Susan, that he had let the fingers of his left hand get soft; he no longer had the guitarist's calluses he had developed painfully while playing with Matt. Yet Steve's guitar fingered so lightly that he barely felt the strings.

"What'll it be?"

Paul nodded, billowing smoke. "You go ahead, whatever you like. I'll follow. You want a pick?"

"Uh—do you have any finger picks?"

"Sure." Paul's guitar case was on the floor beside him. He gave Aaron the three picks and watched him fit them on, glancing at Steve, who was busy folding up the scattered maps. No one said anything, and Aaron thought a moment and began an elaborate version of "John Henry," singing the verses and pausing for extended periods of soloing on Steve's guitar after each verse. It was an arrangement he had worked out long ago with Matt, and though he had not practiced it for some time, it came back to him easily and he had no trouble.

Paul grinned at the solos, following and blowing smoke, laughing once, and at the end he said happily, "Somebody else doesn't kid around, does he?"

Steve, sitting now amid the discarded maps in his T-shirt and clean white Levi's, dark glasses in place, shook his head. "I guess he does not."

Aaron did "South Wind," a song with a calypso beat that he had always liked, with a good solo in the middle, and then

Paul did a Judy Henske piece and Steve a blues tune while Paul backed him up.

Aaron watched them play. It was obvious that Paul loved to have fun with the guitar, varying the beat and throwing in occasional leads, happy as long as the music kept going, he was not particular where.

But Steve worked over his guitar as if he were praying to it, his eyes tightly closed behind the glasses, an intentional blind man. He seemed to be participating in—if not conducting—a religious ceremony, and his playing was impeccable. Only after the piece was finished did he relax, his breathing slightly audible in the silence, his chest slowly rising and falling beneath the T-shirt. He would purse his lips and make slight noises of approval, tuning the guitar a bit after each piece. Yet none of this struck Aaron as affectation: Steve seemed equally in rapture when Paul or Aaron sang to the guitars' backing. The act of what they were doing was enough for him, it was what he *did*, and after one piece he smiled a long relaxed sighing: "Yeahhh . . ."

"I guess," said Paul. "I guess so. You know what I think?"

Steve bent over the Martin. "Sure. Sure."

"I think we oughta go get some beer."

"Right."

So they chipped in and Paul went for it, creeping his Plymouth out the pocked gravel drive and whining off down the highway.

Steve and Aaron snapped on a little bed lamp as the twilight seeped out of the bottom of the sky, played some more, fell to improvising, and then Steve set his guitar down and lighted a cigarette. He leaned back against the wall on his bed with his legs crossed like an Indian. His skin had already darkened from the sun and, contrasted with the T-shirt and white Levi's and tennis shoes, it made him a rich mulatto in the dim light of the bed lamp. They could hear crickets sparking up outside.

Aaron fiddled with Paul's guitar, watching Steve drop ashes into an empty Coke bottle.

"You have a guitar?"

Aaron played several odd chords on the Gibson and stopped, looking at his fingertips. He nodded. "A twelve-string. A Harmony. I didn't know guitars from kazoos."

Steve smiled with his mouth, his eyes hidden. "I like twelve-strings," he said, ignoring the reference to the inexpensive make. "When I was a kid I went to summer camp up by Petoskey. Guy up there, one of the counselors, had a twelve-string. We used to sit around campfires and sing like boy scouts, but he played that goddamn guitar . . . he *played* it."

Aaron hammered-on a few chords and Steve laughed. "Yeah. That guy could make 'Jimmy Crack Corn' sound like 'How Long Blues.' It was the only thing about the place I really liked. First time up there, I went grumbling around, hating everybody—Holden Caulfield Goes to Camp—and this guy saw me making eyes at his guitar, and the bastard bribed me with it. I became Tom Rover and he taught me to play." Steve grinned.

"The way you play now," said Aaron, "the guy must have known what he was doing."

"He was sharp, all right. He was sharp."

"Did you know Paul then?"

Steve shook his head. "Nope. I don't know where he learned. Must have always known how, I guess. He's been around more than I have."

"Paul?"

"Sure. Before he ever got to Michigan State he did a hitch in the Army. He's been all over California. Been to Mexico. Doesn't like the East; he tried that too. I met him—what? four years ago?—when I was at State for a year before switching to Ann Arbor. He was about ready to drop out. I think this summer will be the longest time he's stayed in one place since I've known him."

"I like Paul," said Aaron.

Steve's face went sober and he said with an exaggerated conviction, "Paul Maloney is the greatest guy in the world. There's nobody else like him."

It sounded almost like a catechism, and Aaron was puzzling over it when they heard the Plymouth grinding the stone drive. Steve dropped his cigarette into the bottle and watched it fill up with smoke as if a genie were about to appear.

"That'll be the water boy," he said.

Paul had two six-packs of Hamm's. They pulled the rings on three aluminum cans and Steve and Aaron drank a beer apiece while Paul warmed up his guitar again, singing "Codeine" in a wordless wail around his cigarette, pronouncing the one word and calling it "code-īne" like Buffy Sainte-Marie.

They pounded strings and sang in beery voices until midnight, when the manager asked them to stop.

5.   The next day Aaron went by before dinner. Steve was shaving, and Aaron and Paul did a couple of tunes, Paul taking off on an English madrigal and then a blues piece Aaron could only chord with.

Finally Aaron looked at his watch. "I better get George; he's probably starved by now."

"Hey, listen—" Steve had come out of the bathroom and was digging in his suitcase. "You doing anything later?"

"I don't know. I guess not."

"We're gonna hit the bars again and see what we can find. Want to come?"

Aaron hesitated. "Sure. I'll have to come back here first. I'm driving, and Dooley—"

"Come on over after dinner. We'll be screwing around with the guitars." Steve pulled a sweater over his head. "Then we'll go out and booze it a little. See if George wants to go."

"Okay; sounds good. See you later."

He met Dooley around the corner, coming after him.

"You want to hit the bars tonight with Steve and Paul?"

"Well, not really. This is my favorite TV night," said George Dooley.

Owosso is a somnolent town at night, as it is in the daytime. Most of the bars are just bars; when they finally hit a place from a previous night with a pool table and a jukebox and enough people to get up a respectable noise level, they decided to settle in.

"This place was dead as hell the other night," said Paul. "The people must circulate around in shifts."

"It's dead as hell *tonight*, if you ask me." Steve shrugged. "Oh, well. There's booze."

They got a table and ordered beer, and Paul put his quarter in the coin slot of the pool table, where a couple of kids in Levi's were playing. The bar was a dark, odorous place and most of the people were either young and tough looking or old and squeezed down into complacency or desperation; those sat in corners and drank liquor as a business, watching nothing out of rimmed eyes and creased faces like used paper bags.

Aaron, depressed by the look of it, went over and fed two quarters into the jukebox, tapping out all the songs he could find that he halfway liked. The beer was there when he came back, with Dean Martin starting up on "Bummin' Around."

"I got it," said Steve, when Aaron reached for his wallet.

"Okay. Next one's mine."

"What a town." Paul grinned. "I got to play me some pool so I can stop thinking about it. Play, Aaron?"

Aaron shook his head, drinking. "I'm lousy. You guys play so I can see how good you are, and if I think I can beat you I'll try it."

"I'm very good," said Paul. "Not that you could tell from watching me play Stevie. Man needs real competition to look his best."

"You got to watch Maloney. He's a goddamn hustler. He'd cheat his own mother out of her drawers."

"Damn right."

"Now, I realize it may *look* like he's outmatched when he plays me, but—"

"That's going to cost you, fella."

Steve drank his beer. "What's this *fella* jazz? You been sleeping with Vanneman?"

"No, fella, I just want you to understand, fella, what you're in for, fella."

"Yeah? Well, come show me; there's our game."

The other two had quit and now Steve and Paul racked the balls and broke, verbalizing at each other about the havoc each was about to create.

Aaron drank beer and watched them. This evening, playing the guitars, he had felt easy and good, but now this place and its people wore on him and he felt vaguely disgruntled. He decided that maybe he would get drunk.

He watched Steve leaning over the table in his tan sweater, with his long carelessly combed hair and regular horn-rimmed glasses. Steve's face, except for the glasses, reminded him of someone but he did not know who, and this added to the irritation. He ordered a pitcher of beer and began to drink seriously, watching the pool table. Paul was circling it warily, looking for the best shot.

He drank a great deal of beer in the next two hours, Steve

even more so in an effort to catch up, and Paul least of all. Aaron was seeing their faces through a rippling film between jaunts to the men's room, where he would grin at himself in the mirror as he washed his hands. He knew that he was drunk and had best control himself and say nothing. But he felt that he *was* in complete control of himself, and somewhere behind his eyes a case was building up with brilliant logic.

They had started to talk about the war and Aaron had tried to change the subject. He had no opinion on the war, and with the beer he had drunk it was not a pleasant subject for him. Steve had kept talking and a kind of exasperation went through Aaron until he knocked over a glass of beer and told Steve for God's sake to shut up. Then he went to the john and was sick, and when he got back Paul was talking and Steve was drinking harder than before, and the spilled beer had been mopped up. Aaron started drinking again, but he had not really relaxed.

Now they were talking about women. Steve told about the time he had been awakened in a motel in Flint at three in the morning by the telephone ringing, how when he answered a voice had said, "Would you like a taste of coffee?" and how that had led to the best lay he'd ever had, even if it did cost him twenty dollars. He held his beer up to the light and sighted through it. "I ask you, gentlemen: what comes after sixty-nine? Listerine!"

He laughed and Paul laughed, and Aaron looked at both of them and almost remembered something. He was still angry at Steve, angry at Paul for laughing with him, and as Steve kept on and kept on Aaron began to build his case—not on a basis of anything he actually believed any more, but merely to spite them.

Steve propounded that what a man wanted, by God, was a woman who had been around and was not wet behind the ears but in better places and best of all if she was about thirty years old because that was the best sexual age for a woman anyway and what were they sitting around here jawing about it for when they ought to be out looking for it?

"We work tomorrow," said Paul, only a little foggily. "Try to hold off till Friday."

"I'm the boss. I can damn well do what I want, and if I want to get laid—"

"Wait a minute," said Aaron.

They both looked at him and he paused to drink manfully and let the suspense build while he made ready to throw off the cuff his logical and carefully constructed irritant.

But when he set his glass down he had started to cry. This surprised everyone, infuriated Aaron and ruined his revenge.

"What's the matter with you?" Steve leaned across the table to see if those were real tears. "What are you crying about?"

"I'm not crying. Listen—"

"You are too."

"Listen to me—"

"Why are you crying?" said Steve.

"Goddammit, I'm *not!*" Aaron wiped his eyes. "Now about this crap about experienced women and how they're better and all that—they aren't better at all, and you want to know why?"

Steve only looked at him, and it was Paul who mumbled, "Why?"

"It's because you can't have an ideal form of love with a woman like that."

"Gaaa . . ." Steve took a drink and started laughing into his glass.

"It's true; it's simple." His eyes were drying now but his argument had left him, his cool logic was gone. He had not intended to make Steve laugh.

"They've been around; okay. They know all the moves; all

right—but that's only just one little small part of what it's all about. Don't you know that?"

"Nope." Steve was grinning. Paul looked interested. And he no longer thought of making Steve angry. All he wanted to do was erase the smile from his face. It was not funny at all.

"I've got a girl," he said, caution gone, logic gone, "her name is Susan, and I'll be honest with you and tell you I've never touched her—"

"Fool," said Steve.

"—and I'm a little sorry about that, of course, but there's more than just that. You see," he said very patiently, "I think I'm in love with her, that crazy practical little girl, and when you're in love with someone—really in love with someone like that, like I am with her—then what you want—let me see if I can say this right—what you want with someone like that is something that grows out of the relationship, all unique and everything, something all unique with you and her and each other, you see. Not just sex—a goddamn *dog* can have sex—but what you want—I don't know how to say it—"

He drank his beer.

"—it's something that the two of you have created out of each other and for each other; it's what makes you part of each other and it's something that really should be unique with you. I mean, it seems like, you don't want this new morality crap, somebody who's already had this seventeen times, and you don't really want to have had it either—because then it's less unique, it's diminished just that much. I mean, it seems like—"

They watched him pour beer from the pitcher into his glass with one hand, spilling it over the top, wiping his eyes again with the other.

"You're crazy," said Steve.

"Steve," said Paul quietly.

"You're out of your mind. If everybody held out for that they'd have to be a goddamn virgin most of their lives."

"Steve—"

"That's what he's saying, isn't it? For everybody to be a goddamn virgin—"

"No," said Aaron, "you don't understand. We're talking theories; you were talking in theory—"

"Theory, hell."

"Listen, I'm just talking about the best there is. Listen, my parents—"

"Screw your parents."

"Take it easy," said Paul. "Let's all take it easy, now."

"Then go ahead, damn your laziv—lash—damn your black heart, be a goddamn stud; see how happy it makes you."

"I'll *be* happy."

"And I might as well tell you," said Aaron, sipping his foam-topped beer and not noticing the spilled wetness that dripped from the glass, "I might as well tell you that I'm holding out for what I know, and if you guys want to go screwing around on this job it's your business, but I'm not going to be along—"

"So who asked you, fella?" said Steve with beery aloofness.

There was a long silence as they looked at each other, and Paul coaxed them, "Easy, easy; we're all pretty loaded. It's getting late, Steve, boy."

"Because I'm committed," said Aaron with exaggerated simplicity. "My parents had—they had the best of it, and I don't see why I should settle for less, even if you—if Susan—I'm nuts about her. I'm committed—"

"So *be* committed to her already!" Steve grinned drunkenly. "Is she committed to *you*, is the sixty-four-thousand-dollar question. What's she doing right now, tonight, old buddy, defender of virgins?"

"I don't have to worry about Susan."

"Well, fine. As long as you keep believing that, you're all right."

"Aren't you?"

Paul finally got them up and out into the air. The night was cool and they stumbled across the rutted gravel of the parking lot to Paul's car, with Aaron and Steve going on at each other and Paul soothing them.

"You gonna be a priest?" Steve was saying. "A saint maybe? Hold it all in your hand and yell 'Unclean!' at every babe who smiles at you? You're just nuts. A man can't live that way, and what's more, he's not supposed to. I want to tell you—"

"You *remind* me of somebody," said Aaron, as thoughtfully as possible under the circumstances. "I wish I could figure out who it was. All I know is it was some sonofabitch talked just like you; some damned hedonist—"

"You better believe it." Steve halted at the car and stood with the wind blowing his hair, wagging a forefinger at Aaron. "You had just better believe that, old buddy. Like the hippies say: 'If it moves, fondle it.' "

"That's a lot of crap—"

"I want to tell you something, kiddo—"

"Steve, for God's sake get in the car." Paul was holding the door open from the inside, where he sat behind the wheel. "You're gonna freeze us all."

"I want to tell you something—"

"Don't wave that finger in my face, or I'll bite it off."

"The *car*, fellas?"

"You're going to go around holding yourself in, toeing the old line like a Sunday school kid, until one of these days, sooner or later—sooner if you're luckier than you probably deserve—it'll hit you, just like that, that your goddamn *life* is passing by while you stand and watch it with your finger up your butt."

Paul said, "Steve, God damn you—"

"All *right!* —That's going to be one of the saddest days in your life," he said, giving Aaron a little poke in the chest. "The day you find out there isn't that much difference between what you're holding out for and what you can get. Maybe you'll still have time. 'If it moves, fondle it.' "

Steve crawled into the back seat of the car and immediately fell asleep. Paul had the engine running. Aaron got in and they pulled out into the street and drove in silence for five minutes.

"He's a regular counselor, isn't he?"

"You should talk."

Aaron looked at him and rolled the window partway down. "Do you believe all that?"

"All what?"

"All—*that*," said Paul.

Aaron wavered a moment and chose not to get angry. "I don't know. I wanted to get back at him. I don't know whether I believe it or not. Part of me does and part of me doesn't. I was raised to believe it. And I have really seen it."

Paul nodded. "So have I. But he hasn't. You picked the wrong man to lecture on chastity."

"Not *chastity*—"

"All right. Steve is the wrong man."

Aaron breathed deeply in the stream of air. "I shot off my mouth."

"Yep. I doubt that any of us will remember in the morning, though. Steve is married, Aaron."

Aaron looked at Paul for a long moment. "I didn't know that."

"You don't know Steve. Or me, for that matter. We met last week."

Aaron shook his head, cleared somewhat by the cold air. "Something happened to me once when I was a kid. . . ." He stopped. "Funny what a little beer will do, isn't it? I feel like I've known both of you for years. And Dooley. It's weird."

They stopped at a red light and looked at each other under the street lamps. On the radio they heard a saxophone playing softly, "Shenandoah."

"People aren't all that different. We've all met each other a few times before. Except I'm beginning to wonder if I've really met you. . . ."

"How much difference does it take? To make a difference? When I was a kid—" Aaron shook his head again as the car started up. "So Steve is married."

"Separated. She lives in Detroit; Steve's from there."

"How come the breakup?"

"He had a job in his father's business for a year after high school. Married her. Got accepted by State and they moved to East Lansing—that's where I met them."

"I know."

"Then he decided he wanted to be a lawyer. He applied at the University and they moved to Ann Arbor. She was working in an office. Got bored; people can get bored anywhere. Steve started chasing around; so did she. They got fed up."

"That's rotten."

"It happens."

"Sometimes I wonder if it ever doesn't happen."

"That's because you're lucky. I think. Or maybe not. Anyway, it happened to Steve's parents. They started shipping him around to camps and places; you can figure how that works."

"Yes."

When they stopped in the driveway Paul said, "I can get him in. Go on to bed."

"All right. See you tomorrow, Paul."

"It'll be a hell of a morning, but I'm going to get the bastard up. Serve him right."

Dooley was snoring and Aaron undressed in the dark, sitting wobbly on the side of the bed. He was thinking of some children, trying to piece together a memory that barely eluded him.

6. Early in the morning he lay thinking that there is a time when all things come into the beginnings of their final forms, the beautiful and the harsh blending before your awe and causing a part of your small death that follows after, as you run for the beautiful, flee the harsh and know that both are there and real and are you.

Aaron Young, eight years old, sat on the lawn in front of his house, singing to himself and playing with a number of metal disk-shaped objects. Overhead, the sun burned down on Indianapolis, 1953, spread out beneath it in summer acceptance of heat and burning. A warm wave of air moved over the brown-tinged green of the lawn. The day was hot; the sun was hot.

But Aaron sat in the grass in the shade of a tree, and did not notice the heat. He often did not notice unpleasant things, and now he was happy, singing his song and playing with his toys.

The toys, the metal disks, were lids from peanut butter jars: not the screw-off kind, but those you must pry off, and so were smooth and shiny on the undersides, without grooves, and three of them having a single clear dent near the center from the pressure of the opener.

Three days ago Aaron had been taken by his father and mother to see *Peter Pan* at the Garfield Theater, four blocks

away on the corner, and Aaron had come away awed at the
story and the music and the people who were in it. It was a
cartoon feature, yet he had never seen anything like it before,
nothing so real to him, ever. It was the best of all movies,
better than Roy Rogers or Flash Gordon—was not to be compared with anything else. He had made it his world, and it
outdid all the others he had had.

There were four peanut butter lids. He had known since
having only one that they were nice, but not until he came
out of the theater with tears in his eyes from having to leave
did he realize what he really had.

For on the top of the peanut butter lid, standing in a
white circle of light, green costume ablaze with fresh fire,
stood the figure of Peter Pan himself. And Aaron had not
known, had not known until then what it really was. Before,
a tin lid with the picture of a boy. Now . . . an object of
love, an artwork of incalculable value—and more, when he
looked at the picture and remembered what that green-clad
figure had done, cavorting over ship deck, sailing the night
sky without wings, arms outstretched in substitute, the picture
on the lid transformed from junk to sacrament, from tin to
gold. He took that picture to bed with him now instead of
Joe the panda bear.

The next day his mother went to the store, and at her son's
respectful petition ("the one with Captain Hook on it,
please") bought another jar of peanut butter. And he pried
that lid off without denting it, without so much as bending
the edge or pressuring the center, where stood the child's
villain incarnate, compatible evil, in his scarlet coat and
black hat, his needle-point sword and that fascinating pro-
tuberance where once an arm had been, but never really. He
must always have had that hook.

In the park that same day he came across a hot trail and

followed it. One of his acquaintances had *two* of the priceless items. As it turned out, both were the same, but Aaron acquired them anyway, both of them, by trading off five airplane cards, five of the fabulous "Wings." It was worth the small loss for the greater gain.

The two pictures were of Tinker Bell, the winged fairy who trailed a golden dust behind her. Aaron knew what that dust could do.

Sitting in the grass that summer day in 1953 in the burning city of Indianapolis, Aaron looked at his four disks and sang to himself and was happy.

And down the block came a sound of voices carried on the heavy wind, and behind the voices three boys, loafing along as only boys can loaf. Aaron recognized them: it was Jim and Brian and, a little step ahead of them, talking, Roger. They *ambled*, they swaggered like sailors, the one stirring up air with his soft voice and the others, as always, listening. Such was the basis of their friendship. Roger talked, Jim and Brian listened and made responses. A piper with his flock of two.

All the boys were older than Aaron, Jim and Brian by two years, Roger by three. Here too was a basis of relationship, a rank and file more solidly founded, more adamant, than that of any army, an inflexible order based on age that exists universal in the child's world and goes unquestioned, save occasionally by the youngest, whose silent wonder at the intricacies of justice is of no consequence at all.

So Aaron knew the three, was acquainted with them, but they were not his friends. There had been a time when Brian and Jim were his friends, before Roger came along to lure them away with whispered promises of things that lay ahead, away in years, as yet beyond the thoughts of such as Aaron. But Jim and Brian understood and went away from him, away with Roger toward that far-near place from which they would not return. Aaron stood on the shore, uninvited, and watched them go away to sea, in search of voices he had yet to hear.

The boys saw Aaron, and Roger as always ignored him. But Jim, forgetting, smiled, and Brian waved on his own, and as he waved back over that distance, the distance receded for an instant, and Brian seized the moment and broke away, and his white tennis shoes crushed grass and ants and, so doing, moved him up the shore, up the little hill into Aaron's front yard, into Aaron's world. Jim, perplexed, turned and leaned after Brian, breaking the spider web, and followed, leaving Roger in midsentence, his mouth open as he watched his pilgrims slack away from the sidewalk trail.

"Hiya, Ar."

"Whatya say, Aaron?"

Aaron smiled and said quietly, "Hi."

"We been catching bees." Brian held up the jar that Aaron had noticed half a block ago, but did not want to notice. Once he had caught bees with Brian and Jim. But not for a long time now.

He looked at the jar and heard the quiet power hum that came from it, and his smile widened in spite of himself.

"Pretty good bunch."

"Not like mine," said Jim, holding up his own jar. "I got *more*. But you should see Roger's!"

Aaron's smile lost whatever had caused it to be on his face, and it faded and was gone. He looked at the grass. "Does Roger catch bees?"

"Sure he does," said Jim. "Why wouldn't he?"

"I just—wondered."

"Dumb question." Jim turned to look at Roger, who was standing on the sidewalk watching them. "Hey, come here. Show Aaron your bees."

Roger stood a moment, not used to being told, not liking it, and then he grinned and came up to stand beside the others, looking down at Aaron. "Hello, Aarie. How's life among the children?"

"Hi, Roger."

Roger held up his jar of bees and said, more to himself than to them, "Kind of dumb, you know. Catching bees. But what the heck. . . . What you got there, Aarie?"

Aaron tried to make himself small, but he already felt as small as he would ever feel, and there was no place in the world to go. The grass was not long enough for him.

"What've you got?"

"Nothing—"

But Roger was down on his haunches, reaching, and Aaron could not refuse the grasp of an older boy. He could only submit, wishing he had stayed in the house today.

"Can lids," said Roger. "No, hey. Peter Pan!"

"Oh, I saw that," said Brian. "Gee, that's a good show. I read the book too. You get those off peanut butter jars, Ar?"

Aaron nodded, thankful for Brian.

"Hey, Captain Hook. What ho!" And Roger was slicing huge swaths in the air with his cutlass. He ran-through Jim in an embarrassing place, and Jim laughed. Jim always laughed.

"That's a good show," said Brian.

"Aaaa . . . Fairy tales. You like fairy tales, Bri?"

"It's—a good show."

"Do *you* like fairy tales, Aarie? Oh, *I* do. I just *love* fairy tales. Don't you, Jimbo?"

Jim laughed. Aaron felt that the day had suddenly grown much hotter than he had ever thought it could be. He wanted to take his pictures and go into the house. But Roger had them.

"Now, Tinker Bell," said Roger. "There's one fairy I don't mind. She's okay."

"Let's see," said Jim, and then, under Roger's eye: "Yeahhh."

Aaron looked at the grass and wished they would go away and leave him alone.

"Isn't she, Aarie?" Roger was smiling at him, but Aaron did not see it. "Isn't she a cute one, Aarie?" And then, "What's the matter, Aarie? You don't *believe* in this stuff, do you?"

"Hey, come on, Rog." This was Brian, nervously.

"I'm just kiddin' around. Aarie doesn't mind if I just kid around with him, do you, Aarie?"

Aaron looked at the grass. "Come on," said Brian.

"I wonder if these things would sail. I bet I could send one of these things clear across the street, into that vacant lot. What do you think?"

"No, you don't," said Brian. "Now, lay off him, Roger. These are Aaron's."

"Take it easy; I won't hurt his fairies. Hey, fairies . . ." Roger looked at the picture of Tinker Bell and smiled broadly. "These fairies don't even exist," he said. "Aarie, these things don't even exist."

"I've heard of fairies," said Jim.

"Yeah," said Roger, looking at him, perhaps not really knowing, impressing Jim, irritated at Brian, contemptuous of Aaron. "I said *these* fairies don't exist. But fairies do. My brother goes to the university in Bloomington. He knows a couple of fairies there. You guys know what fairies really are?"

And Roger told them what fairies really are.

He laughed and Jim laughed in response, nervously, and Brian did not laugh at all, with Aaron just sitting there looking down at the grass. Slowly his eyes had filled with tears, and now they coursed in big drops down his face.

Roger looked at Aaron. "Hey, what's the matter, Aarie?

Didn't you know that? I bet he didn't even know it," he said
to Jim. "I bet he thought fairies really were like this one."

"Roger." Something had happened to Brian; all of them,
even Aaron, noticed it. He was younger than Roger, but he
was also bigger and for some reason his discomfort had
grown acute. The line had been crossed; something in him
responded, making him act. "Give Aaron his pictures and let's
go. Come *on*, Roger—" and he took Roger's arm and was not
gentle.

Roger looked at him for a moment, and then let his smile
save his face, as he always did.

"Okay. Don't get tough." He gave Aaron the lids and without turning said to Jim, "Come on," and picking up his jar,
stepped down to the sidewalk. Jim followed.

The two of them, one tall, the other not so tall, waited on
the sidewalk for Brian. "Hey, come on," said Jim.

Brian ignored him. Instead he put a hand on Aaron's
shoulder and said, "Hey. Hey, don't cry. Roger was just
playing, he was just—kidding. He didn't mean any of that, Ar.
Really, it isn't true."

"Let's go," said Roger.

And even Brian could not ignore Roger. Roger offered
him too much to ignore. Roger offered too much that Brian
hungered for, that Brian needed.

So the boys walked on away, each of them knowing, perhaps, what had happened, but not speaking of it, for boys do
not speak of such things.

And Aaron, beginning his great confrontation, sat quietly
in the grass in Indianapolis, 1953. At the very beginning, he
had no thought for what lay ahead of him, years away in
time, the ghosts and voices that would confront him. He
knew only that something had started, something was always
to be lost, as he unscrewed the lid of the jar Brian had left
there, to watch bees blow away on the warm wind, before

standing up and going into the house to press his own lids back onto two other jars, and throw the rest away. Outside, the sun burned the grass and the wind blew for a long time.

7.   The three of them were foggy in the morning, but they all got up. Steve did not seem to remember what they had argued about.

"I—you know, it's all *there*, but I can't—I must really have put a load on. Something about women, wasn't it? That was *you* that was with us?"

"It was me," said Aaron. He did not have a headache, but carried the slight nausea that resulted when he drank too much.

"I wish I could remember."

"Don't waste your time," said Paul. "The talk wasn't worth the price of the beer that brought it out."

"It'll come back to me."

So it became a habit, playing the guitars in the evening or going out to drink in Owosso's dark taverns, where they kept peace after the first time and argued in friendlier tones. Aaron worked his second week in the heavily overgrown country north of Owosso. Steve had given him a township map of smaller scale, encompassing as much area yet to be covered as several of the section maps. He spent each day writhing under electric fences, which seemed to abound in that part of the state, ducking clouds of emerging mosquitoes from the warming and humid weather. He had not received an answer yet to his letter, and he kept thinking about his impassioned speech, wondering what had caused it. Irritation with Steve, too much beer, but what else?

Living in Ann Arbor and seeing Susan every day, acting more than thinking, it had been easy to ignore his twinge of—

whatever it was: jealousy? He was not jealous of Susan. Susan was not promiscuous by any stretch of the imagination, but she was realistic. She had told him how involved she had been—probably she had been in love—and she had been burned the way everyone is burned sooner or later. Should it bother him, he thought, that he had not been burned, that he came from parents who never had been burned? It seemed to him that he was beginning to fluctuate between his sensibilities and his reason—the best, which he had seen, and the lesser, which he knew was more realistic. Or perhaps, he thought, there was something else, though he could not see what it might be.

And then something happened and he wrote to Susan:

Hello again. We're almost finished in Owosso, where we've been working for two weeks. The country is rough as hell and I'm getting many, many muscles—the better to squeeze you with, my dear. Why haven't you written to me, Susie? Do you realize I haven't seen you or heard from you for a whole month? I'm lonely and I miss you. Please write unless for some reason you don't want to.

A very, very strange thing has happened to me, and the only thing I know to say about it and be honest is that it scared me badly. That sounds funny but it isn't. I was driving in from work yesterday at a little after five, going fast to get in and finish dinner so I could have time to do some reading. We got paid for the last two weeks yesterday morning and for some stupid reason I cashed all the checks—four of them, for two weeks' pay and expenses—and I had two hundred and fifty dollars in my billfold. I was about six miles out from town with the sun behind me to the right and the day all gold and yellow, and feeling pretty good and everything, and I saw a man and a girl and a little baby, by the side of the road, hitchhiking. I don't usually pick anybody up because I'm chicken, to be honest, but these people were standing there, and the guy had the baby on his shoulders with the feet hanging down, and for some reason I stopped and picked them up.

They were a pretty sorry-looking family. The guy had on old

dirty Levi's and an old shirt with the tails hanging out, and hadn't shaved for a couple of days. The girl looked like a farm girl, in a shapeless dress; her face was a lot older than it should have been, sad eyes and a mouth that hadn't smiled for a long time. Both of them were young but looked older that way, and the kid was just a kid of two or three, babbling and swinging his feet and dirty and wearing little old dungarees and dirty shoes.

The girl took the kid and got in the back and the guy climbed in front. They didn't say thanks or anything, and I asked them where they were going.

"Inta town," said the guy, looking out the window. That's about the only thing he said all the way in, except once when I tried to be sociable and said, "Weather's really turning nice," and he said, "Yah." The girl kept her mouth shut, but the baby gibbered and talked baby talk; he had the best personality of all of them.

We were still a couple of miles out and had been driving along in silence except for the baby when I got this funny feeling in the back of my neck. It sounds crazy, Sue, and I have no idea what caused it, but I've never liked to give rides to people because a lot of people have been murdered that way, and if *that* sounds corny, it's still true. So I got this feeling like the girl was *looking* at me from the back seat, and I glanced at the rear-view mirror and of course she wasn't (nor the kid) but I couldn't get rid of this feeling. Then for the first time I remembered I was carrying all that money and here was this big silent guy beside me, and I thought what a perfect setup it would be for a guy and girl to take a kid along when they hitched rides and then rob whoever picked them up and maybe even kill him or something. I know, I know, Bonnie and Clyde stuff, but still . . . Here was the guy in the front seat and the girl in back and me loaded with cash—and I really got scared, Susie, I mean I started to sweat.

You don't understand—I haven't made it clear enough. I wasn't just *uneasy* or *apprehensive*, I was terrified. Something a lot deeper in me, apparently, than the idea of being robbed started to come out. I started thinking about how they would do it, how the guy would turn and shove a gun into my ribs, or the girl would put one at the back of my neck, and they'd have me turn off on a side road and just shoot me and leave me in a field or a ditch and take the car and everything and probably never be caught—and it was really that I started to realize how afraid I am of dying—and it got to where I *knew* they were going to do it, and all I could do was wait for the move.

We got into Owosso and stopped at a light and the guy said, "We'll get out here," and they got out without another word and walked off. The last I saw of them they were looking in a store window and the guy had the baby on his shoulders again and the girl was pointing at something in the window.

And that's all. I'm ashamed as hell, but I can't get over it, I've felt weird ever since—couldn't read last night and thought about it all day today. It's never happened to me that way before. I must be getting old.

If you get a chance to take time off from whatever you're doing and write me a letter, I'd like to hear from you. Tomorrow evening I head back for the weekend. Be good.

AARON

1.   Aaron Young met Ann Campbell in a restaurant across the highway from the motel where his crew was staying, a mile out of Fenton. Ann was a waitress in the restaurant. It was not because of Steve that Aaron met her, but what happened shortly afterward was at least partly due to Steve, and what eventually happened and failed to happen was caused by a number of things, none of them tangible.

If Aaron had consciously evaluated his conflicting opinions of Steve Garrett at the time they turned Owosso over to a cleanup crew and moved on to Fenton, he might have decided that Steve came awfully close without quite making it. The *it* consisted of various images of what Aaron liked in his friends, combinations of intelligence, wit and something else—perhaps labeled *humanness*—which Aaron in his harshness of judgment, in his caution, allowed to move him to genuine friendship. Sam Lowry had it in abundance; Huston Reeve had enough of it. Paul had it. Rod was a question mark. Vanneman probably did not, nor Dooley. And it looked as though Steve did not quite have it either (this was a slight spinning of Aaron's original conception of Steve) and it was too bad. It was, in its way, quite sad, for Steve had all the *other* attributes: looks, which were close enough to perfect so the difference made no difference; talent, with which his guitar playing showed him well endowed; and personality, the thing that made him one of the best crew chiefs on the survey. Yet the quirk that Dooley had noticed was a real one, and it forced Aaron to shy back. Steve was not an open case like Paul; Steve was not the type of person you could be sure of—was not the type that Aaron could quite bring himself to trust. Because Steve, like that boy Roger, was a man who broke dreams—there was always one somewhere. Dreams were not a part of their lives, and because of that they did not like to see them in the lives of others. There was always a Steve or a Roger somewhere.

That Steve liked Aaron was obvious; while Paul was Steve's closest friend, Aaron made it a threesome that was together more evenings than it was apart. And Steve outwardly seemed to respect Aaron's somewhat melodramatic stand: he chased his women when Aaron was not around.

So there was a friendliness but not real friendship. Aaron had brought his guitar along this time, intending to sit up late over beer in Steve and Paul's room, improvising with them as he once had done with Matt. He did not know yet that what he had had with his brother was gone and would never be replaced by anyone. His unconscious attempt at building something was never to develop—for Steve was not Matt: Steve built his own image, lived each day as if it were his last, filled his life with things, with a *style*, which looked good but was to Aaron a second-rate satisfaction, a palliative of the disillusioned. Yet he watched Steve hungrily, sometimes unsure of his own feelings.

He met Ann on the first evening in Fenton, having waited the usual hour for Dooley and then crossed the highway on foot to the restaurant. Aaron had become increasingly irritated with George as a roommate, and had thought of asking Steve for a switch. But he decided against it; everyone else in the crew was satisfied and there was no use causing trouble. Instead he suffered nobly, with a twinge of self-pity, and lately had had other things on his mind.

The weekend had been a frustrating one. There was no letter from Susan. Sam worked late Friday night and Huston was out of town and his father and uncle and aunt were visiting. Aaron moped around, out of the mood for reading and with nothing on television, and went to bed rather than wait up for anyone. He saw his family next day, but by the time he got over to Sam's apartment, on the lower floor of the old house, Sam was getting ready for a date. They talked awhile and Aaron came back home and spent the evening watching television with his family. Sunday was another ineffectual day. He went to church with his family and saw some of his old friends—none of whom he really knew any longer—had dinner at home and spent the rest of the day with Sam.

Sam Lowry worked afternoons until midnight as a janitor, cleaning in an office building uptown. He was twenty-five years old and divorced, had gone to college in Indiana, and now lived alone in his part of the old house, occasionally bringing in some girl or other. For three years he had been writing a mammoth "poetic novel" that he claimed would set the literary world on its ear. Composed of both poetry and prose, it featured a picaresque hero caught in a time and space warp, who bounced around the world and history, and an absurdist black humor plot that had no real beginning and went on and on as he added to it. He would read interminable sections aloud to Aaron and Huston, carrying parts of it around in old typing-paper boxes and keeping the original in a forty-pound steel box he had got somewhere. Parts of the manuscript were good; meanwhile he had sold a half dozen stories to the pulp magazines.

Aaron and Sam had met at a poetry reading at the junior college, became immediate friends, and took turns counseling each other, Aaron in that role when Sam had got his divorce during that bad summer a year ago, and Sam in it now that Aaron was restless and unhappy on a fine Sunday afternoon.

"Why so sad, chum?"

They were sitting on the floor in Sam's living room, in front of the record player, drinking cold beer and listening to folk music.

"I don't know. Several things, I guess. Susan—I haven't had a letter from her in a month."

"Maybe she's tied up with her job."

Aaron shook his head. "I wouldn't think so. She told me she wasn't much of a writer, but—I'm afraid she may have found other interests."

"Well, it happens."

"Yes, but—not with her. It shouldn't happen with her, Sam."

"Come on. It can happen with anyone."

"Thanks for the encouragement."

"Well, she probably hasn't had time or hasn't gotten around to writing yet. She doesn't know you're pining for her."

Aaron nodded. "Yes. Maybe so. That's probably it. It isn't just her, there are a couple of other— That hitchhiking thing and—"

"Don't make that something it wasn't."

"I guess." He thought a moment. "But, Sam—" He looked up at the poster art and the old furniture. "Sam, I've got a lot invested in that girl."

Sam said, "I know you have."

So in the little restaurant outside Fenton, Aaron slid into a booth across from Dooley and did not say much, after a poor weekend and a hard day. He had little to say to Dooley anyway and to say anything at all to him often started one of George's monologues on electrical engineering or plumbing. Aaron was tired of those.

The girl who served them was friendly and energetic, a striking girl with long blond hair and a wide mouth. They were out of the steak Aaron wanted, and she bantered with him about a substitute, standing with one hand on her hip, smiling. Aaron brightened and when the girl left he said quietly, "Wow."

"Hm?" said Dooley.

The girl came back, having run out of customers. "You're not from around here, are you?" she said to Aaron.

"How can you tell? My accent?"

She laughed. "No; I just haven't seen you ever before. I'd remember. Anyway, the motel's across the road."

"Well, you've got me. I'm from Saginaw. I go to school in Ann Arbor."

"To the university?"

Aaron admitted it and told her about the job. She was fascinated, and surprised him by sliding into the booth beside him. "That must be wonderful; traveling around all the time, all over the state."

"It's a good job."

"I never get out of Fenton," she said glumly. "Would you believe I've never, ever been out of Michigan, even to visit? Even on a vacation? I'd love to live in Ann Arbor, where there are things going on all the time, and close to Detroit. I have a cousin who went there."

Aaron talked a little about the plays and concerts and mixers that he sometimes went to, and the good bars and lounges with dancing, and the movie houses he attended more often. She listened to him with her eyes intent, as if she were hearing an important newscast, her blond hair close to one eye and her uniform crisp and white. She was a beautiful girl.

"Lord," she said quietly, when he finished. "I'd love to get out of this town. You can't *do* anything here except go to the show or play pool in one of those dumpy bars. If I had any courage I'd take my babies and just leave, just go anywhere. Maybe California. It's supposed to be great out there."

"Are you married?" said Aaron.

"Divorced. I have two darling little girls. Want to see? I'll be right back."

She got up and Aaron watched her walk into the kitchen. She did not look like a woman with two children.

She came back with her billfold, but had to take another order from a trucker who came in. Then she sat down with Aaron again.

"By the way, my name is Ann Campbell."

"Aaron Young. This is George Dooley."

"You fellows really have it made. Men have all the best of it, I guess. Here—" She showed Aaron and George a Koda-color snap of two little blond girls. "This one is three. Karen. And Debbie is two."

"Cute," said George.

"Ann, they're beautiful."

"They really are, aren't they? Isn't it strange how a foolish bad marriage between a couple of dumb kids can bring something like this? They're all I have in the world."

"You don't look old enough to have two children."

She flashed him a white smile and said, "That's a nice thing to say. Thank you. I'm twenty-four, though."

She looked at the picture again and snapped her billfold shut. "Well, I'll get you gentlemen some food. With a job like yours you're probably starving."

After Ann brought their meals Aaron said, "You know, I like her."

"Yeah," said Dooley. "She's sure built."

"That too."

"Steve'll be after her," said Dooley, taking a bite.

Aaron looked up from his plate. "What?"

Dooley chewed for a minute, swallowed and said, "Steve isn't gonna let a babe like her get past him. As friendly as she is . . ."

"They're eating in town, aren't they?"

"Tonight they are. But if they ever come over here and Steve gets a look at her—good-bye, baby."

Aaron looked at him and then slowly began to eat.

When Ann brought the bills she said, "Are you going to be here long?"

"Probably two weeks," said Aaron.

"Oh. Well, I guess I'll be seeing you around, then. Do you play pool?"

"Not very well," he said, thinking of Steve. Steve played pool. "Maybe—"

Ann looked at him.

"Uh—what time do you get off? We—"

"Seven-thirty," she said. "I get off at seven-thirty."

"Look. Maybe we could go out someplace. Dance or something."

"Oh, I'd love to. There's a place uptown where they have dancing."

"Okay. Why don't I come back? Do you have to go home first?"

"No. I have another dress here. I can call my mother and ask her to keep my babies tonight."

"Great. I'll see you later, then," said Aaron, and he and George left their tips and paid the bills.

Outside, crossing the highway, Dooley said, "You did a smooth job of hustling on that one. Gonna get into her tonight?"

FOUR: *Fenton* | 127

"I'm going dancing," said Aaron. He was thinking that Susan had not yet bothered to answer his letters and that she was no doubt seeing a lot of men in Seattle. Besides, he wanted to put a prior claim on this girl and keep her away from Steve until they were through in Fenton. He liked this girl and he thought that one thing she did not need was someone like Steve.

2.   So they drove uptown and danced in a dark little bar, nicer than those in Owosso, with a jukebox that played automatically for the several couples who were dancing. Ann moved in his arms as if she was at home there. It was a quiet place and when they were not dancing they sat in a corner booth and talked and drank beer, Ann getting a foam moustache on her upper lip like a little girl drinking milk, laughing when Aaron copied her. She was good company and quite lovely and Aaron liked her. He had dated only college girls for the past two years, and it was a strange relief to be with someone who was not faintly in competition with the male sex, someone who did not talk about her future career or her father's business or, like Susan the psychiatric social worker, about "relating" to people and "adjusting" to social environment—talking with a hard-eyed dedication that sometimes made him uncomfortable.

Ann had been born in L'Anse, Michigan, a small town on the upper peninsula, and had never been south of the Straits of Mackinac until she was fourteen.

"You can probably imagine how I wanted to come south. The *world* was down here and I thought I was being strangled up there. That's funny—now I'm here, and there still doesn't seem to be any world; I'm strangling even more because I don't have anyone—only my babies. It seems so lonely all over. It can't be this way everywhere, is it?"

Her look was so honestly questioning that he felt sorry for her.

"I don't think it's a question of where you are," he said. "It depends more on who you are, what kind of person you are. And it depends most, I think, on who you're with, who you have to depend on. Ann Arbor is a very active place, but like anyplace else it can be the loneliest town in the world if you're lonely. Some of the saddest times of my life have been spent in Ann Arbor."

"Are you lonely?"

He looked at her and said without thinking, "Not any more." Then he did think, and he modified his answer. "That is—I don't know. I don't *think* I'm lonely. I think—I think I'm very *lonesome*."

"There's a difference?"

"Well, yes. Lonesomeness is kind of a temporary thing, but loneliness is really a state of being: if you're a lonely person, you're in rough shape."

"I guess that's me," she said. "And yet you're right—about being with someone. Even now, talking to you, everything is—so much better."

He smiled. "How did you get away from L'Anse?"

"I married Jimmy. I stuck the place out until after high school and I was going with Jimmy by then. He worked in a lumberyard. My father died before I graduated and it looked like Mama was going to stay there for good. But I couldn't, Aaron, I just couldn't. I wanted to see Detroit and go to big theaters and dance in nightclubs and all—stupid little things. So we worked it out, Jimmy and Mama and me. I couldn't just leave her. But we had an aunt Joanne, Mama's sister, living here. I had only seen her twice, that I remembered, when they came up to visit. Her husband's name is Carl. So we

wrote to them and talked Mama into it, and we all moved
down here. Mama lives with Carl and Joanne, and Jimmy
and I got married.

"I've been here ever since. We didn't get along too well
after Karen was born; Jimmy had trouble getting work—
he hadn't finished high school. When Debbie came it was just
too much for him and he left me—I guess I can't blame him.
He went to Detroit and was living with some girl, so I divorced him. The last I heard he went west. I never did get to
Detroit."

He started to say, *There's not much there*, but thought
better of it and said simply, "God, Ann, that's rough."

"Yes. To be stuck in a place like this with two children and
no husband—and the worst of it is it's so lonely—I mean
lonely—it's terrible. After you've lived with somebody and
slept with them for years it's horrible not to have them there—
not to have *someone* there any more."

"I wouldn't think a young, pretty girl like you would have
trouble finding someone."

"You're sweet. But in a town like this—and working in that
restaurant . . . You never meet anyone who'd be willing to
take on somebody else's family. And anyway, they're all as
little and mean and hicky as I am—"

"You aren't hicky."

"Yes, I am."

"You're beautiful," he said, taking her hand.

"When somebody hasn't ever had a chance to live, he's a
hick. You're so *lucky*, Aaron. Just being with someone like
you who knows what life is—it's so nice, so exciting. Somebody who doesn't drive trucks or live in Nowhere."

"Well."

When it got later and they had drunk more beer, the music
stayed slow and they did not talk, but danced very close
together on one small section of the floor, and Aaron no

longer thought but simply drifted with her in his arms, her long blond hair over his hands and their bodies tight and he quite willing to take whatever came. There were three or four other couples left; the gaudy red and green lights from the jukebox outlined them with faint auras as they stood almost motionless, arms about each other, no longer really dancing.

Ann nestled against him with her eyes closed and said, "We ought to be going. . . ."

"Yes," he said, feeling very light-headed, and he kissed her cheek and said, "Let's take you home."

They woke up somewhat then and smiled at each other, both thinking the same thing and realizing they were pleasantly high for it.

They came out of the bar and stood in the yellow light that seeped through a darkened window, framed with green neon. Across the street there was a small light in the rear of a restaurant, otherwise dark. The street was dark-faced now too, the buildings stooped in their small-town night lit only by street lamps and a corner drugstore, and the faint garish lights of bars intersticed along the darknesses.

"Come on," said Aaron.

The June night was warm and humid; the sky had clouded and they saw it boiling. No moon, no stars—only the dark mass like heavy fog rolling above them. A wind had picked up and came in little chattering gusts and then a long drawn-out exhalation of breath. Ann hooked her purse securely in the crook of an elbow and took Aaron's arm, her skirt billowing as she moved against him.

"It's going to rain!"

Aaron looked up as they neared the corner. "Look at that sky."

"Let's hurry. I don't want to get wet."

"It feels good, though, doesn't it?" They crossed the street and passed the drugstore and he thought, *I should get something there—* But Ann was pulling him, holding down her skirt, and there was no way he could have done it and he thought it would not matter anyway; he was only taking her home.

"Ooo—it's so *hard!*"

The wind was blowing away the heat and the night felt good in it; the night was doing something, had lost its summer passivity, and with the girl there beside him they reached the car on the dark side street and Aaron let her in and walked around to his side and got in. It was so dark now he could not see her face, but she slid over to him and he put a hand on her shoulder and kissed her, sliding his other hand around under her sweater and pulling her close.

"Mmm . . ." She put her arms around him and said, "Aaron . . ." and he kissed her again feeling very hot, and then relaxed, feeling how calm and relaxed she was, enjoying it, and he moved his hands over her, kissing softly and insistently.

A few drops of rain tinned on the roof of the car and Aaron looked out to where the wind was whipping the trees, holding her tight.

"We should've brought a bottle or something."

She kissed him under his ear and whispered, "I have plenty at home."

He started the car and flicked on the headlights, revealing the world in a torment of wind and leaves. The tinking of rain came again on the roof and a soft pattern of it blew into haze in the yellow headlight cones as Ann told him how to find her house.

When they pulled up and Aaron cut the engine and lights the tympanic drumming came louder and a heavy growl rolled out of the sky somewhere far off; it followed up with a streak of lightning that flashed for an instant and was gone.

"Come on," said Ann. "Let's get in before it really hits."

Aaron got out of the car and the wind had died some, the rain no longer misty but coming, slowly still, in large wet drops that grew heavier. He opened the door for Ann and she was out and rushing him across the lawn to a dark house under the trees at the end of a walk.

"Take it easy!" He laughed. "I *like* this!"

"Shhh! The people upstairs." Ann fumbled in her purse for the key and let them into a hallway, pointed to the stairs in the blackness, and led him on through and unlocked another door with another key. Then everything was blacker as she closed that door and he heard it lock. They were in a living room, but all he could make out was a lamp near the window. Ann clicked on a high-intensity reading lamp in the corner, stood grotesque in its white light, black-shadowed on the ceiling, then turned it into the corner until it muted down to a glimmer across one space of wall.

"How's that?"

"I'll show you."

He moved toward her but she laughed and dodged away, said, "Follow," and went into the kitchen. She turned on a dim light over a cabinet, opened a door and took out a bottle and glasses. "Would you like to fix the drinks? This is bourbon. I've got Scotch if you want."

"Bourbon is fine."

"Good. I'll put some music on." She slipped away out of the kitchen.

Aaron looked at the bourbon and carefully read the label. He unscrewed the cap and poured some into the glasses, filling them a third of the way. He held them under a faucet and filled them, then thought a moment and took a sip from each glass, went to the refrigerator and found a tray of ice in the freezer. He held it under the faucet and dropped two ice cubes into one glass, spilling it over. He mopped it up with a dishcloth, drank the other glass down a little and dropped in two more. He was thinking that this was nothing that thousands of people had not done before, hundreds of thousands of times, probably thousands of others doing it right now. The feeling in his stomach, he told himself, was only nervous fear at this being his first time. There was nothing to worry about. They might not even do anything, and if they did then she would know all about it. This wasn't high school kids in the back of a car. She had been married. She had two children.

He drank off his bourbon quickly and refilled the glass. He had made them too strong—what did he know about mixing drinks?—so he sipped Ann's and put some more water in it, testing until it tasted decent. He carried the drinks into the living room and sat down on the sofa, sipping the whiskey and feeling the ice with his tongue, watching Ann. He had turned out the light in the kitchen and now the reading lamp paled out into the room off the wall, spreading long shadows. The room was small and neat. He looked around and noted the television set, the phonograph in a corner beside a large chair, two end tables with lamps, the coffee table with artificial flowers as a centerpiece, the shelf built into one wall to hold books. Except for the absence of any pictures or paintings on the walls, it was very much like Susan's apartment. But he was not thinking about Susan.

Ann put the music on softly, accepted her drink from Aaron and sat down beside him on the sofa, drawing up her legs and looking at him sideways with her head tilted slightly.

"Is it all right?" he said.

She nodded, drinking. "Tastes fine."

They watched each other for a moment. The storm was

beginning to hit outside; several long thunderclaps cracked and rolled down the sky like Hendrick Hudson's ninepins down a long hallway in the clouds. It was raining in sheets that held out beneath the thunder, an almost subliminal roaring, a vibration through which the explosions came and blue lightning flashed. The lamp in the corner of the room was so dim that part of the room lit up for an instant with the electric blue, like a burning fluorescent light that had almost stopped working, flickering sporadically. Ann's face changed color slightly each time the lightning came, her eyes suddenly darker, and they seemed to be looking deeper into him in the instants of blue light. This made him uncomfortable, as if during those flickering instants she became a different person, one who could see him better than he saw himself, by lightning—a different person from the one he half knew, was at least acquainted with: this one waited and watched him in the eerie light, a changeling who saw him held in the rain's rhythm, the vibrations softly dulling his ability to react to what was happening. For a moment he felt that if he did not speak he would find himself unable to and sit helpless while something was done to him—and when he spoke the mood was broken and everything was again the same.

"So you're a L'Anse girl."

She nodded. "And you are from Saginaw."

"Yes, ma'am. I—hope you make it out of here, Ann. Go to California or somewhere, if you really want to."

"Well, I want to. But—"

"What?"

She looked away and said quietly, as if she were informing herself and not him, "I'll never do it. I don't think I'll ever do it. I'll never leave."

"Why not?"

"Because," she said, "I'm afraid. I'm a L'Anse girl; I wouldn't know where to go or what to do anyplace else."

"That's crazy. It isn't that hard."

"Maybe for a man. For me it's—I just—all the people I have in the world are here. My mother, my aunt and my babies. Unless, sometime, somebody *takes* me away, I'll never leave."

She looked at him and seemed to be waiting. *Crack!* went the thunder. He drank some more and looked at the patch of light on the wall. He did not want things to slow down like this; he knew things must keep moving. But he could not move them.

She said, "Would you like to dance with me?"

"Yes."

They took their shoes off first and he felt things speeding up again through his feet on the soft carpet with her in his arms, at first not touching and then barely touching as if she was teasing him, then dancing close and then not dancing but embracing in the middle of the room. And then back to the sofa.

After a while she stopped him and said, "Let's go into the bedroom."

As he got up and followed her into the darkness, it was as if he was watching himself, curious to see what would happen.

They stood looking at each other in the dark across the bed, a double bed that had been slept in alone for too long. The storm crashed a little and began to ease away into nothing but rain as Ann undressed, sliding the sweater up over her shoulders. She zippered her skirt down the side and stepped out of it, unhooked her stockings and slid them off, sitting down on the side of the bed. She unhooked the bra and slipped it off her shoulders. Her body was young and smooth and she turned to look at Aaron with her hair down her naked back and brushing close to one eye.

"Shall I leave the rest for you?"

Aaron looked at her and realized with surprise that he

was no longer nervous. His hands were calm and his heartbeat fast only from looking at her and he was not at all afraid. He was, instead, slightly puzzled.

"Uhhhmmm . . ."

She looked up at him. "Is something wrong?"

He waited with a strange look on his face in the darkness that his eyes had grown used to. He hooked a thumb into his belt and said, "I don't know—"

"What do you mean, you don't know? What's the matter?"

Part of it was toying around at the edges of his mind, the easy part, and for an answer he grabbed that.

"I'm not in love with you, Ann."

She laughed and said, "*What?*" and then saw his face and broke off with a half smile, thinking she knew what it was. "You don't have to be in love with someone to love her. It doesn't take all *that* much involvement."

"Well," he said, beginning to feel stupid. "I don't know."

"Well, *I* know. That's one of the things I do know. Come on. I'll help you, for goodness' sake."

"I don't—think so."

She twisted around a little more and said, "Are you kidding me?"

He stood there.

This irritated her, and she got up and came around the bed after him, talking. "Good *God*, Aaron, love is the easiest thing in the world, even if some people do go through their whole lives making it as hard as they can. That's only because they think it takes something from them, instead of the opposite. People don't want to see what it's all about."

"I don't know if I know what it's about," he said, backing up.

"Well, I think you do. I think you'd know very easily if you'd just let yourself. If you would just undress and get into bed with me and let me show you. *Aaron—*"

"I don't know," he said. "I'm—I've never—loved anyone that way."

"Then you haven't started to know what life is about. This is life. This—" She took his hand and pressed it to her breast, and Aaron felt the warmth of flesh and firm nipple, felt his own desire driving up and out, removing any fear that might have remained. But it was not his fear that was holding him.

"This—" said Ann, and pressing herself close to him she moved his hand down between her legs and for the first time in his life Aaron felt, through her underwear, what a woman was made for, knew for the first hot moment what he was made for.

Yet what had stopped him continued to stop him, and he withdrew his hand and stepped back, sitting down, suddenly weak, on the edge of the bed. Ann looked at him as if she could not believe what was happening, caught somewhere between frustration and mirth.

"Well, I'm damned."

"I'm sorry," he said. "I know this must seem pretty stupid to you. It seems stupid to me."

"You shouldn't be afraid!"

"No; I know that. It isn't that, I don't think. I don't know what it is."

She moved her hand to his groin, felt his heat and hardness, and he pushed her hand away. "God, *stop it*. It isn't that, either; believe me.

"It's my life. It's my whole life that's built up behind me and is looking over my shoulder right now. My head and my body say Yes, all right, go ahead, it's good. But there's something else. I want to, but I won't."

Ann sat down beside him. "This is the craziest thing that's ever happened to me. You know," she said, leaning against him, breast against his arm, "all of this wasn't just for *your* benefit." He looked at her and she stopped and said quietly,

"I'm sorry. You're—I guess you're bogged down in something, aren't you?"

He sighed loudly, thinking how ludicrous this all was, how foolish he was, what a fool he must seem and be.

"I'm sure as hell bogged down in something."

Ann said, "Are you in love with someone?"

He did not hesitate."Yes. I am."

"Oh. Well, maybe that—puts a different light on things."

He began to talk about Susan, and if there was still some trace of doubt in his mind concerning love, there was none in his voice, and it was obvious enough to Ann so that she got a robe from the closet and they lay down side by side on the bed while Aaron talked and Ann smoked a cigarette.

"You're nuts about this girl, aren't you?" she said then.

"I guess I am. I guess that's why it bothers me she doesn't write. I don't know what she's doing or who she's seeing—"

"Does it matter?"

"No. Except it does. Ann, can you see how I feel?"

"I can see, yes. I can't understand it."

"Neither can I. My Puritan past gets tangled in with my liberal present."

"Aaron, I was laid when I was fourteen, in the back room of my church. Does that make me all ruined? Doomed to unhappiness?"

"No. Of course not. It's only this perfection business. I guess I can't explain it to anyone who hasn't seen it. I have this *feeling*—this urgent thing about my parents. You would have to have seen my parents before my mother died. I have to have that, what they had, or I'll never make it, Ann. Anything less, compared with that, would be intolerable."

"So why compare?"

"Try not to. Be me for a while and try not to."

"Perfect marriages are rare."

"So what? What do I care how rare they are? I know it

can be done, because I've seen it. *I've seen it.* I can't be interested in how rarely it's done; I can only be interested in its being done twice—the one with my parents and the one I have to be damn sure I have. Nothing else matters."

"All right," she said. "I wish you luck. But why do you have to have someone who's never—"

"I don't *have* to. But my *mother* was like that and my *father* was like that—no new morals for them, oh, no—and together they built a family so good I can't believe it myself, when I see other people. The *conditions*, Ann, I'm trying to recreate the conditions so I can have a chance. I've got to replace them; you can see that. Families break up, people die—"

"Shhh, all *right*. Take it easy. What will you do about Susan, then?"

Aaron did not answer the question. He was not thinking about Susan, whom he had claimed he loved without thinking about it, as if to hesitate would open his mind, the conversation, to other topics. He was thinking now of this perfection business, and of what other possible reason there might be for his refusal to love Ann. He had wanted to love her and the perfection thing and his church background had inhibited him, but he wondered if it was that that had stopped him finally. It had not seemed so at the time. It had seemed that they were only filling in for something that was not clear to him. It had seemed almost that he was refusing her *because he wanted her so very much.*

But how could that be?

Ann said something that broke his chain of thought, and they talked and finally Aaron looked at the luminous dial on his watch. "Good lord, five o'clock. I have to get up in two hours."

"Stay here. In a while I'll make you breakfast."

"Ann, I'm sorry about all this. I surprised myself as much

as you. Don't think—I didn't want to. Don't think you aren't—"

"—the sexiest thing you've ever been to bed with. I know."

"It's just me—crazy Aaron building sacred golden cows."

"It's all right. We had a good time. And you are in love."

But that was not it at all.

When he finally left her it was full light, and fresh from the rain. She had fed him eggs and bacon and toast and orange juice and coffee, and he went on out to work without seeing any of the crew.

All day he thought of Ann and Susan and his mother's death, with a mixture of tenderness, sadness, apprehension. And the hitchhikers had not really left his mind. Whenever he saw someone thumbing a ride he was reminded again of his experience. He never carried more than twenty dollars in cash now, although he knew the money had nothing to do with it. He glared at all hitchhikers with a singular look compounded of wrath and remembered fear.

Later, when the other members of the crew began to bait him (Dooley had, of course, told everyone that Aaron had been out all night), he ignored them and then avoided them. He did not go into the restaurant for dinner or see Ann again the rest of the time they were in Fenton.

3.   Paul finally came over to Aaron's room one evening while Dooley was in the shower. He stood outside the screen door with a cigarette in his mouth, squinting into the room and shading his eyes from the sunlight.

"Hello, Mr. Young. Haven't been seeing you around much."

Aaron was lying on the bed with a book of poems. "Come on in. Been catching up on my reading."

Paul nodded, smiled, closing the screen behind him, and lapsed into a fit of coughing, dropping his cigarette on the rug. He had developed the cough over the past few weeks and had not been able to shake it.

"Want a drink?" said Aaron.

"What've you got?"

"I mean water."

"Oh. Skip it, I'm okay." He picked up the cigarette and put it out on the inside of a wastebasket. "Aaron, why haven't you been coming around any more? Why have you stopped eating across the road?"

"I don't care for the food. Besides, I get antisocial when the remarks begin."

"Oh. Those guys . . ." Paul sat down in a chair by the door and lighted a cigarette. "You don't let stuff like that bother you? Vanneman—"

"Are you kidding? Vanneman and Dooley? I can live around them and not know they're there. But Rod. And Steve. They're something else."

"You know they were only kidding."

"Some people don't care for some types of kidding. Steve especially knows that."

"Of course, you dope. Rod didn't mean anything; he was just joining in. He likes you."

"How can anyone tell what Rod likes?"

"And Steve just wanted to get you riled."

"He got me riled."

Paul inhaled and let out a great cloud of smoke. "So," he said, "you going to pout it away? Or you going to come on over and have supper tonight?"

"I'm going to pout it away. Paul, I don't want to eat over

there anyway. Not at night. I'll see you tomorrow at break-fast."

Paul looked at him thoughtfully and said, "All right. How about this: you want to go out tonight? We got some girls lined up."

"No, thanks. I'll just read tonight."

"You know something," said Paul, contemplating the glowing end of his cigarette, "you are a very mysterious fellow, Mr. Young. There are those who wonder about you."

"Good. I'm a mystic."

"Mm-hmmm." Paul got up and stepped outside, looking around at the sunset and the summer-colored light that seemed suspended over the trees. He turned around and said through the screen, "One more thing. Uh—you know Steve."

"What about Steve?"

"He's going to try to hustle your girl. I think. If you have any claim on her—"

"My girl, hell. I don't own her."

Paul stood there with his face close to the screen, filtering smoke into the room and looking at Aaron on the bed. He started away and came back.

"I'll see you at breakfast," he said. Then he hesitated, shrugged one shoulder, and walked away.

That night there was a party in Steve and Paul's room. Aaron heard it, waking up in the night, above Dooley's snoring—the sound of a record player and laughter. He lay there listening, sweating under the covers in the warm night. There was a clattering, and someone became angry; a door slammed, and opened and closed again. He heard a man's voice and a girl's. Then someone was sick in the parking lot—it must have been the girl because the man was still talking. She stopped being sick and they got into a car and left. Then only the music, in disjointed bursts of sound on the breeze, and finally silence.

The next morning Aaron crossed the highway with Dooley to the restaurant. He gave his order to the morning waitress and looked around for the others. No one else was there.

"The other guys leave?"

Dooley leaned back to look through the window at the motel. "Cars still there."

"They must be sleeping in, the bastards."

"Steve said something about having a party last night."

"I guess they did. Didn't you hear it?"

"Uh-uh. I sleep pretty good. They musta had Sievers and Vanneman in."

A few minutes later Vanneman and Rod came in, looking haggard.

"Agh." Vanneman sat down and put his hands over his eyes. "Oh, oh, oh . . ."

Rod yawned and nodded to Aaron and Dooley. "Morning. I guess."

"Had a good one, huh?" said Dooley.

"Oh, God."

Paul and Steve came in ten minutes later.

"Good morning, good morning," said Rod with false cheer.

"Up yours," said Steve.

"Oh, boy. Coffee." Paul grinned weakly in greeting and sat down by Vanneman, who still had his hands over his eyes.

"I want to tell you boys," said Steve, "this stuff has got to stop. My whole damn crew is coming apart around me. I'm coming apart myself. How we gonna get them poles, we keep screwing around like this?"

"Screw the poles," said Rod. "Back to bed, everyone. Combat leave."

"I think it's going to rain today," mumbled Vanneman hopefully.

"You get yours home okay?" said Paul, grabbing a menu shakily.

Rod closed his eyes. "How should I know? I can't remember anything except she was sick as a dog. I think I took somebody somewhere."

Vanneman said slowly from beneath his hands, "Was I drunk last night, or did one of those guhls have a wooden leg?"

"You were drunker'n hell," said Paul, "and it wasn't wood; it was some kind of plastic."

Vanneman looked up. "You mean it really was artificial?"

Steve grinned. "I wondered about it till she took it off."

"Damn. I thought I dreamed that or something—about this guhl taking off her wooden leg when she crawled in bed with somebody. Did somebody lay her?"

"Sure. You did. Didn't you? Don't you even remember?"

"I don't know. I think I remember laying somebody. . . ." He thought a moment and said, "Son of a bitch. I screwed a one-legged guhl."

Aaron had finished eating. He left a tip and paid the bill, and as he was starting out the door Steve hurried over and said, "Sorry you missed the party, old buddy."

"I wasn't in the mood."

"Well, it was your loss."

"Just what you needed, huh?"

"You should know," said Steve.

Aaron looked closely at him. "What do you mean?"

"I mean the women sure get lonely around here. Somebody has to give them what they want. If it were left up to you—" He grinned. "What are you, a one-shot fellow? Take that girl Ann, now, that waitress—"

"You son of a bitch."

"It wasn't my fault," said Steve. "Can I help it if nobody else would—"

But Aaron had gone out.

He worked that day with a coldness in his head and his insides churning, stalking across the muddy fields in his heavy shoes. After the rain the fields clung to his feet like lead weights, and he moved like a deep sea diver and kicked up clods of mud, not trying to avoid the crops. He cursed himself for a fool, cursed Steve, cursed Ann—but especially himself. Susan had not written to him, was letting him down, and it seemed that Ann had let him down too, or vice versa, and Steve was getting it all. What good did it do to have values if you kept losing all the time? Why be a lousy— stupid—*clod* (he kicked) and let everybody else win every- thing?

In the afternoon he followed a line of poles to a farm and climbed over a wooden gate into a field of young steers. He was not paying much attention, thinking about Ann and Steve, and when one of the steers lunged at him he panicked, slipped in the mud and fell into the barbed-wire fence. The fence was a hot one and he convulsed, grabbed all over by huge hands, and he cut his wrist on the barbed wire and rolled under it, shocking himself again and tearing his shirt. He was covered with mud and the thought of tetanus im- mediately occurred to him, and he wiped the muddy hand on his shirt and sucked at the bleeding wrist, tasting copper and thinking: *God, God,* knowing that farms were ideal for getting tetanus through a cut, and he tried to remember when he had last had a shot. He thought the university required one of all students, but he was not certain it was a tetanus shot he had gotten, and he closed his eyes, trying to remember.

Finally he calmed down and sat there thinking: *What is the matter with me lately? I'm nervous as a kitten and all I ever think about is sex and death.*

The cut had stopped bleeding and was clean from his sucking at it. He took several deep breaths and picked up his clipboard and slid under the fence and checked the pole, after waving his arms and yelling at the steers to drive them back across the field, as he should have done in the first place.

4.   Driving in at five o'clock, he heard the country and western radio station that pulsed out of Big Oak and blanketed most of the lower peninsula. He did not listen to the radio much, and when he did it was usually WJR in Detroit, the only decent station he had ever found. But occasionally he listened to the Big Oak drivel precisely because of its banality; it made him feel magnanimous if he could tolerate the mash of sentimental piety, sex and violence that made up country music. The announcer was a former disk jockey from Flint who had somehow picked up the necessary twang for his new job, and he wheedled his audience in a syrupy voice:

"Well, if yer ridin along out ther in yer cors, we'd lak ta thankya fer allowin us ta rad along withya. En if yer listenin' in t'us in yer homes ther we'd lak ta thankya fer havin' us in. . . ."

And then he played as his final song the old cornball of lost love that Aaron could not help liking—and Aaron was reminded as always of when he had first heard the song, with the little guitar piece at the end—and thought of Matthew, his brother, and of the summer and fall they had spent as a team, brought about by a common interest and a common agony. That was when their mother still lived, and at first there was no sign of what would come, for Aaron and Matt had been close and then, strangely, not close.

He could not have said when the break began. Probably there was no point in time at which the finger could be pointed and the word "here" uttered. Probably it had not been a break as such, and there was no point—only stages of development. For that was it: they had developed away from each other. What Aaron sought in books, Matthew found in a football. Aaron had gone to plays at the junior college while still in high school; Matt went to drive-ins with girls. For Aaron, poetry; for Matthew, comic books and sports magazines. Matthew was an athlete, got hurt, suffered at being left out of basketball games, threw out his arm early in baseball season. It was always, it seemed, Aaron reading about life, gaining theoretical perception of its nuances and heartbreak, while Matt lived in the grossness of it, unaware of its deepest sorrows and loving the smell of it, the taste of its blood, the feel of its bite.

So it had not happened at any time; rather, one day the sun rose clearer in both their faces, but especially in Aaron's, and he realized that something had burned down to a low flicker of what once had blazed like tigers' eyes. And nothing to do, no way back; the wheels were lashed for each of them and they watched each other going away.

That spring their mother became ill and went to the hospital for the removal of a tumor. They thought then that she would not recover, she was so ill, and Aaron's life was a nightmare. They spent much of their time at the hospital, their father most of his time there, and Aaron sensed a creeping uneasiness that had to do not only with his mother, but with all of them, and he watched them with a vacant feeling and tried to reach somehow to something he could not touch, but needed.

Their mother recovered and came home and continued to improve, and outwardly there was a slight relaxation. But not for Aaron, and he was watching Matt now, and waiting. And finally something happened.

Matt came home late after school, one hand clutching tight the warped throat of an old crone of a guitar that looked as though someone had kicked it around the block every day for ten years. He had bought it for nine dollars of his twenty-dollar bank account from a boy who had taught him to play four chords, and he sat down on the floor in the living room, where Aaron was reading Conrad, and sang "The Escape of Old John Webb," chording as he sang, more or less to the beat:

> He had eighty-weight of Spanish iron
> Between his neckbone and his knee—
> But Billy picked Johnny up under his arm,
> And lugged him away right manfully.

Aaron watched him and then said, "Where did you get the guitar?"

"Bought it from a guy at school."

"You learned to play it quick."

Matt looked up from the guitar. "Well, it's not really playing it. He taught me some chords; you can play chords and strum to accompany yourself if you sing. It isn't really playing, but it sounds like it. How did it sound?"

"It sounded good," said Aaron.

Matt smiled. "Not too bad, was it?"

"Hey, look—" He wanted to ask Matt to teach him the fingering of the chords, but the old distance slipped back and he said instead, "Don't stop—play some more."

Matt added a chord he had found for himself, thumbed through a ragged folk song book he had wheedled along with the guitar, and launched into a solo version of "Everglades."

As Aaron watched his younger brother sitting there on the floor, banging one hand on the steel strings and grimacing as he clumsily fingered the simple chords, singing with a pure and unself-conscious voice that surprised his brother, Aaron felt a crack of light glimmer through the increasingly felt wall that separated them, as the fresh beginnings of a common interest toyed within his reach. He had listened to Matt's folk song records, had found himself liking them. He had never known anything of music and was no farther along that road than Matt—probably a good deal less along it, for Matt and several of his friends were beginning to avow themselves folk song buffs. Now Aaron felt a touch of the excitement that had inflamed Matt, and something else along with that, a glimpse of possibility, of filial sentiment and desire and sense of duty, of "family," suggesting in the thrumming old strings that all was not yet gone, that a discovery lay there at their feet to be picked up and grasped gingerly, blown on and fanned into reality if only they could do it.

How things progressed from there it was hard to recall later, after all of it was past. Aaron listened to Matt play and sing, and Matt became rapidly better on the guitar. Eventually Aaron was singing with him, the two of them in the basement recreation room, listening to the records, comparing arrangements with the song book, and working out their own style. Aaron learned chords, and practiced them, toughening his fingers on Matt's guitar, and then they switched off playing as they sang.

Summer came and began an eerie sublife for Aaron. He had finished his first year at the junior college, and got a job for the summer working the midnight shift at an automotive parts factory.

Why he took that third-shift job Aaron never really knew: it seemed later that there was a dark appeal to it that coincided with his adolescence turning to manhood. The idea of working through the night while everyone slept excited his imagination, and his father talked of wartime production and how he had made bombsights at Mallory's in Indianapolis during the forties, the factory turning out full around the clock, and this led Aaron to want to do the same—to want to have that experience under his belt even if it was automotive parts and not bombsights, to be able later to say, "When I worked the midnight shift . . ."

So the summer became a first in his life, a kind of duplex living he had not experienced before. He found himself keeping a highwayman's hours: sleeping through most of the day, playing the guitar and singing with Matt in the evening, then going to work when everyone else went to bed. Very soon the romance fell out of the midnight shift and he was left with a summer flashing by before his eyes, of gold sundowns and silver guitar strings and a gray-green tappet assembler that *tik-tik-tik-tik-tik*ed away the long nights as he stood over it in the hot and oil-heavy air of the factory.

Fortunately the job paid well, and Aaron bought himself a yellow Ford, and finally, one evening, with Matt tagging along to give advice, he went down and bought a guitar, brand new. It cost something over a hundred dollars and was not a particularly good guitar at that, but it was good enough for Aaron. It was a twelve-string guitar, exactly like an ordinary instrument except that each of the six strings was doubled, paired with one string tuned an octave higher than the other, so that when it was strummed it sounded like silver and each chord played twice as full as on an ordinary guitar.

They would spend the evenings working over the folk songs and occasionally now singing for some of their friends. A fellow Aaron had known discovered that he and Matt played, and invited them to a party, where they performed several tunes and got a good response. From that point, it began to slide into a way of life that lasted all summer and into the fall.

The response to the brothers as a team was curious and largely dependent upon their past reputations. Most of the curiosity centered on Aaron, but the interest, understandably, was with Matt, for Matt was better known to more people and his popularity was set. He had a natural cool, without having to think about it, without particularly bothering to try. Both were quiet boys, but where Aaron's brooding had brought him, with his dark hair and haunted eyes, a reputation as a "brain"—a self-sufficient type to be respected and not bandied with—the response to Matthew's reticence had labeled him a "nice guy," a shy but friendly mover. There was no arguing; they accepted their roles and played them without complaint, without comment. When Matt would sit in silence, fingering his guitar and lost to those around him, it was, they said, a touch of his brother; and when Aaron flew into a manic state and knocked out songs for an hour straight, it was Matt's influence that caused it. The brothers were labeled and marked; both were liked and both respected—but it was generally agreed that Matt was the easier to reach. And seldom, at first, did anyone try to reach Aaron.

While their mother was convalescing from her surgery, the hospital tests came back. And one night Matt and Aaron sat in the basement and heard their father tell them what it was. They knew before he said the word, knew from the sound of his voice and the look in his eyes, and after Dad and Aaron had talked it out, of X-ray treatments and drugs and a great deal of hope and much prayer, while Matt listened in silence, Dad went back upstairs and the brothers sat looking at each other, and then Matt went up into the bedroom and closed the door, and Aaron heard the sharp sounds of Matt's new banjo that he had bought on time, as his brother took his own private anesthesia alone in the failing light. For a while the distance was there between them again, huge and impenetrable.

The illness added a new dimension to their music, a kind of desperation and a need to plumb to the utmost the joys that could be grabbed from this part of their lives, as if to ease and make more bearable the harsher side. They both felt guilty and ashamed to be having fun, yet strove for it all the harder, as if only by leading dual lives could they keep some tenuous grip on their lives at all. To think too long on the changes bearing down upon them, to contemplate the future, was close to impossible for them; they grasped at what was reachable as their former home life, their foundation and security, crumbled beneath their feet.

Autumn came with its usual fire, in the trees and at the burnt edges of the horizon early in the evenings. Aaron quit his eerie job and began his second year of college, and Matt his final year of high school. Almost, once in a softly-held-breath while, things seemed normal, as if life were stable and not teetering on the crazy edge of chaos.

There was a time when they went on a hayride in late September with the young people of the Baptist church, rolling out on a wagon over old roads and farm trails with the year just turning copper and the air starting to feel clean in the strange sharp cold-filtered way of autumn. Aaron sat in the middle at one end of the bouncing sweet-strawed wagon, back against the old boards with his twelve-string in his lap. He felt in that time and place how strangely different it was to be with people who liked him, who admired him for something good that he could do, nice people who could make him feel that he too was nice—and he liked them all very much, the sweet pretty girls and the friendly guys, and felt at home with them.

Matthew sat cross-legged at the other end of the group, the hay, the wagon, looking soberly up at the extended neck of his banjo, poked above the sides of the wagon, over the heads of the group like a slender, stringed, pegged animal of sorts peeking over the side at all of autumn out there with sunlight falling down streaked and dusty across it. His old brown guitar lay close by.

They sang easy, well-known songs: "This Land Is Your Land," "Blowin' in the Wind," "500 Miles." Aaron strummed, occasionally finger-picked folk style, quietly. Matt had caught onto the banjo easily, had learned the tricky art of frailing, had already known three-finger picking, now alternately hammered-on, pulled off and played straight the tunes with a rolling, galloping rhythm, face intent, pouring out a metallic ringing sound into the evening. Occasionally he launched into something of his own, "Old Joe Clark" or an intricate and fantastic arrangement of that banjo classic "Cripple Creek." Aaron could only hold on and try to fathom the convoluted passages, strumming a few chords in support of his brother's flight. For this song Matthew loved; he played it incessantly, constantly adding to its intricacy, breaking it down and rebuilding according to his whims. The crazy notes jangled off his fingers, and the wagon bounced on down the road behind the horses, enveloped in a canopy of song.

Afterward, the sun melted down along the horizon and spread itself in a puddle of paint through the gray and blue clouds there, and they watched it go through the windows of the back room of the church, with brown doughnuts in their hands and the pungency of cider in their nostrils, talking, with Aaron participating—slightly awed, as he had lately been, at how popular he was becoming, at how easy he was beginning to feel with these people, how he liked them: how, after so long, he could feel the shell loosening, beginning, perhaps, to fall away from him, to make him easy and not alone. And for it he had to thank his happy brother, who was moving him into a different life, a new life of shared feelings, understood emotions, simple friendships. At this rate, he felt, with a delighted amazement, it would not be long until he could make it on his own, without Matt's gentle prodding. He would have learned the ropes of this kind of thing, would then have the best of both worlds; and how good that would be.

And then everyone sitting in a circle on the floor, kids learning to be Indians, cross-legged, while the Brothers Young took over for some serious folk singing, not serious at all but easy, loving it, all of them loving it and them—and the scene played itself out in variations of the summer gone, the new-arrived fall, a pattern of life that stayed rattling in Aaron's head for years, and quilted out to a patchwork form like this:

Matt wears old corduroy pants and a flowery shirt with the tails hung out; Aaron, white Levi's that aren't, and a sweat-shirt faded by time and washings, with MICHIGAN across the front in big letters, that he has picked up somewhere. Both of them in tennis shoes, Matt seated on a high stool with chrome legs and a blue seat, Aaron on the floor with his yellow-tan guitar butted in his lap, its neck poked up like a periscope aslant, twelve silver-and-bronze strings tight and gleaming and vibrating impossibly to sing out the strange fine songs in rhythm to Matt's particular picking way up the neck of his battered guitar.

Start with a fast rhythm, light, high up on the top strings and up the neck a bit, skipping three fingers over the strings rapidly, so the silver sound soothes out fast but soft into the room, letting everyone know there's music here:

Vrrrrrrzzzzz

and then up to add in the bass strings and pick up speed and all of it louder now and suddenly drop into your rhythm the blue-grass style of fingering that sends a swift chill to the spine, hitting a chord on the beat and then in between that and the next beat chopping down the finger on an open string (hammering-on) to skip up the note with a sliding sound:

Dowwwwoooo

hitting it fast, over and over, always on the off beat, until the
room is filled with silver, hand-beaten out of a wooden box
with fingers:

Vrrrrrrzzzzz
Clang, ta-chang, chang, chang
Dowwwwoooo
Clang, ta-chang, chang, chang
Dowwwwoooo

softening. Swing into the words then, as if you've been waiting an eternity of long black nights in somebody's cellar of
the soul, crying to let out with the words:

I'm gonna send thee,
How shall I send thee?

and thinking: *How* can *I send thee? Man, you got* ears?—and
you're already long gone down the hall from anyone who
can't hear, who can't feel:

Vrrrrrrzzzzz
Clang, clang, clang, ta-chang
Ta-chang, ta-chang, chang, chang
Dowwwwoooo

all fading off and gone and them with it.

And when their hips and thighs ached so badly they knew
they would not sleep for the rest of the night, but lie feeling
the fruit of their efforts, with the mind still spinning out the
tunes long after the body had grown tired—when they felt
it was that time they would glance at each other and grin
apologetically and—

" 'Bout had it?"

A nod. . . .

—slip into the rail-haunted patterns of their favorite, the song to end evenings with and send them all—performers and audience—to bed with a clatter of iron rails in their dreams, the spirit-ridden ballad called "Fast Freight":

> As I listen for the whistle, lie awake and wait,
> Wish the railroad didn't run so near,
> 'Cause the rattle and the clatter of that old fast freight
> Keeps a makin' music in my ear*

Aaron clipping out the basic freight train rhythm—*clickety clack-a-tat, clickety clack-a-tat*—and Matt ranging up and down the strung throat of his brown battered discovery, improvising, until a final soft fading out and the metallic train twang of an E string said it better than either of them could have, so well no one ever needed to ask, said: *That's it. There isn't any more.*

And by that time there never was.

Then tiredly home to the lonely house and the other side of life that was there waiting.

So life opened that summer and fall like a dark flower Aaron had never seen and was afraid of, but could not resist. He took out several girls from the college and from the church. Through the week he and Matt dutifully made their trips to the hospital, where their mother had returned late in the summer, and on weekends they sated an increasingly large circle of friends with their brand of folk music. They were invited to all the parties now; their type of singing was hitting all over the country and they were much in demand as entertainers, increasingly popular as individuals. Aaron's gamble, it seemed, had paid off. His last-chance effort at saving a relationship had succeeded and more, bringing dividends he had not expected. Aaron and Matthew were a team now, the Brothers Young, moving together, working out songs and routines, hamming it up, winning friends and influencing people. . . .

Once they had an argument while practicing—only once. After ten minutes of losing patience, Aaron looked at the floor and said tightly, "You've got to come in *strong* with the tenor there."

And Matt answered heatedly, "I'm doing this *my* way; if you don't like it you can go on away and leave me alone."

They looked at each other and Aaron said, "All right. We'll do it your way."

"No—" said Matt reluctantly, with a disgusted look on his face, but not at Aaron. "No, let's—try it both ways, and then work it out. . . ."

Aaron thought, almost screamed inside his head: *We're making it. God, Matt, we're making it, like brothers, can you see? You can see it, can't you, Matthew?*

And with summer gone, autumn followed after, rolling like a pebble down a dark hole and ending with the rattle of death.

On a Sunday morning they were called by the hospital. Their mother had gone into a coma. By the time they got there, driving silently through the streets of yellow leaves, she had died.

"But she was getting better," said Matthew, as the three of them stood in the special room for next of kin in the hospital. "I really thought she was getting better. . . ."

Aaron put a hand on his shoulder, but his brother shook it off and went to stare out at the trees.

There was no more music after that, except once. After one of the difficult days that followed, Aaron came home alone from the house of some relatives where his father and he had spent the evening. Matthew had not wanted to go.

Matt had said little since the day in the hospital, and Aaron, feeling his success slipping from his grasp just at the crucial time, had tried in vain to repair the ties that seemed somehow to have severed.

When he came into the dark house he heard a sound from the basement that chilled him. And that was the moment he was most aware of human suffering and the soul-ache of loneliness. It was the sound of a banjo.

Aaron made his way through the darkness and stood at the top of the stairs, in a fall of moonlight from the kitchen window. The sound came from the bottom of the stairs, in the recreation room, and, standing there at the top, by the light of the moon he could just see the silver glints of light flashing off the chrome as his brother sat, invisible to him, on a high stool in the middle of the room. The music came like idiocy, tortured frenetic monotony designed to dull the nerves, ease the pain, a scattering of tossed notes so wild he almost did not recognize the tune. Silver flashes struck his eyes from the dark.

There was a pause in the madness, and Aaron heard a soft sound of breathing pulse up to him in the echo of the notes. He stood without moving.

"Matt?"

There was a long silence of held breaths before he said again: "Matthew?"

A pause, and then: "Yes."

"What—are you doing, Matt?"

Another pause.

"Nothing." The voice did and did not sound like his brother.

"You shouldn't be down there all alone in the dark." He took a step. "Why don't you turn on some lights?"

"I don't want any lights. Don't come down."

Aaron stopped with one foot on the step and felt with

a horror something that he needed badly beginning to leave him.

"Why not? Don't you want some comp—"

"No. Aaron—don't come down."

And then a long silence and then a final blow, like something settling over him and squeezing him until he could not breathe:

"Go away. Just go away."

His hand began to tremble on the door frame, and the shattered notes began to flow again, hammered up from below.

I've let him down, thought Aaron, in that moment before turning. *He needs me, and I need him, but we can't reach. I've failed in some way. I've failed him and me and all of us.*

Eventually he realized, as the bond slowly rebuilt itself, that he had been wrong at that moment; it was not a question of failure or success. He saw that Matt had only played out his personal grief, a thing that no amount of closeness could alleviate or share in. When Matt turned eighteen and enlisted, he was exorcising his own demons and beyond the ability of anyone to help, to predict, to feel responsible for. Aaron saw, finally, that the difference had been there always, that it was not his fault, that his only failure had been in trying the impossible. He realized it and yet did not realize it, did not stop the silent hurt each time he called back the flashing banjo in the darkness, the aborted notes of "Cripple Creek" that rang on and on somewhere to painlessness, a strange and final serenade in the night.

5.   Before supper, while Dooley was showering, Paul came over again. Aaron was lying on the bed, watching the fading light change the ceiling from patterned white to gray.

He turned his head to look at Paul against the screen, but did not smile or speak.

"You got a minute?" Paul hesitated, fingering the door handle.

"I guess. Unless you want to tell me about the great time you had at the party last night."

"No. I don't." Paul came in and sat down in the chair as he had the day before, lighting a cigarette. Aaron wondered why he smoked so much.

"Thursday. Tomorrow we take off for home."

Aaron said nothing.

Paul watched him, then settled back in the chair, seemed to consider, and almost imperceptibly nodded. "I think maybe I'm going to tell you a little story," he said. "About something I did when I was in the Army." He brushed his sheep dog hair out of his eyes, squinting at a curl of blue smoke from the cigarette. He coughed once, but choked it down.

"I was stationed in Germany, you know."

"No." Aaron looked at the ceiling.

"Yeah, well, I was. I was. And one Friday night I was in Berlin on pass. I was sort of moving around from bar to bar, getting decently high, looking for a girl, and I ran into this girl and started buying her drinks. She was maybe in her late twenties, built like hell, and I was all of twenty-one. She spoke English, so we talked. Her name was Regina—Gina. That sounds Italian, doesn't it? but she was German. I guess it's German. She was from Frankfurt, but out in the country someplace, away from town, and she'd left home with this guy and come to Berlin. He was going to marry her, he had *said.* Only he didn't; after a couple of weeks he ran out on her and now she was broke and looking for somebody with a car to take her back home. She was willing to pay.

"Well, I was always a gutsy kid. I told her I didn't have a car, I'd ridden in with another guy, but I could probably borrow his on Saturday and take her home. I couldn't guarantee it. She said that was all right, she'd take the chance. I said of course she knew how it ought to be paid for, and she said oh, yes, that was fine with her.

"So we went back to my room and stayed there all night and all day Saturday until late in the afternoon, and then I called this guy at his girl's parents' house. He was there but he needed the car. He said I could borrow it in the morning though, so I told Gina and she said yes, great, fine—so I hung up and we went to it again, all night until late Sunday morning. Then I called the guy again.

"Well, one of those crazy things had happened: he'd totaled his car out the night before; somebody had piled right into him. Nobody was hurt or anything, but we'd have to hitch a ride back any way we could get it.

"I told Gina I was sorry, and she said that was all right, I'd tried, and anyway it had been fun. So I felt bad about it and I gave her some money to eat on, just in case, and she left. I saw her again later, in some bar, playing up to a sergeant. I don't know if she got back to Frankfurt, or whether she decided to stay in Berlin; she didn't seem very worried about it one way or the other."

Paul put out his cigarette and lit another. Aaron rolled his head a little to look at him in the darkening room. They could hear the *swish* of the shower, and light traffic passing on the highway.

"Now, tell me, Aaron," said Paul, looking over at him in the twilight. "Was I a bastard for taking advantage of that poor girl? Am I a bastard?"

They looked at each other. "No," said Aaron quietly, "I don't think so. I guess not. No."

There was a pause. "Then," said Paul, "what about Steve, and what about Ann?"

"That's different. That's different."

Paul sighed. "You don't seem to get it, do you? Steve isn't any saint. He's married and separated. He learned it early from his parents. See, he didn't have the kind of family you seem to have had. And he doesn't quite work on the same value system. All Steve knows is that he's going to die one of these days when he isn't expecting it. He's doing his living now and not betting on the come."

"I know that. Paul, you don't have to apologize for him."

"But that's not—"

"Or for yourself either. You don't have to justify anything to me—why should you? I'm hung up about something; it's me, not you. I don't even really know what it is. . . . Why did you come over here?"

"I want you to understand Steve."

"*Why?*"

"For the same reason," said Paul, "that I want him to understand you. Because both of you keep building up cases against each other, based on your own cockeyed viewpoints. You're a strange product, damn it. You seem to come from a genuinely happy background. So do I. But Steve has had it completely different. And Steve is hung up worse than you are, I think. He's playing some kind of game with you, Aaron. He's fascinated, he's pushing to see what you're really made of. He doesn't believe you."

"Well, that's rough. I don't believe him either."

"I know it. I know that."

They both looked around the room in frustration. Paul recovered first and said, "I heard what he said to you about Ann."

"I don't care what he—"

"I think you deserve to know," said Paul, "that he was lying."

Aaron looked at him.

"He just made it up. Ann wasn't here at all last night.

Whatever you do, you make them loyal. Steve never even got started with her. But he expected you to show up, after the other night. It kind of threw him when you didn't. So he said that to see what you'd do. That's the way he is—playing his game for keeps, taking the pieces right out of life."

"And why me?"

"Because he likes you—yes, he does," added Paul to Aaron's look of contempt. "And because he's fascinated and because he doesn't believe you. He doesn't believe you. Rod and Phil showed up last night. He knows them, he's met them a thousand times. Dooley is predictable and dull, he's obvious. There's just you."

Aaron was about to answer that there also was Paul—but Paul was on his feet, stretching. They could hear Dooley, finished with his shower, grumbling in the bathroom. "I'll tell you," said Paul, yawning with his big fist over his mouth, "Michigan is all right, but I've been thinking. I know a guy who went up to Canada, prospecting for uranium. He hasn't found any, but he's still up there, and he wants help. You ever fish? The fishing is unbelievable in Canada. I think *next* summer . . . except . . ." He grinned at Aaron. "You know, sometimes people give me the coolie jams. Just people in general.

"Think I'll mosey over and get some food. Turn in early for a change. See you."

The screen door closed and he was gone.

6.   They finished up the area on Friday and Aaron drove home. There was a letter there from Susan; he took it down to the recreation room, turned on the heater and sat down under a lamp.

DEAR AARON,

You're probably trying to remember if you know anybody in Seattle, so maybe if I apologize first and remind you of some things, you'll know it's only me. I told you I'm a poor letter writer—that isn't much of an excuse, but you always were understanding. I've been working in the psychic void of the bank (remember The Bank?) and have been too out of it at night to write a line.

Bankers' hours must have changed, he thought.

All right, so much for excuses. Another reason for my not writing was that I don't completely trust anyone, even myself, and I couldn't believe that what happened on our last day could have been as good as I remember it. I decided maybe we shouldn't be much in contact during the summer. Looking at it in the cold light of reality it seemed best to put things on ice for a while and let this serve as a cooling-off period for both of us. I know what you think of things like that, but you're so impractical that somebody has to pay attention to these things, so I decided it ought to be me.

Good old Susan, he thought. If ever anyone came close to being Salinger's "breathtakingly level-headed girl" it was Susan.

Anyway, damn it, I miss you in spite of myself, and your last letter hurt too much to ignore, with that "if you get a chance, write" business. And what are these weird things that seem to be happening to you? Hitchhikers indeed!

That was the only mention in the letter of what he had written about, this one oblique reference. It disturbed him a little, but he was so glad to have a letter from her that he overlooked her lapse of interest. And when he got to the "With love, Susan" ending he read the whole thing over once more and folded it away, thinking: *What a girl, my Susie,* thinking that things now were really going.

1.   On Monday they moved into Durand, a town whose
sole distinction, apparently, judging from the signs in parks
and other places, was that its high school band had played in
the Rose Bowl a few years before. It was a nice town, Aaron
thought it prettier than Owosso or Fenton, and for once he
had a room to himself.

It was not much of a room. They signed in at the Durand
Grand Motel, with Steve telling them hopefully that it was
the best place in town. It was a step down from what they
were used to. The Durand Grand was owned and operated
by an old lady who smoked cigars and eyed them with a
half sneer that made it plain *she* knew the things that were
being planned—maybe she would squelch them, maybe not.
She made everyone pay a week in advance.

The rooms themselves were ancient and cramped, with tile
floors and thin walls; Aaron's bathroom was tiny and contained a concrete-floored shower stall whose nozzle trickled
out a single bullet shaft of mineral-hard water that would
barely make suds. There were no television sets but, in some

eldritch attempt at modernity, there was a swimming pool. There was no air-conditioning.

It rained all the first day and the crew did not work. In the early morning only one room had been vacant and the crew sat in muggy abjection and watched the long slant of rain streak out of the gray, tumbling clouds. The rain beaded in the open screen-covered windows and everyone sweated and moped, throwing glances at Steve and mumbling about their "stellar crew chief." The sky grew very dark and grumbled over the rain, cracking shafts of blue light at the town so that everyone was afraid to swim in the pool. They argued about the war and watched the rain pebble the surface of the pool as if it were being slowly boiled, and later Steve and Rod and Dooley played knock rum while Paul fiddled with his guitar and Aaron watched out the window and listened. Vanneman spent a long time sitting in the john with the door open, vocally cheerful as always. The room filled with an earthy scent that should have caused a poet to think of mortality, and Aaron appropriately brooded. Later everyone went swimming in the rain except Aaron. They called to him from the pool, falling like dead weights off the diving board into the peppered water.

"Hey."
"What."
Pause. "You shouldn't speak with your eyes closed."
"Why not?"
"Just doesn't seem like a good idea."
Aaron rolled up on one elbow and opened his eyes. He had sunk into a depth of sleep unusual for him, dreamed his old dream, slept too long, and his head felt dizzy and weighted, like a diving helmet. His mouth tasted like cotton and his eyes crimped shut so that he had to force them open, as if he had

been dead for years and was coming back to life, a heavy-headed, hollowed-out mummy.

"My God, it's night."

Paul was slumped inside the door, arms folded in the darkness that was not black but gray and heavy, more a fog than a darkness. "It's only seven o'clock."

"Is it still raining?"

"Yep."

Aaron sighed and fell back on the too soft bed. It had a faint erotic smell of must and urine. "I feel like I've died. I always sleep crazy when it's raining. What day is it?"

"Still Monday."

"I slept all day."

"Yeah." Paul stretched and lighted a cigarette. "You're making me sleepy."

"I feel all dead. Thanks for waking me up."

"I banged on the door, but I guess you didn't hear. I thought you might want to go eat with us."

"Oh. Yeah." Aaron swung his legs over the side of the bed and put his head in his hands. "Wouldn't you know I've got a headache?"

Paul nodded. "I don't feel so great myself. This rain does something to my lungs—it's like I can't breathe. I ought to go back to the West. Mexico." Aaron groaned. "What the hell. Didn't you sleep last night?"

"Yes, I just—this rain—it always puts me right out, when I'm lying around and that soft rhythm is out there. When I was a kid I used to love to hear it tin on the roof. I had this built-on room and I could hear it."

Paul coughed. "Listen, would you rather I brought you something back? I can—"

"Oh, hell, no. I'm okay. I just feel like I'm made of lead or been run over by a truck, that's all. Like I've been drugged. Are you all going to eat together, or what?"

"Well, I thought you might like to go with Steve and me."

"Where's Dooley?"

"He went with Rod and Phil. I guess he figured—I don't know—"

"He's getting chummy with Vanneman; I don't care. I haven't paid much attention to him lately. Give me a minute to clean up."

Outside there was an insistent summer drizzle that seemed colder than it really was. It made Aaron feel miserable but helped wake him up a little as they walked down to the other room to get Steve.

"Great weather you drummed up for us, chief."

"I aims to please," said Steve, putting on his waterproof jacket. "Vanneman likes it, anyway."

Paul laughed. "He'd like it if he saw the ark come floating past."

"It'll be lousy working when this stops."

Aaron sneezed, said, "Oh, great," and they got into Paul's car.

Durand's "business district" is shaped like a letter T. They drove the three miles into town and found the others in a restaurant along one of the short arms, seated around a huge circular table that was large enough for all of them. Aaron was finally beginning to wake up, and realized he would probably be awake all night.

The girl brought their food and when she left Vanneman said, "Hey, Aaron, you going to hustle that waitress?"

Aaron looked at him and said nothing and Steve said, "Let's knock it off, Phil. I'd rather hear about your war plans, if you want to know the truth."

"My *plans*, as you so succinctly put it, fella, are to stay out of it. This man's hide is too sacred. Anyway, the Air Force can handle the war."

Paul looked at Aaron uneasily. But Aaron continued to eat,

listening to the opinions as they were picked up from that morning, and fitting each of them into the category his view represented. Vanneman and Dooley were for bombing the hell out of everything, and differed only in that Phil wanted no part of the war himself—"I just want the bastards to give up before my two-S runs out"—while Dooley, patriotic, thought he might enlist if his engineering program did not work out. "We've gotta go sometime. I could probably get a pretty good job if I enlisted."

Paul was a pacifist. For some reason, possibly that Paul had served his time, this surprised Aaron. "It's lousy," said Paul simply. "It's immoral, illegal, anything else you want to call it."

"Strange coming from you," said Rod. "You were in."

"Don't give me that, either. This is a bad one; it's a wrong one and we're going to get burned."

"Well, hell. You know what I think." Rod shut up.

Dooley brandished a fork. "I think we gotta stop them somewhere. It's either there or on the California beaches. That's what the President said."

"On the California beaches," mused Paul. "That's interesting."

"They better stay off our beaches," said Vanneman. "Surfing's crowded enough the way it is."

Everyone had an opinion on the war except Steve and Aaron. In the bar in Owosso Steve had been high and had argued for the sake of arguing that *something* had to be done, either winning or pulling out, he did not care which. But sober, Steve did not seem even that interested.

"I'll tell you, gentlemen," he said when pressed. "I am a law student, and the entire matter is below my dignity. Besides, it doesn't apply to me; they aren't going to be drafting any law students."

Paul grinned. "You hope."

"What about you, Aaron?" Steve looked at him and there was scarcely a flicker in his eyes; maybe he did not remember.

"I don't have any opinion," said Aaron. "I don't think about it much."

"Great. Welcome to the clique of the noninvolved." Steve gave them all a sweeping look. "You see, gentlemen, it's simply a matter of having other things on our minds. Aaron and I have other problems to worry about. Deeper, more personal questions, of subtler skein."

"Subtler *what?*"

"The warp and woof of existence, gentlemen, the fine points of universal morality."

"You're a couple of asses, is what you are," said Rod, summing it up.

2.   When they went outside the rain had stopped.

"Think maybe we ought to bang the old git fiddles to-night?" said Paul.

Steve and Aaron glanced, did not glance, at each other. It was not certain to which of them Paul was speaking.

"Don't both of you answer at once."

Aaron said, "I didn't bring my guitar."

"I'll tell you something," said Steve suddenly to Aaron. "You keep talking about that damned guitar, and you never bring it. I'm beginning to think you don't *have* any guitar."

"Well. I do too."

"Why don't you ever bring it, then?"

Aaron sighed. "Listen, boss, can I play yours and Paul's tonight?"

"Well, since you didn't bring this legendary twelve-string of your *own*, I guess you'll *have* to."

They picked up some beer and settled into the cramped

room Steve had drawn. The place was already falling down around him; clothes and maps were everywhere, and they soon added beer cans to the assorted refuse. Aaron and Steve had become wary again; they treated each other with a polite impoliteness and Paul, watching them both with scarcely veiled amusement, made them nervous. They were careful of what they said, carefully careless in their manners.

The room was heavy without air-conditioning, and they soon moved out onto the steps. Rod and Phil had gone to a dance they had seen advertised somewhere, but Dooley came over, lost without his television. Rod and Phil were back soon, bringing more beer.

"How was the dance?" Steve paused, executed a melodious and intricate maneuver, and slipped back into the standard beat where Paul was waiting wryly.

"Not so good," said Rod, popping off the tab and handing a beer to Aaron.

"High school guhls, mostly." Vanneman sat down on the curb beside the gravel drive, draining most of a beer at one pull. "S'matter, George, how come you aren't watching— Oh, I forgot."

"Yeah, rub it in," said Dooley.

"I forgot, I forgot."

"Hey, I saw the old lady watching you boys through the window when I pulled in," said Rod. "I don't think she likes guitarists."

"That lets *them* off the hook," said Vanneman.

The sky had remained heavy after the rain and there was no movement of air. They sweated and began to slap at mosquitoes.

"Little vultures," said Rod.

Paul handed his guitar to Aaron. "They're always around, aren't they? They can smell people for a mile and they come out of the grass like demons. Things never get so good for a guy that some damned mosquito somewhere isn't waiting to bite him behind the knee."

Aaron agreed. "You can have this back. I'm getting inside."

"Let's *all* go in," said Steve, scratching.

So they moved into Steve's room, dumping maps and clothes off the bed and two chairs, moving suitcases and guitar cases and rolling beer cans under the bed.

Then they played, and Vanneman organized a four-part harmony to accompany the guitarists, and they sat on the bed and chairs and on the floor and sang "Hang Down Your Head, Tom Dooley."

They ran out of beer about the time Vanneman took advantage of a lull in the music to ask Aaron what he *really* had done with that waitress all night, and Aaron was rearing back to hit him when Paul grabbed Aaron from behind and said, "Let's go get some more beer."

The night was cooler now. They crunched across the gravel to Paul's car, feeling a thin rain begin to fall again. "Who knows?" said Paul. "Maybe we won't be able to work tomorrow, either."

"One of these days," said Aaron, "big-mouth Vanneman is going to push himself too far."

Paul grinned at him, flipping on the headlights and windshield wipers. "With all due respect and affection, Mr. Young, I doubt if you could put a dent in Phil's armor. He's a spongy one."

Aaron laughed and shook his head. "All right. Wait and see. You saved his hide a minute ago."

"Well—somebody's."

They drove through a twilight zone of rain like a billion needles in the headlight beams. Paul tuned in the Big Oak station and they listened to truck driver songs and hillbilly laments poignant and saccharine, warm and dry, in the car with the highway empty and the town deserted.

They got the beer and started back, and when they were almost there Aaron said quietly, "Are you really a pacifist?"

"Of course," answered Paul, as if they had been discussing this for an hour. "So are you."

Aaron gave him a quick look. "What?"

"Well, aren't you?" There was a pause. "That's why it was so funny to me, your almost taking a poke at Phil. You don't want to do things like that, Aaron. Somebody who *likes* to fight will kill you one of these days."

"Wait a minute—" Aaron shook his head, as if the beer were only now clouding his brain. "Look, I'm not sure where you got all this wild information of yours. . . ." They drove in uneasy silence for a few moments. "I figured out why I slept all day."

"Oh? I thought the rain—"

"Well, that too. Yes, sure, the rain. But it was after I heard you guys discussing this goddamn war—"

"Sure. You hate it."

"Now *wait*. Wait a minute. I don't hate it. That is—I don't *know* whether I hate it or not. I don't—all you guys have these violent opinions on this thing, on lots of things. And I—don't. I just—like I said at dinner tonight—I don't *think* about it. I don't think about anything like that."

Paul turned down the radio on Tex Ritter.

"What do you mean?"

"What do I mean. What *do* I mean? I started thinking today, when all of you went swimming. This girl of mine—"

"What is her name? Susan?"

"Susan, yes. She's like all of you, only more so. She's so involved in social issues I—sometimes I can't stand to listen to her. I think I'll scream."

"Go ahead."

"I mean, when I listen to her. Sometimes."

"Oh."

They pulled into the motel drive and sat for a minute, listening to the rain on the roof of the car. Aaron wished they had not gotten back so quickly. He was beginning to feel that he was onto something. Not the war, no—it was not simply the war that bothered him so he could not think about it, and there were special reasons for that, if he cared to admit them. It was something else; something was keeping him from being able to care about anything outside himself and his own experience. He had something to clear up before he could pay attention to any of that. And how, he wondered, did that bear upon his relationship with Susan, his feelings for her?

"Hey. Hey! Come on, get that beer in here!"

Vanneman was standing half out of the door, yelling at them through the rain.

"God—damn—him." Aaron turned to Paul. "Tell me this: why do you go through all this?"

Paul looked at him curiously. "All what?"

"Steve's hard-driving hedonism. You don't like it all that much. Not like Steve."

"Maybe I do. Besides," he added, grinning, "somebody has to keep tabs on the activists."

"All right. All right—but one thing, though. I don't know where you got this crazy idea that I'm—a pacifist, or anything like that. But I wouldn't count on it. I think maybe I'm something else completely, Paul." He looked out the window. "And if that son of a bitch keeps it up, you may find out. Both of us might."

Paul was looking at him.

"Come on!" called Vanneman.

"Well, maybe," said Paul.

They still did not have enough beer to get more than pleasantly high, enough to make them loud enough and late enough for the old lady to bust up their party at twelve-thirty. It was still raining.

Aaron went back to his room and, due largely to the beer, slept for three hours. He woke up fully clothed lying on the bedspread, listening to some extraordinarily early-rising bird outside and unaware of how long he had been awake. He could no longer hear the rain and the room was chilly. He undressed and jumped into bed before the spot where he had lain could cool off, but he was awake now and he was busy thinking and he did not go back to sleep.

How was it, he thought, that he could have gone with a young woman for five months now—been in love with her yet—and it had not occurred to him that the things that mattered most to her meant almost nothing to him. How could that be?

The answer was, of course, he realized, that he *had* known it.

It was not that Susan was such a great one for personal involvement, anyway. The difference between him and Susan was that Susan loudly espoused causes but never, or seldom, became really involved in them. But Aaron (due to his inability to *keep from* being involved? No . . .) Aaron refused or was unable to align himself with one side or the other. With any side. Why was that?

Susan had dragged (yes, well, practically, *dragged*) him to a Cinema Guild film on the McCarthy hearings of the early 1950s. She had taken him to see a documentary on China, and a film on therapy for retarded children, and a film on the Watts rioting. He had found them all interesting, but there came a point in each following discussion at which he listened more than he talked, at which point he had become (well, yes, he thought, lying in the night) *bored*.

On one of their ill-starred picnic attempts, they had driven out of Ann Arbor and into a thunderstorm so heavy they could not see the road in the rain. Parked by the side, they had necked until—haphazardly, it seemed to him—Susan had become irritated at his unwillingness to discuss the war (the war, the war) and they had had their own minor thunderstorm inside the car.

And he could see her viewpoint. Every thinking, intelligent person, as well as many others unthinking and/or unintelligent, was worried about all the things Susan was concerned with, whether they got involved or not. If you did not worry about these things, what in God's name did you worry about? The new morals? Ridiculous. He accepted the new morals. What else, then? What else?

That was it. Nothing else. Nothing that he could see or think about.

And this disturbed him most of all, because he knew there was something.

3.　　　It rained off and on all week, but they worked every day. Aaron usually had to go into a field of wheat or alfalfa right at the beginning, and that soaked him well enough so that anything less than a good drizzle never bothered him. It did make him uncomfortable, being wet and cold early in the morning, and irritable when he brushed against the fireweed plants that grew sporadically all over the state. They burned through his wet Levi's like hot needles, and he griped to himself.

But the following week was sunny. It was late June now, and the summer heat began in earnest. He slept without pajamas or a T-shirt because of the heat, and sometimes he would stand nude before the dresser mirror and look at himself. He had been working hard for over a month now and had never been in better shape. Sam said he was disgustingly healthy, and it was true. It felt good to be in shape, strong and able to feel the muscles in his arms and pectorals, to see the deep rich color the sun had given him. His groin was a great proud thing of velvet softness and iron hardness and he was proud of it, thinking of things he would do with Susan in the fall, wishing he did not have to wait.

The three weeks in Durand comprised the best part of the summer for Aaron. Susan's letter had almost carried him out of the doldrums and he worked hard and fast in light farm country that was ideal for outdoor work. The corn was high above his head now and some of the wheat had already been cut, leaving stubble fields that were easy to cross. He constantly reminded himself that never again would he have so good and healthy a job, and he made himself enjoy it.

He came across all kinds of animals. Walking down a dirt road with woods on both sides, he came upon a large snapping turtle, and spent several minutes determining the strength of its jaws by having it clip off assorted twigs. After a rain there were always frogs around the ponds and creeks he came across. And one day, as he was crossing a cut field of wheat, a hen pheasant had squawked and whirred away from him, gliding low with a dropped wing into the woods. A few steps farther he found a freshly hatched chick, still with its eyes closed, so weak yet it could not hold its head up, covered with a fine down. He did not touch it, but looked and moved on.

There were also snakes in abundance. On some wooded road, where the trees arched together overhead, he could expect to surprise some snake or other, sending it into the woods with more of a crashing sound than he would have thought possible. Since there are practically no poisonous snakes in Michigan, if he found one near a stream he would often go chasing off after a better look until it disappeared in the weeds. But he only wanted to look and did not care to get too close. He had never really cared much for snakes. Once he almost ran over a big black snake that was stretched across the road in the sun; he hit the brakes instinctively and the snake moved off so quickly that he was not even certain it had been there.

There were other odd and more disturbing things about the summer. He would come across deserted ramshackle farmhouses amid overgrown brush and weeds that reminded him of the experimental film made by George Manupelli of the university, in which a girl explores such a house until at the end all the doors close in on her. Remembering this, alone with the house and no people in sight, only fields and trees and one dirt road as far as he could see, Aaron would hear the breeze blowing old boards, see the trees bending in it and a wooden-handled pump with a rotten platform above the well, feeling an eeriness hard to imagine at other times. The sense that once people had been there who now were gone was acute to him, and at such times he would stand in the weeds trying to grasp something that eluded him.

Three things happened in Durand that served as preludes for what was to come. The first was a growing hostility of the birds. All summer, as he waded through alfalfa or swam through blowing wheat or tramped on plowed land, the birds had been with him, sitting on the wires with their armored toes, flying above him and jabbering, a vociferous conglomeration of sparrows and grackles. They had entertained him at first, and later he had paid them no attention.

Then as he was crossing a field of weeds and brush one morning, he heard a slight *whirrr* and something went *flap* on the back of his head. He turned to see a bird rising up ten feet over him, hanging in the wind. It was so ludicrous a situation that he thought of the Hitchcock film and almost laughed in spite of his shock—but the bird wheeled and came down again, and he swung at it with his clipboard. It flew up and sat on a wire, shrieking.

From then on he was forced to keep an eye out when walking in fields, for the birds followed a few feet over his head, and occasionally one would dip at him, like a tiny black warplane. He knew it was because they nested in the brush and stubble, that it was normal for them to react with violence toward someone threatening their nests; nevertheless it was disconcerting, and at times he would stop and yell at them, throw stones or clods of dirt at them, alone with them far out in some field beyond the road.

As he was driving out to his area one morning, a flock of something rushed out of the woods by the road directly in front of his car; quail, he thought, or pheasant chicks. He stepped on the brake, but the birds tried to run parallel to his course, and he hit one of them. When he got out to look, picking up the dead bird and spreading out its wings, he saw that it was a young hawk—had the sharp hooked beak and hawk tail feathers.

He was suddenly stupid with grief. He had hunted as a boy, with his father, although not for some time now, and that had never bothered him; he was not in the least squeamish about things like this. Yet all he could think was that here was a hawk, a beautiful thing that would soon have been hovering far up on a high wind, and he had killed it. He looked at the fact of death in his hands and could not realize it. He laid it on the floor in the back of his car and was halfway out after his first pole when he became aware of himself. "You idiot," he said aloud, and after checking the pole he came back and tossed the dead bird off into the brush.

They did not go out or play the guitars every night, and

Aaron was able to do some reading: he was involved early in July in a copy of *In Cold Blood* that Sam had given him. He had been a fan of Truman Capote since high school.

But he had never seen anything like this. Reading alone at night by the narrow-shafted bed lamp, he immediately identified with the murdered family: his parents, himself or Matt as the son, and Susan as the daughter. With the dark warm around him, he would lie in the night picturing his youth disrupted by a horror such as this, torn from his sleep, tied up, his mother and father and brother and Susan all blasted away by shotguns in a nightmare that he could not conceive actually happening, yet had happened. As they finished up Durand his days became unrealistic sojourns through an eighteenth-century-like glorification of nature; his nights were tumbled away in dreams and a bewilderment at what was happening to him. He wrote in his notebook:

> Capote's book has had an unusually strong effect.
> Fear of death. Fear of terror occurring in an environment of, supposedly, contentedness—& the knowledge that this did happen, & could happen. I keep checking to see that the door is locked.
> Hitchhikers.
> Tetanus.
> Birds.
> Ann and Steve.
> Am *afraid* all the time.
> Personal vulnerability & the insanity of everything—
> I keep thinking of these. Why?

Then they were finished in Durand and he went home and wrote to Susan:

This won't be a letter, probably, but more like a note to myself which I hope you will keep for me. It's 12:45 and I've just spent an evening with Sam, drinking his beer and coffee and talking about everything from home videotape recorders to C. S. Lewis.

I'm home now, and a strange thing has happened that I want to get down while I have it. I pulled up in the driveway, got out and looked at the sky, which is incredibly clear and star-filled tonight. The garage light was on, so I turned it off and came inside, into the living room. "Hi," I said, but nobody answered, because Dad was asleep on the sofa and Ashley, my uncle, in a chair. They'd been watching a science fiction movie on the late show, and as I stepped into the room a dinosaur was chasing a little Mexican boy across the screen (he escapes; I've seen the picture)—and right then I had one of those strange and jarring clicks of memory I sometimes have. I remembered; that crazy movie, that dinosaur chasing the kid, brought it all back in one surge, and I was suddenly melancholy—just for a few seconds, until it faded. But I remember so well that Friday night late show, always a science fiction movie for the last five years or so. I remember three things specifically: first, there was a time I used to watch that damn movie with my father and my brother—not every week or anything, just sometimes. We would sit and watch those really bad pictures & would point out to each other sometimes the inconsistencies, the improbabilities, the bad dialogue, etc.—even as we enjoyed the show, & we were never vicious about it. It was sort of amusing & sort of a game.

Then that passed, & a couple of friends I used to hang around with in high school got into the habit of coming over on Friday &/or Sat. nights & staying late, & we'd watch that show—turn all the lights out & watch, all together, the three or four of us, if my brother watched, & we got a real kick out of it. Except, my Dad had sort of been cut out of the pleasure, & he got to the place where he & Mom would go to bed around eleven & leave the living room to us. That makes me sad now, sort of, but I never thought of it at the time.

Anyway, that time passed the summer I worked nights in a factory, because I had to work Friday nights then. I remember going to work every Fri. night all that summer, & I'd leave for work about 11:30, just as that show was coming on—& the strange thing is that even though I'd outgrown the show (or thought I had), I missed it that summer more than anything else. I probably wouldn't have watched the thing even if I'd been free to—but the thought of not being *able* to watch it any more, of going to work just as it came on, made me sad, made me miss it a lot as if it were something valuable. I swore when the job was over I'd start watching it again & it would all be the same. But I never did & it never was. My mother was dying by that time, & I was always too busy growing up fast and also not growing up & being sad after that to let myself have the luxury of watching that show again. It was gone, cut off from me, forever, I guess.

Anyway, that's what hit me when I got home tonight. For what it's worth. More tomorrow.

But he sent it off the next day without adding anything.

4.   Then they worked four weeks in the Muskegon–Grand Haven area, far out on the west coast of the state. On Monday mornings Aaron would get up early and drive all the way across the state on bad two-lane highways and check in at the Holiday Inn near Muskegon. Then he would work in his area in the suburbs of that city while others worked farther out among the hills and sand dunes that have blown up high along the lake. Muskegon is one of the largest and nicest cities in Michigan, and with the state park and its beach a few miles away in Grand Haven, the plush Holiday Inn, and a room air-conditioned against the July heat, a half-stone's throw from the pool, Aaron should have enjoyed the four weeks very much. In some ways he did—but in other ways and for several reasons he did not.

He was back in with Dooley, and after the privacy of a single room in Durand, he was not happy to be listening to Dooley's tedious monologues again. This, his television pro-grams, the shared bath and a growing irritability on Aaron's part made it difficult for him to put up with Dooley. Fortunately, George had become Vanneman's friend, and now spent part of each evening watching television in his room, while Rod, Vanneman's roommate, had taken to hitting the bars with Steve and Paul, since Aaron had again stopped going out at night. After dinner in the adjoining lounge, he would go up to the room on the second level and pull one of his books out of the suitcase. He would stretch out on the bed and read until eleven and then go to sleep. With the dining room close by and the pool, which he used only a few times, Aaron did not have to leave the motel once he got back from work; thus he spent his four weeks in Muskegon. He heard rumors from George about what the others were doing; Rod, strangely enough, seemed to be more than equal to any carousing that Steve planned. He threw himself into it with a seriousness that surprised everyone who had not known him before, and between the two of them, with Paul's ever-tolerant presence, they were turning Steve and Paul's room into a part-time orgy chamber, as Steve and apparently Rod too pursued their pleasures fiercely like doomed Romans.

Working in town was new to Aaron, and it was an interesting change. If his map covered a suburban or residential area he would leave the car and walk for blocks down the tree-lined streets with his clipboard, checking an average of three hundred poles a day. It was pleasant work unless he struck an area where the houses were not served by alleys behind the back yards; then he was forced to walk through the yards and the resulting detours caused by fences and hedges, the suspicious housewives and occasional husbands who came out to see what this stranger was doing, and the dogs, who often caused such a racket that he really did feel sinister—all turned the job into an unpleasant chore that, once begun, seemed unending. Relatively little of his time was spent in districts like this. The rest of the time it was enjoyable.

He spent the days now with his mind drifting, seldom concentrating on anything in particular, refusing to focus on the things that had been bothering him. He was determined to sleep his way through the problem until it disappeared, though he did not know this. He thought he was enjoying an easy job, a vacation from rural work, a good summer, a promising summer with Susan waiting at the end of it.

On the weekends he had found two letters at home from Susan. One of them consisted mostly of a tirade against her parents and the bank, wishful thinking about what she *ought* to be doing this summer, and a good deal of her sensible didacticism on the reasons for urban rioting and the pseudo-fascistic elements that seemed to have taken over the destiny of America. Again she had practically nothing to say concerning his letters. Then in her second letter she hinted darkly that her suspicions about him were possibly confirmed, due to his constant talk about his family, his past, etc., etc. She did not like to talk or listen or read about wonderful families (these being all alike, as the Russian had said). Her way of looking at things irritated him and he took it out on Sam.

"Why the hell does she have to be so objective? Sometimes I get the feeling she isn't even human. She's a product of the University of Michigan School of Social Work and she thinks like some kind of machine that makes graphs on a long sheet of paper."

Sam was sitting at the kitchen table drinking coffee out of a huge brown mug with *Papa* lettered on it. He gave Aaron a mock-sympathetic look. "Aren't you being just a little bit maudlin?"

"Do you know," said Aaron, ignoring him grandly, "on our third—no, second—on our second date she stood back and looked me up and down and said: 'You know, I'm going to *enjoy* analyzing you. You seem so normal and healthy, and I'm sure you aren't.' Can you beat that?"

"Well," said Sam, who was not feeling particularly magnanimous today, "what did you fall in love with her for, then, if you don't like that?"

"I don't know. I guess she has other qualities."

"Maybe you wanted to be analyzed."

"Hell. Maybe I did."

But most of the time he did not think about Susan. Most of the time he was paying attention to the map, or telling himself what a wonderful healthy outdoor job he had, or thinking about books or movies. His main area began right at the lake and extended into the city dozens of blocks. He wandered up and down alleys, ate lunch in whatever convenient restaurant he could find, and tried not to think about anything unpleasant. He tried to think only good things of Susan.

When he was in a good mood and thinking of Susan, he would plan things to do with her in the fall when they got back to school. He decided that he would take Susan up north across the Straits to Mackinac Island, the summer resort. They would take a weekend and go horseback riding, loaf through the antique stores and gift shops, and wander on foot over the trails and rocks and hills and woods of the island. They could get a motel cheap in Saint Ignace on the upper peninsula (for which he would make her pay half, as a symbol of what they were doing *together*) and they would sleep together and make love and be *in* love and it would be daring and exciting, like a honeymoon.

He played a game sometimes, imagining that he would look up and see Susan there in Muskegon, by some miracle transported from Seattle to surprise him, and he thought what it would be like to see her, crossing a street and coming toward him, so unexpectedly and impossibly there. But she never was there, and he did not play the game too long.

Once he sat at a corner in his car, ready to head back to the motel, caught in the middle of his drifting by a picture of Ann wanting and needing him in her loneliness, and he wished then that he had helped her and in the process helped himself, learned something of love so that he and Susan could understand each other better in the fall, but not only for that—

And suddenly his senses grew sharp: as he had found himself in the middle of a road, skirting a stand of woods, pushing into the breast of a wheat field, so now he noticed a yellow lawn sprinkler in a yard seen through his right window. It was almost close enough to wet the side of the car, spraying out past the sidewalk to the street—if it had been on his side he could have put out his hand and touched the water—and he smelled the very sweet, clean freshness of the water flung out upon the air. He watched a row of transmission poles that marched from somewhere uptown across the back of a drive-in theater, behind the screen, and straight off through the fields and into the woods—each of them fifty feet tall and branched at the top like a Martian. Nonconformists, those boys, he thought. Transmission poles went where they wanted to go, paralleled no roads except by chance, and did not give a damn whether they could be got to or not by such as him. He wished then—this was his day for wishing—he wished he could be like that, simply *break away* and move off where he wanted to go, concerning himself with important and relevant things (not the things Steve had mentioned: "personal questions, of subtler skein"—he did not give a damn for subtlety, he hated subtlety by now and wanted frankness, openness). He wanted honesty and he was not getting it and the bad thing was that he knew where it could be gotten, the only place it could be gotten. And Steve and Paul and the others had nothing in the world to do with that.

So now he was living a self-imposed exile, and it deepened one day when he was lying on his bed after work, watching the news on television while Dooley showered. He always watched the news in the same way, if he watched at all: he watched with a vague half awareness, and half of that not really interested. This left a one-quarter alertness that was in turn half preoccupied with the personality and presentation of David Brinkley or Walter Cronkite, the remaining one-eighth involved in the news itself. For a long time now he had been unable to make himself really care about what was happening in the country or in the world. The current crises, foreign and domestic, were carbons of earlier crises that had involved him and, supposedly, others, crises about which he had been unable to do anything except worry and talk, specu-late upon, become bored with. Eventually his helplessness had not mattered anyway, as the affair either was solved or faded away out of the news and therefore reality. Only immediate things remained to involve him, only matters that affected him, *personal questions, of subtler skein.*

And now he lay in fascinated horror as he learned of the murder of eight student nurses in Chicago. Mouth open, eyes widening, he gazed like a paralytic at the screen, where the camera moved over the apartment house and then, briefly, showed a photograph of the lone survivor. He watched within a cloud of unbelief, unable to take his eyes from the picture, unable to move and turn off the set. When the program went on to other news he did not hear or see, though his eyes were locked onto the screen as Dooley, trying to whistle, hopped out of the bathroom.

He did not eat much supper that night. He told Dooley he was sick and walked back alone, leaving George to his dessert. Then he tried to read, but his mind would not take in the words and he kept going back and going back. Finally, as darkness chipped away the light from outside, he lay without a lamp, using the television as a flickering blue-white light that lulled him to sleep. Dooley did not come back early, and he got up at ten o'clock and went down for a hamburger, but moved on into the bar instead and drank two double bourbons. Then he came back to the room and went to bed. He had stopped sleeping properly since the final week in Durand, and now, beginning a recurrent horror that would last for weeks, he woke up in the night, seeing girls die in the muffled dark and listening to Dooley breathe, choked and tortured in sleep as if he were being strangled.

5.   He kept writing in his notebook; the deaths he had heard about had shaken something loose in him, and he was unable to continue his banal progress through the summer. So he scribbled in his unintelligible hand because it was better and easier than brooding upon the thoughts that came to him; he hoped that by putting them down in ballpoint ink he could close the notebook cover on them and they would be gone and no longer in his head.

He was thinking about Matt again, about the way Matt always went out for athletics and especially baseball. Matt had played in the Little League at Hoyt Park every summer, and when Aaron did not work or worked part time and was off in the morning, he would drive with his mother and Matt and some fellow players over to the games and watch his brother play, feeling a family pride that no one would have tried to suppress, because that was his *brother*. He wanted to write about that now for some reason, so he scribbled away in the evening when Dooley was gone and he was alone in the room:

We would go to those baseball games in the morning, spreading out a blanket on the green but trodden grass behind and up a hillside from the diamond. We would sit on the blanket on the grass and watch Matthew play, and sometimes I would walk down the hill to the green park building and buy popcorn for us and we would sit on the hill eating popcorn and watching the game.

A bit Hemingwayish, he thought, but not bad, and that was the way it had been. *Besides*, he thought, smiling, *why not Hemingway? Am I not a psychological Jake Barnes?* But he realized that he was only posturing for himself, so he went on:

My brother Matthew was the best second baseman in the league, and almost never would a ball get past him. His only problem was that he could not hit well, and this hurt him. It hurt him with the team because they needed hitting, and with himself because he tried so hard and wanted so badly to be good at it. Still, he was popular with everyone, respected by the kids on the other teams because he was so friendly and he worked at his position, and, of course, also, there was that fast glove of his.

Aaron stopped and read it over. It was pretty good, but of course it was not really the way he remembered it, the way he had it in his mind, with the warm sun that was not too hot in the morning, with the cool breeze and the wide-leafed trees of the park and everything green except for the gray-suited players and the colored trim on their uniforms. Maybe, thought Aaron, he should try to write a poem about it. But he felt that a poem would be even more abstract and removed from the actuality of it than his prose, and he was not trying to memorialize it or any such thing, he was trying only to say it so exactly that he could get rid of it, like so much useless junk that kept getting in the way of his summer and his life.

Well, what else? he thought in his father's voice. *Spit it out, boy.*

His mother was simple and childlike and totally innocent, and he loved her. And because he loved her he took her for granted until very very late—indeed, until too late. After that, for the rest of his life, he would call himself a fool for this crime, universal and childish though it was, natural though it was. And the universality of it and the naturalness of it would comfort his guilty soul not one bit. He would never think of her again without chastising himself, and because of her he would never consider himself as highly as he had always thought he would. He hoped that he had at least profited from the experience in wisdom and would never fail in the same way again, but in all honesty he could never claim even that. For the rest of his life he never would think himself one-half the man he should have been.

Well, he thought. *If she was all that innocent, where did you come from? And what was this "never"?* As a matter of fact, what in God's name was any of that? Had he really been cruel to his mother? (Wait—it said: "took her for granted.") Well, perhaps that was the truth. But he had started out to write about Matt, and now he was expanding that to write about his whole family, and in terms he did not care for, in ways he did not care to remember. What would he write about his father?

But no. He had nothing to write about his father.

Well, then, he thought. *What else? Ashley?* His uncle Ashley, who had moved from Indianapolis to live with them because of something that had failed in himself? *Ashley had it too,* thought Aaron unconsciously, half-consciously, for some of this was at the quite open level where truth is faced and recognized, accepted; he was not *there* yet and so could think about Ashley's near-fatal attachment to his family— could think, actually, of making a little story out of it, just the way it had happened, and then, if he did it right and well enough (and in the first person—no tricks like that last entry), he would no longer have to think of Ashley or any of this. *Yessir, boy,* he thought, *art is great, if it works.*

So he wrote his little story:

A BAG OF FRUIT

That summer I worked nights in a factory. My mother had gone into the hospital in April, becoming so bad so fast that we spent the spring in a daze, expecting her to die at any time. Then the cortisone brought a remarkable improvement, and in late May she came home. Soon afterward she was up and around.

Everyone held his breath that summer as she continued to improve, but I did not spend as much time with her as I should have. Suffering from that adolescent inconsideration that, like all selfish diseases, came at precisely the wrong time, I lived with the outward appearance of a normal teen-ager, did all the things everyone else did, bought myself a car and a new guitar. Behind the selfishness was an attitude combined of forced belief that everything would be all right if only I did not think about it too much—and a deeper and crippling certainty that things would not be all right, which I did not want to think about.

When the summer was almost over the cortisone lost its effectiveness and my mother went back to the hospital, knowing then that she would die but refusing to give up hope. Our relatives took turns caring for my father and brother and me and everyone visited her, and I quit my job and tried to concentrate on school.

Ashley worked in a factory in Indianapolis and did not begin coming up regularly until that fall, when he would bring his family for the weekends. He was my mother's brother, a tall thick-haired man resembling the young Paul Newman, and he had, like all the brothers and sisters and their husbands and wives, grown up in the Depression without much education—for all of them including my parents had been poor, surviving through ingenuity, cheerfulness, hard work and the WPA of Franklin Roosevelt.

Ash, the youngest of eight children, became one of the most-liked uncles when the next generation arrived. He had a soft smile and an affability that won people to him, and his outlook was simple and practical and human. All of us liked to be with him; we would wander through cut-rate stores, Arlen's, K-Mart, laughing at his comments on the special sale merchandise as he held up an adjustable screwdriver or a ten-cent plastic flashlight. "You know," he would say, "that's useful, for the price. . . ." The comments were delivered in a soft and twangy Indiana voice, and more often than not he would end up buying some worthless tool or piece of junk because it was "too good a bargain to pass up." Sometimes Dad and Ash would start a routine in some grocery store, Dad as a customer inquiring something of Ash, who immediately became a voluble know-nothing clerk for the amusement of us and nearby shoppers. But they did not do this that autumn.

Like many Depression families, my mother's was extremely close, and no one I have ever seen had as strong a feeling of kinship for his family as Ash. Because of the number of relatives who were always around, it was necessary to take turns, no more than four at a time in the hospital room; had it not been for this, Ash would gladly have stayed through all the visiting hours. He was especially close to my mother and, though no one could read his feelings accurately, I was to learn that autumn, better than anyone, I think, what Ashley was facing.

Ash had always hated hospitals. His mother had died in one at the age of seventy, and he was convinced that that was too young, that being in her own bed in her own home with family love and care would have made a difference. The first time he came into the room at the hospital, I was there. After greeting us, Ash looked around and said disgustedly, "Couldn't you have got a drabber one than this? Good Lord—we got to brighten this place *up*. Who wouldn't be sick in *here?*"

The next time he came he brought an armload of flowers and a bag of fruit and some magazines and a portable FM radio. "Now we'll see!" he said, moving into the room like a force of nature. He found some soft music on the radio and opened the brown paper bag. It was filled with apples, oranges, tangerines and grapes and bananas and grapefruit. "I forgot to bring a bowl," he said, presenting my mother with a bright miniature sun of a tangerine. "Bite into that, kiddo. A little fresh fruit works wonders. Smell that, that *natural* smell—think *I'll* have one, if you don't mind." Then he moved around the room, eating the tangerine, peel and all, putting flowers in vases and water glasses, humming with the music. Everything was suddenly brighter, including the patient, and as Ash sat down to read aloud a story from *Better Homes and Gardens*, he smiled triumphantly. "Ha. Now we'll see."

When he was with us that autumn the weekends were divided between trips to the hospital and games of basketball on the concrete driveway in front of the garage. No one ever came alone; there were always five or six uncles and cousins to make up teams. Ash was still fit—he had played first string in high school at Terre Haute Tech and his coordination had not deteriorated much—and the teams would argue over who got Ash, sometimes tossing for him because his side usually won after a high-scoring marathon that left the cousins sweating and the other uncles winded, while Ash went ahead and practiced free throws.

These games were such an ingrained part of us that no amount of solemnity could have stopped them—probably it contributed to them, as a release from the apprehension that built as the illness became worse. Ash would play as long as there was competition, even if it was only for a game of twenty-one. And I was always willing to play with him.

We went to the grocery store late one Saturday afternoon and bought a bagful of fruit: apples, oranges, bananas. We looked for tangerines but could find none, and this upset him. "Your mother can't stay up there and just eat hospital food all the time," he said. "She needs good fresh fruit. Tangerines or not, this should cheer her up and help her too. . . ."

I looked at Ash because of a tone in his voice I had not heard before and could not recognize, and because he should have known his sister was too ill now to care anything about fruit. But he smiled and said, "Tomorrow I'll show you boys how to play basketball. Maybe tonight, if there's time." And because I wanted to, I took the bait and said, "Well, you can *try*."

Ash had got a fruit bowl out of the kitchen and brought it with us to the hospital. Dad was there. My mother was asleep and Ash carefully arranged the fruit in the bowl. "She'll like it when she wakes up and sees this. I wish we could have got some tangerines, though. She likes them and a bowl of fruit isn't right without good tangerines."

Then we sat and Ash and Dad read the paper they had bought from the boy who peddled them to the rooms. I watched my mother for a while and then looked out the window until Ash was finished with the comics and the sports page. I had started to realize finally about the wasted summer when I had been too busy being young and hiding from reality to face what I knew was coming. I wished that I had waited another year before getting that job, had not worried about the car or spent so *much* time playing the guitar, had spent more time with her, just a little more time with her.

She did not wake up before visiting hours ended; the drugs they had been giving her kept her asleep much of the time now. Dad took two of my aunts in his car and I rode home with Ash.

"I wish she could have woke up while we were there," he said. "I wanted to show her the fruit and how it looked in the bowl. Food like that works wonders with people. None of this phony canned stuff; that's *real* food. People don't get much real food any more."

We went on for a while in silence through the night and the air came like sweet breath through the open windows.

"Ash," I said then. "It doesn't look good, does it?"

"I wish I'd come up here more before this fall," he said. "August. Why did I wait till August to start coming? Because your Mom was doing so well, I guess. It's an eight-hour drive up here." There was a pause. "Oh," he said. "Don't worry, boy. Things'll get better. Things'll be all right."

"Ash, I think Mom's going to die."

"No," he said. "Oh, no, no. Don't ever say that; don't even think it. She's going to be all right. She's just sleeping a lot. She needs to sleep a lot." He kept his eyes on the street, driving carefully. "It's the food, though, a lot of it," he said. "I *wish* we could have got some tangerines. Your mother always did like tangerines. Damn it. Tomorrow we're going to have to go out and find some tangerines somewhere."

I almost said, *The stores are closed tomorrow*, but I did not. I had recognized that same tone of voice, understood it now, and said instead, "Sure, Ash. Okay."

He did not speak again until we got home. Then he grinned at me and said, "Let's turn on the garage lights. I'll wipe up the court with you."

"No, you won't," I said, knowing that he would. And we played basketball until midnight, when the mosquitoes finally drove us in.

6.   Aaron thought about that story as he worked the next day, trying to keep it straight in his mind as other things crowded in, things he had not put into it, had deliberately left out—but they wanted into it.

He worked on the edge of town, checking poles on some busy streets and in urban neighborhoods where the houses were large and old and beginning to show signs of desertion by white middle-class families.

A couple of Negro children, a boy and a girl, were playing on the walk in front of one of these. They watched him curiously as he circled around for a pole at the rear of the house, ceasing their game until he returned to the sidewalk.

"Hello," said Aaron.

The girl looked up. She was six or seven, dressed in a purple skirt and off-white blouse, and she wore a shawl around her head and shoulders.

"I am a poor old widow lady, and this is my little son."

Aaron stopped. "Is that right?"

"Yes, sir. I work my poor old fingers to the bone so we can eat."

The boy, a year or two younger, grinned at Aaron. "Hi, sir."

"Hi yourself. May I ask you, ma'am," he said to the girl, "about how old you might be?"

"I'm old. Twenty-eight; and I ain't getting any younger."

"I see. Tell me this: do you think it would help a poor old widow lady and her little son to get along if somebody was to buy them a Dairy Queen from that place over there?" He nodded across the street.

All three of them smiled, but the girl stuck to her role. "It would help make ends meet, sir."

"I wanta mi'kshake," said the boy.

So he took them across the street and bought the boy a mi'kshake and the girl a cone with chocolate on it and himself an ordinary cone. They stood around watching each other and he thought it would be nice to have some kids.

That was the day a man climbed a tower at the University of Texas and, with a high-powered rifle, shot forty-five people on the surrounding campus. Aaron heard about it on the radio, but he did not watch the news on television that night, and his reaction at first was one of disbelief and then a stunned inability to realize that so much death could be surrounding him this summer. Everything seemed to be crumbling into an insanity of death and violence; he thought about it only a little and then repressed it, adding it to the material that ran wild through his mind at bedtime or when he awoke sweating and cold in the air-conditioned dark.

He dragged out his notebook again and reread the story. It was true, it had happened this way, but he had made the story as much about himself as Ashley, and he knew that the story of himself was by no means complete with such an innocuous account.

He had left out too much, and he would always leave it out, for he was slowly working around the edges of something now and he could not bring himself to actually put it down in cold factual words on paper. That was why, he thought, with a realization, that was why he had not really written of any of it to Susan—because it was impossible for her to believe or understand, useless for him to try to tell her.

Oh, Susan was an example of a type, all right (he wondered what she would think of that—his fitting her into a category the way she always did others), she was another one like Steve, another one of those who live to break up people's dreams for them—*wham*, and nothing left but firewood. She was an example, a type of product of a type of family, and their ways were predictable and set. Upon meeting someone like Aaron, they first reacted with suspicion toward the home itself, and then, since that was in the past and closed to investigation, with a feeling of skepticism toward the product of that home, because *he* had been there, yet—and this infuriated them—he was apparently unable to see that the ideal he believed he had known could not have been.

What had he done, Aaron wondered, that made him different from people like that? How had his family been so different? His family had done only the usual things as he grew up, explored the mad dream of the fifties, that sad insane somnolent decade when do-it-yourself and togetherness and pray together and backyard barbecue and move to the suburbs and and and and had all conglomerated into The Good Life that the parents of his generation had worked hard for and fought hard for all their lives to reach and now, having reached it, found they had raised up a generation of children who told them they'd been wrong, gone wrong, followed the wrong American trail and now had reached a dead end. And yet so much of all that had been innocent and understandable and good.

Perhaps his problem, he felt, was primarily one of excessive recall—he kept *remembering* things. They were in themselves, most of them, innocuous memories of things he had no particular reason for recalling; it was only that they were finer and sadder and worthier than things that had happened since, things happening now, so they kept coming back. People have a way, he thought, of coloring the materials of their

pasts so that they would be there and ready, of correct satu-
ration, necessary hue, when they were needed later, for whatever psychic reason. And now he was calling them in, little
bits and scenes like embroidery that had psychic cash value,
as it were, for him: it was like a bank account or a good stock
to lean on in hard times, and these were hard times.

Speaking of embroidery, for example, that was one of the
things, a quick flash scene *zip* of his mother at her embroidery, putting flowers and birds and trees into the fabric of
their pillows and sheets, little green leaves and men and maid-
ens courting, and red strawberries. *Zip, zip,* all gone but there
still. . . .

His father gardening (it was rare and frightening to recall
things about his father, for that man still lived and was vulnerable in a way even Matthew could not be, for Matt was
only his brother) placing those fabulous craftsman's hands
deep into loam, shaking dirt from dangling roots, dropping
bulbs into holes spaced evenly along their little Indiana
house. . . .

His brother, age ten, with a cub scout cap and a yardstick,
playing cavalry all over the living room, chasing Cochise. . . .

None of it meant a damn, except that there was enough of
it, strung end to end like motion-picture film and recording
tape, enough of it to make twenty years, the twenty best
years he felt he would ever have, twenty years and four quick
trembling lives, and it had been short and happy and filled
with love.

Oh, they had taken a trip to Florida when Aaron was
eleven, a good age for crawling over the cannon in the Spanish fortress at St. Augustine, for riding the little train through
"Africa U.S.A.", where the animals were freer than he'd ever
seen them, and where he had been afraid to have his picture
taken beside a real "native," black and near-naked and loin-

clothed and holding an African spear and shield—afraid, but slightly too old and yet too young not to do it, to stand grinning with a frozen gut beside the huge black man while the shutters clicked and there he stands today in Kodacolor, eleven and grinning as only a scared boy can grin. They had got lost on a bad road in the Everglades, had gone in and in for what seemed hours, under the trees hanging Spanish moss over the road until it seemed dark for early afternoon, he and Matt sincerely wondering if there were a way out, and then they found a town and soon after no more swamp. They had passed a chain gang working on the road, fierce-looking men in gray, the first convicts Aaron had ever seen and he half-expected them to make a break for it while the red and gray Dodge was passing by, a beautiful new getaway car with four innocent hostages, but they did not. In South Carolina he got a jar of red dirt such as he had never seen in Indiana, and in Georgia and in Florida too they could see wild boar grazing in the woods and stubble fields beside the roads, mean tough animals with tusks that could mess a man up or even kill him. And at Silver Springs three beautiful ladies breathed from an air hose dozens of feet below the surface of the amazing clear blue water. And at Marineland they saw sharks and eels and barracudas and sting rays and watched a porpoise leap fifteen feet to take a fish right out of a man's hand. He had seen this much later on television and it was not the same, because he was older and it was television. But then it had been the four of them, two days driving south, south, wrestling in the back seat with Matt, the two of them leaning out a window into the hot wind and singing a nonsense song Aaron made up:

> *We're riding away on the old Mississippi,*
> *Riding away far to go—*
> *We're riding away on the old Mississippi,*
> *Riding away far to go, go, go.*

The four of them heading into the American dream, togetherness and the summer vacation, nineteen fifty-six the perfect year for it, Ike in power and Dulles holding back the Russians, prosperity everywhere and cars starting to sprout fins, no recession yet and no Sputnik, Korea settled if you didn't look close and Viet Nam just getting started, though to most it was still Indo-China and nobody would know it well for ten years, "Qué Será, Será" on the radio with Doris Day, and Gogi Grant with "The Wayward Wind," and Elvis with "Love Me Tender," "I Want You, I Need You, I Love you." Oh, Jesus, America and boyhood and the family.

Oh, Susan didn't *believe* in the family, his family; nor did Steve or Ann or anyone but Paul, who had been there maybe in his own way and knew better, knew maybe that what they had done was of little importance, of no importance—that it was a combination of sensibilities and tradition. What had Susan claimed? That the Western family unit was practically gone among the upper-middle class in America. Yes, but, yes, but, *but.* Aaron had not come from an "upper middle-class" family, at least not until fairly late. Far from that, the roots that bound his family together went so far back there was no tracing it, and only now, only with one member dead and another retired from life and another prostituting himself into murder to salve his wounds did he, the fourth, see it as a breakup of a family, and a way of life, and therefore, since he had participated in the best of it and now too in the worst of it, the very death of it, did he see it as a tragedy that would drive him forever. Because Aaron had come from an ideal home—that is, a family unit of the sort that is rare in practice but not in theory, and not in desirability according to the long-standing ideals of middle-class America. Everyone would like to have come from a family like Aaron's, yet so few actually did that he was unable to find any of them, except maybe Paul—indeed, people thought him a pretender, distrusted him instinctively for their own protection.

And now what do you do, with your mother dead and your father building irrelevant furniture and your brother killing people who were possibly closer to being honest and right than those who had hired him—and yourself busy correlating all of it like Susan herself and chasing down ghosts at the same time? What do you do—when you have been educated away from such a life, when your sights are systematically raised over the heads of people who love you and have not changed on you—when your religion has lost you, your family has lost you, you have come a long way, you think sometimes, toward losing yourself? What, thought Aaron, do you do?

Well, he could not write about it, and especially about the end of it. He could not write about his true feelings that calm and eerie summer, his attempts to believe all would be well when he knew it could not be. He had attended the family prayer sessions with the pastor of their church, asking God to heal her with His love and mercy—and Aaron fluctuating between belief and unbelief, faith and apostasy, praying on his own each night as he drove to work, to let her live, just let her live. The folk singing with Matt, alternating with times he sat alone in his new car in the park at Ojibway Island, trying to *realize* it, trying to prepare himself for something he had not experienced, could not believe would ever happen. How in the fall his father had told him to let the college officials know where he would be each hour of the day, in case the call came—and he never did it, because he did not want to be called; it was as if by his being unavailable there could occur no reason for finding him, until that blind Sunday they had stayed home from church for no reason his father could name, and Aaron had dreamed, the night before she died, dreamed that she had died.

The images fell on him like a black rain, the carefully put-away feelings and unwanted memories: How his parents had taken drives through town on cool summer evenings when they thought she was improving, driving through the nice sections of town, the newer sections to which they had once talked of moving, past the home of their doctor, and he—a man after all, a human man—would be in his front yard on his hands and knees, working in his flower beds. They would blow the horn and wave to him, and he would wave back, but never as gaily as they. How the ambulance had come to take her away for the last time to the hospital, and Aaron had not been there, had been playing somewhere with Matt while their lives crumbled and their world turned upside down. How they had gone to a movie when their father worked late once, before she went back, rather than stay home with her because it was the final showing of—something or other he had since forgotten.

How they kept her drugged and sleepy and when he visited her and spoke to her she would wake up, and her eyes would be wild for a second and then turn to him and recognize him and she would relax, and her eyes would show only tiredness and love.

How they entered the funeral home, which needed no description because they are all the same, evoking a sweetly nauseous feeling of death, a sensation as much felt as smelled in the flowers and heard in the low talk and seen in the objects there—Aaron thinking that there could be no more horrible place on earth than a funeral home—and everyone crying except him, and if he had had the power he would have let them all die right then, but especially Dad and Matthew and himself, because it was a kind of pain that even humans should not have to endure. As he stood there useless and helpless and unable to realize himself or any of this, the horrible security of his family suddenly left him, leaving behind only a new-old kind of sad wisdom, and he saw that his family was not really a great and omnipotent protector at all, but only some grieving people crying out their hearts, which were, after all, very much like his own. In that brief and drawn-out moment, for the young man poised at the edge of his crisis, God Himself became a little less than God.

He would not write any of that, he *would not think about it* or any of his failings. He slapped the notebook shut and buried it deep in his suitcase and then, alone again, he walked through the early August night to the bar and played the jukebox while he sipped his way through a ten-dollar bill.

7.   Steve leaned across the big round wooden table in the Holiday Inn dining room on Thursday morning of their last week in Muskegon. He waited in the expectant silence and then leaned forward a little more and said, "We're going to Greenville."

Vanneman put down the doughnut he was holding. "Oh, boy."

Rod said, "Is that a place?"

"Why, of course it's a place," said Steve jovially. "Oh, yes. It's practically in the center of the state. Over by Big Oak."

Vanneman looked at Steve and then said decisively, "You're kidding. They wouldn't really pull us out of here for some cheesy place like that, would they? They wouldn't do that to *you*. Not to *your* crew."

"What do you mean, 'cheesy'? You've never even seen the place, I bet. You'll like it. Really."

"But *this* area is infested with resorts and beaches and women. It's the only part of the state I really like."

"Me too," said Dooley, working away at his breakfast while

Aaron leaned on an elbow and sipped tomato juice. "Even if I never get to the resorts."

Paul laughed. "Greenville is a kind of resort area too. Only it happens to be surrounded by—uh—"

"Farms," said Rod.

Paul nodded, laughed and began to cough. Everyone else groaned.

Steve looked sincere. "Well, yes, guys," he said carefully, "I must admit the—uh—pleasure cruise is over. But we're all going to work extra hard today and tomorrow and finish up, and Monday I will meet you all bright and early in Greenville. Back to nature, and all that, what? This city life is making you all soft anyway."

" 'City life,' " said Dooley, his mouth full of egg and toast. "I been climbing sand dunes since we've been here."

Steve grinned. "Don't worry, boy—I appreciate that. We've worked hard. But things'll be all better in Greenville."

"Uh-huh."

"Oh, yeah."

"Sure."

Steve's grin became a helpless smile. "Now, boys, boys—this is your crew chief talking. Would I lie to you?"

"He's done it again," said Vanneman. "The bastard has sold us into the swamp for a handful of beads."

Now Steve was all righteous indignation. "Why, you ingrates. You didn't even thank me for *bringing* you here. Why can't you take it like Aaron? Don't hear Aaron sobbing around, complaining, do you? Huh?"

"He's not losing anything," laughed Vanneman. "He's been in his room every night for a month."

"He just hasn't given in to dissolution and degeneracy like the rest of you."

Vanneman smiled. "I think that waitress in Fenton took the fire out of him—"

"All right," said Aaron.

"Listen, boys, my loyal stellar crew: I'll tell you about life. Big Daddy wouldn't lie to you. You got to take the good with the bad, or vice versa. Something like that. We have had us a string of tolerable good luck, mighty parful good luck. Now—we got to take us some of the bad. . . ." Steve lowered his head like a riverboat gambler accepting the whims of Fate.

They looked at him respectfully and Vanneman said, "Shit."

Then they moped for a while. Paul yawned and stretched his way to his feet. "Guess I'll travel. See you guys in an hour at the Blackjack Bar."

"Yeah. Sure."

Paul leaned against the chair, coughing weakly. "I can't figure out why I'm so *tired* all the time."

"I'm sure it can't be because you run around all night," said Vanneman.

"Um. Ciao." And he left.

The others got up. "Listen," said Steve, looking at Aaron. "Paul and me are gonna take a few places apart tonight. As a kind of farewell to the coastal regions before we head inland. Anybody want in on it?"

Rod assented. Vanneman said, "Me and Dooley want to play some pool. We'll probably see you around, though."

Steve was still looking at Aaron. "I don't know. I've got some letters to write and stuff—"

"God, fella, you can write letters in the next world. Call her up and then come along—one entire round on me."

"I don't know, Steve. I'll see you later." Steve gave him a wry and impatient look as Aaron walked away.

It rained some in the afternoon. The weather was erratic on the coast of Lake Michigan; rain threatened every day or two in the summer, and when it came might last for ten minutes or three days, according to whim. Aaron finished up his map and quit early, sat out the time in his parked car, writing on a letter to Susan, and, recalling something Steve had said, pulled into the water-slick parking lot in slightly better spirits than of late. He showered, waited impatiently for Dooley and hurried through his dinner, watching with discomfort as George ordered dessert and took his time with it as always. When they got back to the room Dooley puttered around interminably, finally leaving to go out with Vanneman.

Aaron had been drumming one finger silently on the arm of his chair. Now he jumped up and, rubbing his hands together nervously, stood looking at the telephone.

Call her, Steve had said. Call her. . . . Aaron had thought about it all summer, toying with the idea, but only now did it seem plausible and he wondered why he had not done it before. Letters were all right, yes, but to hear her voice—to actually talk to Susan—

Then he sat down abruptly, suddenly possessed of cold feet. He tried to decide what he would say to her, what he would talk about. He could not call all the way to Seattle and then permit a tongue-tied silence to hang between them. Of course, she would have things to say. But he must have things to say too; after all, he was doing the calling.

He thought about his letter and decided against it—that was all too black and depressing. He did not feel that way now; on the contrary, he felt an elation that made him curse himself for not doing this sooner. Imagine the anguish he could have saved himself during the letterless period if he had simply picked up the telephone and called her.

He picked up the receiver and then put it down again and got one of the white three-by-five cards he used as bookmarks and a pen.

He thought for a moment and wrote:

> Her job.

This gave him another thought and he added:

> Your job.

Then for some minutes he could think of nothing else, but finally he had what he considered a respectable list:

> Her job.
> Your job.
> How is she, and me, etc. etc.
> Does she miss me?
> That "put each other on ice" business.
> The last day in A^2.
> When is she coming back?

That would take up enough time, he thought, what with the spontaneous things that would come to both of them.

He picked up the receiver. The man at the desk said they would put the call on his bill. (The company would not pay for that, but he could deduct it from the expense account.) He dialed the number direct to save money. The telephone rang three times.

"Hello?"

A woman. Her mother.

Aaron coughed and said loudly, "Hello. May I speak with Susan, please?"

"I'm sorry," said the woman. "Susan isn't home yet. Would you like to leave a message?"

There was a very long pause.

"Hello?"

"No, thank you," he said. "I can call back. . . ."

Then the receiver was in the cradle and everything was almost exactly as it had been a few minutes before.

Except that something had broken inside him and all the

despair that had built up over the long summer came hurling at him like the waves on Lake Michigan. He realized that he was losing her. Not that an overwhelming amount of evidence had mounted up: it was simply that at eight o'clock—eleven in Seattle, he thought—she was not home yet; she was out with somebody and he needed her and she was not helping him, had never helped him in her letters or her understanding. He needed Susan and she was out somewhere.

He kicked a wastebasket across the room. Then he went over and picked it up and dropped the torn pieces of his ridiculous white card into it.

Then the telephone rang.

He looked at it, for one insane moment believing it was her, calling him. To apologize? To sympathize?

He picked it up. "Hello."

"Aaron?"

"Who else."

"I thought I'd give you one more chance. You're only old once and all that, and the free drink still stands. What do you say? Want to go?"

"Sure," he said. "Yes. I'll go. I'm ready right now."

"Great. Come on down; we're traveling."

"I'll be there," he said.

So it went, he felt, riding in Paul's car out Seaway Drive south toward Grand Haven, with Steve up front beside Paul and Rod with him in the back—it went right back to his non-involvement (his immaturity) and her awareness of it. It seemed unfair, his losing her (if he was going to lose her, as seemed likely now) because he knew little of her view of life and cared little for it, rather than from having *done* anything wrong. He had not been interesting enough for her, interest*ed* enough, and that had hurt him. Not his sins of commission (for he had made few if any of those with Susan, or with anyone) but his sins of omission. And that seemed to him patently unfair.

They crossed a long bridge into Grand Haven and drove out toward the beach, past the musical fountain with its colored lights, Steve and Paul gabbling on some innocuous subject that eluded Aaron's half attempt to hear in the wind from the lowered windows. Rod looked out his window with his face set in its own peculiar tightness, the nervous appearance of holding himself in that Rod always wore when he was getting ready to release himself. But Aaron could not feel even his usual curiosity; he wanted to get someplace and drink, somewhere dark and noisy and frantic enough to involve him.

Then nothing happened and nothing happened and then he became aware of himself again and they were in a bar. Aaron was drinking Seagram's and Seven-Up, did not know how many he had had, did not consider stopping. He leaned on both elbows at the table and brought his head up to watch them playing pool. It was Rod and Paul, a far distance of some ten feet away and removed from him by a veil of much liquor.

"Hey. Where—"

"Take it easy, fella." Steve was beside him at the table, drinking, his face sharp yet out of focus, depending upon how Aaron looked at him and what he was thinking.

"Dozed off a little, did you, boy?"

"I have not slept much lately. Do you know," said Aaron, "I don't even remember coming in here. I do not remember coming into here. Herein." He leaned forward. "I *did* come in, didn't I?"

"Have a drink," said Steve, bopping him lightly on the shoulder with his fist.

"Good idea." Aaron drank, set the glass down. "Good. Good ol' Stevie. Mm?"

Steve chuckled.

Aaron thought of something. "Steve, boy, do you mind if I tell you something? Something personal?"

"Sure, kid," said Steve affectionately. "What's on your mind?"

"This sort of occurred to me, and since it is the very gospel truth, and tonight I have not only the guts to tell you, but also the inclination—"

"All right. Fire away."

"The thing I want to say, Steve, boy, is that I hate your lousy guts."

Steve looked at him and slowly shook his head. "Well, that's a hell of a thing to say to anyone."

They looked at each other through a gauzy curtain. "Go on. Don't stop now."

"I hate your guts because you're a plain and simple bastard, and you get away with it. I know things are going to catch up with you and you aren't going to get away with it forever—but I get tired of waiting for you to get it, and sometimes I'm afraid you aren't going to get it after all."

Steve looked serious now. "Some guys," he said, "can't take a drink without getting mean."

"Don't change the subject. I hate everybody like you, though," said Aaron confidentially. "It's not just you, anything personal or like that. I even almost really like you, in a crooked sort of way. It's your *type* I really hate. Guys who get away with things."

Steve grinned modestly. "I will admit I'm a lucky sort. You know, it isn't good to drink so much if you're only going to let it make you mean. You only should drink enough to keep a clear head, like me."

"Guys like you don't ever have problems like other people. You aren't afraid of things and you never feel guilty about anything and you just do as you like."

"Everybody's afraid," said Steve.

"Because you don't have any values except to get what you can while you can. The new morals crap was built for people like you. You don't have to feel anything. You don't have to care about people."

"There's a little game," said Steve, "that a guy told me about once, that he said he played whenever he really got scared bad. He said what he'd do was, he'd get in a car and go out on some two-lane highway and get going like hell, seventy or eighty miles an hour, and he'd wait till the road was clear except for one car coming the other way, and then what he'd do was, he'd get over in the left lane and go head on at this other car. And he'd stay there. If the other driver *also* pulled over in the left lane—and they always did, he said— then everything was okay and you got a big charge out of it and for a long time you weren't afraid of anything at all. You only did it when things really, really got bad, because, of course, it was dangerous. I never tried it myself. Everybody's scared, but I never got that scared. Especially after this guy got killed in an accident—I guess it was an accident."

Aaron was silent, looking at his drink, thinking of the time he had seen that game played, or something similar.

"Well?" said Steve. "Is that all? What're you thinking about?"

"Nothing. I haven't got anything else to say to you. I used to like you."

"Oh." They both drank for a while, not looking at each other. They could hear the clicking of balls and the drifting monotony of conversation, and finally Steve said, "Aaron? I want to tell you something. I was lying about what I said about that Ann girl. I made it all up. I never really did anything to her. Those girls we had that night—we picked them up in town at a bar. They were all dogs."

"Why'd you tell me that about Ann, then?"

"See what you would do. After all that shooting off your mouth about ideals and all, and then taking her out and staying all night. I thought it was—funny, somehow. I wanted to see what you'd say."

"I didn't do anything to her, either. We just talked all night."

"Oh. Sure."

"Really. I told you, I was hung up on Susan—I wouldn't have gone back on her."

"Do you mean to tell me," said Steve, "that you really are this way?"

"What *way?*"

"The way you come on. If you really hang that much importance on some girl and stick to what you say—"

"Well, I'll tell you," said Aaron mournfully. "Susan, I guess, isn't all she's cracked up to be, and me neither. I'm the one who had the great family, though. She didn't understand any better than you. I guess she'd make you a better girl than she did me."

"Well, if you aren't a case."

"Yeah, I know. You don't *believe* me. Nobody believes me but Paul. I think he believes me."

"Paul understands you, I think. He understands everybody, the bastard."

"Well, my background keeps twisting me up. My lousy good childhood. I wanted Susan to understand about that, but she sees things her way. Susan has problems of her own, and they're too large to allow her to give me the sympathy I seem to need. And I suppose the reverse is also true. I couldn't give her, because of my problems, the help and concern she apparently needs from me. It's a shame—both of us need help so badly we can't seem to help each other."

Steve said nothing, and Aaron thought of Ann, his frustration increasing. He remembered what she had done in her need and her willingness to help herself and him. Had he acted then, and long before, but especially then, perhaps now he would not be so much worse off.

"I'm a mess," he said, making it sound more like *mesh.*

"You certainly are," said Steve.

And then Vanneman and Dooley were there, Vanneman laughing and pounding him on the back and Aaron hating him, saying tightly, "God damn you, Vanneman, cut it out!" and Vanneman going over to pound on Paul, who was sitting at the bar and coughing. He finally had to go to the men's room, and when he came back his face was white and he drank a quick bourbon straight and relaxed again.

The two of them, Vanneman and Dooley, had had just enough to drink so that they were gregarious and talkative, which Aaron was not. He was not happy to see them. Vanneman had by now commandeered the pool table and he and George began to play.

Aaron leaned toward Steve. "Why don't we get the hell away from those bastards before I kill one of them?"

Rod had sat down with them. He said quietly, "How far is it to Saugatuck?" Rod had given up pool and was seriously working at his Scotch.

"Not very far. Why?"

"I know a couple of girls down there."

Steve leaned back. "You *do?*"

"Sure. Marie and Sandy. They're living in Saugatuck for the summer—it's an art colony, like, you know. They've got a cabin."

"My God," said Steve, "why didn't you *say* something?"

"Well, I knew them at school. And they're sort of friends of the family. You see, my aunt—"

"Why are we screwing around here?" interrupted Steve impatiently. "Let's go."

They caught Paul's eye on the way to the door, and the

four of them were just outside when Vanneman and Dooley came after them. The night was warm, without a breeze, and Aaron was sweating and unhappy.

"Hey! You guys aren't taking off without us?"

"Sorry, fellas," said Steve.

"Little private party," said Rod.

"No, you don't." Vanneman came up jovially, with Dooley behind him. "Nobody goes without we go! Right, Aaron?" He slapped Aaron on the back. "Any little waitresses tonight and—"

Aaron pushed him away violently and Vanneman said, "Hey," and came back. Aaron swung wildly and hit him in the stomach, crashed into him with a shoulder and sent him toppling like a shot elephant into a collection of trash cans at an alley. They made a noise like a train derailing.

"You crazy sonofabitch—" Dooley grabbed his arm as the others pulled out of their shocked hesitation and started forward. Aaron jerked free and swung again, catching him on the point of the jaw. Dooley went down like a sack of concrete.

"Aaron!" Paul got him by the shoulders then. "Take it easy!"

Steve helped hold him. "God, he's stoned."

"So is George," said Rod, kneeling on the sidewalk where Dooley lay, one foot twitching. Vanneman had got up and was holding his stomach. "Agh," he said.

"All right. All right!" Aaron shook off Paul's hands and brushed past Steve toward the car.

"Dooley. Hey, Dooley, boy—" Vanneman slapped his cheeks until George came around. Several people were watching now. Rod and Vanneman stood him up on his feet and he sagged again, his face the color of vanilla pudding in the street light.

"Better get him on back," said Paul.

"Yeah. I'll buy him a drink first." Vanneman supported Dooley with one big hand, holding his stomach with the other.

Dooley mumbled, "That bastard . . ."

"He's drunk as hell, George," said Rod. "He won't even remember in the morning."

"I'll remember," said Dooley, as Vanneman helped him away toward the bar.

When they got to the car Aaron was leaning against the fender with his arms folded, looking at his feet. "What'd you do that for?" said Steve.

"That bastard Vanneman." Aaron did not look at any of them. "Always shooting off his goddamn mouth and shoving people around."

"Take it easy." Paul unlocked the door and swung it open. "You really put George out of it."

"Got in the way. Sonofabitch is always getting in the way." He ducked into the back seat and fell onto the floor.

Rod propped him up in the draft from the window, and by the time they reached the village of Saugatuck, nestled like a Vermont art colony with its antique shops and summer cottages and cabins, Aaron was beginning to put himself back together.

All Rod had was a telephone number, so they stopped at a booth to let him call the girls. There was no answer, so they prowled through town and ended up at a roller skating rink that had been turned into a dance hall. There was a long bar against one wall, tables across from it and a huge crowded dance floor under blinking colored lights with a live group rattling out electrically so that all of it was a press of noise and bodies. On a pedestal beside the musicians, a girl in tight psychedelic pants gyrated in a musical orgasm, her eyes closed and her mouth open in panting ecstasy. The music cracked out and rumbled off the walls with a hard rolling sound that tightened down on them with its pressure.

They could not find an empty table, so they squeezed themselves in at the bar. Aaron watched the girl on the pedestal, wondering if she ever took a break: she moved as if wired electrically for motion, as if wired to an amplifier, living only as the music pumped through her. He began to drink seven-and-sevens again, thinking that if the music stopped, if a wire shorted or something blew, the girl might go out in a flicker of colored light, like a hot blue arc between terminals. But the music went on and on, and so did the girl.

Rod nudged him. "No wonder we got no answer. That's Marie."

Aaron nodded without really understanding.

Rod, looking around the place, spotted Sandy a few minutes later. She was sitting at a big table with two other girls unknown to Rod. He and Aaron and Paul and Steve crowded in on them, and another dancer finally took Marie's place and she came over, as things began to haze again for Aaron.

Everyone had paired up and he was odd man until Marie arrived, and he looked at her hungrily as introductions were made. She was breathing hard, sipping a whiskey sour, flecked with a light coating of shiny perspiration and exuding a faint animal odor that no one seemed to notice but Aaron. He felt the purest lust he had ever known and almost choked on his drink, his head swimming from the whiskey and from Marie, who was finished for the night and ready to pair up. He heard Rod's voice dominating the conversation, Rod, who had let himself go now, forcing himself into a release as compulsive and pervading as his usual composure. He worked at it, but Aaron only half-heard, half-noticed.

Aaron was talking to Marie. She was from Wayne State in Detroit, staying in Saugatuck with her friend Sandy for the summer. She was an art student, a painter and model. Aaron began to talk, laughing with her, and both of them beginning to hang on each other, not making sense now but talking themselves into something.

The dance hall closed up on them and they all went over to the girls' cabin, clinging together in a mass in Paul's car in the sweet-smelling night. They had their own bottles and at first everyone was in the living room with its garish wall posters and abstract art, wild music surging around and through them from somewhere, Sandy doing an imitation of Marie on the pedestal and Marie wearing only a robe and then not even that. Couple by couple they drifted out of the living room and at some point he was alone with Marie without lights or music or, apparently, clothes, talking about something and thinking of something else, thinking of the qualitative difference between the way you felt and acted with a girl you loved and with a girl whose name for the moment had slipped your mind—it must have been a qualitative difference, very subtle, because quantitatively there wasn't any except that now it went on and on. . . .

And then it was like dying, poised there over the hot hollow emptiness of death that he tried to fill with himself, to drive himself into, probing deeply with his dream of life, farther than he would have thought possible or wise, and filling it and feeling himself channel into it and away in this hollow act of life that seemed more an act of his own death. . . .

And then stars overhead and a cool flight home to darkness and a headache in the morning.

8.   He went home that weekend feeling unhappy, and was not sociable with his family. He had made up with a sour and grudging George Dooley and a surprisingly friendly Phil

Vanneman, who had offered to let bygones be traded for a couple of drinks in the lounge, at which time Aaron had finally
heard the Way of the World According to Vanneman, fulfill-
ing all Aaron's misgivings. The gruel composed of Action,
Escapism and Optimism Above All did not help his state of
mind. Fortunately Paul had been along to ease the clash of
personalities.

On Saturday night Aaron and Sam went out and listened
to Huston Reeve play his trumpet in the Winchester Lounge.
They sat at a tiny table by a corner of the dance floor and
moped for a time in silence. Huston played the saddest music
on his trumpet that Aaron had ever heard. Listening to him
and drinking iced bourbon, Aaron began once more an
attempt at piecing together his problem, and Sam listened and
drank Scotch and tried to sympathize. But most of what he
said inadvertently came out: "Maybe it's what you're making
it."

"No; or maybe yes, in a way. There's so much death all
around and I'm so *conscious* of it—I can't stop thinking about
it, as if I'm coming face to face with death for the first time
in my life and never saw it before. I'm like a fifteen-year-old,
confused and twisting back and forth and nothing solid."

"Isn't that pretty much the way it is?" said Sam. "What's
solid any more?"

Aaron nodded. "But it didn't used to be that way. It didn't
used to be. Like that Beatle song says, 'When I was a boy,/
Everything was right.' Everything *was* right. When did it
stop being right, and why?"

"I don't know." Sam took a drink and listened to Huston.
"Plays nice, doesn't he?"

"Yes."

"Put it this way, then. You ask: 'When did it stop being
right?' Well, when did you lose whatever *made* it right? What
was it that made everything go? Innocence? Idealism? I think,

for me, it stopped being right when Barbara divorced me. Not that I didn't have it coming, but I didn't think so at the time, and the pain then was more a localized thing. I try not to think about it now, because the world has looked a little cockeyed ever since. I didn't think it would."

"Lots of people get divorced."

"Listen to you; don't be magnanimous with Samson, boy. The rejoinder is obvious: 'And lots of people are unhappy.' But it's more than that. Sometimes I think if just one of the girls I bring home turned out to be right for me, I'd be luckier than I deserve and everything would work out. But it isn't so, because then I realize that it isn't that these girls aren't right for me, but that I wouldn't be right for them. The one thing I've learned since I selfished myself out of Barbara is to be honest with myself—I think. I'm still selfish enough to enjoy living for myself and not having to give to anyone. When and if I change I'll know it, and that'll be the time."

"Well, then, maybe it's a kind of realization that comes at different times—"

"More than once."

"—when you begin finding out the truth about yourself and about the world, corny as that sounds. But especially about yourself. Or maybe you find it out before you admit it. What happens, I wonder, if you don't ever admit it and learn?"

Sam did not answer, but nodded at the man with the trumpet.

"I can tell you the first time I was really hit by it," said Aaron. "The first stage, I guess, of the uncomfortable truth about the world. Or this country. Or people. It was three years ago, when J. F. K. was killed."

"I'll drink to that."

"I was out at the junior college that day, in the language lab, studying Spanish. It was in the afternoon. On the way down there I remember passing my faculty adviser—a woman, very nice—and she was crying and went on past me. Then there was no one in the lab except the attendant, and somebody came in and said, 'He was shot.' I had a feeling right then that I knew who the guy was talking about, and he said, 'They don't know yet whether he's dead or not.' But I'd seen this guy before, and he wasn't the kind you take seriously. So I chose to think he was either kidding or talking about somebody else—only I think I really knew, and I ducked away from it. So I plugged into my tape and the two of them went out. I sat through the whole forty-five minutes of my Spanish tape, and when I left, I saw that a lot of people were crowded into one of the rooms where a television set was, and I went in. Chet Huntley was on and the first thing I heard him say was, 'John Fitzgerald Kennedy is dead.' I drove home right then. I didn't cry until much later.

"You see, I had only the vaguest idea of what really was happening. I had followed Kennedy from the beginning of his campaign; I was in high school then and in a way I overrated him, idolized him, I guess. But it's impossible to say how his death affected me—not so much at the time as later, when I realized that a corner had been turned for the whole country in the sixties, and Kennedy knew it and, I think, would have gotten us through it the way—the way I don't think we're going to get through it, Sam. I was *involved* then, everybody was beginning to be involved in what was happening, in a way they hadn't been. When he was murdered it was like a thirty-year step backward just at the wrongest possible time. Things started going wrong with people's attitudes—those riots in Watts last summer and the mayor's refusal to get involved, and this war, this God-damned war. It was like everything was a lie; and maybe that's why I can't really get involved even about the war or the things a social worker professionally cares about. All of that—the disgust and the sadness and personal sense of outrage, the feeling of being sold out—I had already suffered all that before, and not enough was left to be much affected by this. At least, that's part of the reason."

"I know another part. Matt."

Aaron nodded. "I just can't think about it; I want *out* of it because I don't trust anyone any more. It was like the first outpost of idealism and youth and concern being blown away from under my feet when that man died. I didn't think of it in those terms at the time, but that's what it was.

"And then," he said, pausing to drink, seeing Sam's face intent, his eyes awake and thinking, "then there was my mother's death, and Matt leaving. She didn't deserve to die, she was too young and too good a person, and she had never hurt anyone in her life. On the contrary—she was open to being hurt by lesser people; because she was so good, she was in many ways vulnerable and defenseless to the really bad things in life.

"After two years, I still mark the beginnings of realizing my own weaknesses from the time of her death—or I should say her illness. Because she didn't deserve to die and I didn't want her to, I refused until very late to believe that she could. I ducked it again—always ducking, shying away from pain, from reality, Sam. I tried to live another life that summer and not think about her. I was afraid. It was like being lied to by all the things I'd ever believed in. That's the only way I can say it. Like being lied to by myself too, because I refused to face it, avoided thinking about it, avoided the extra little kindnesses I could have shown her. I wanted to forget. I wanted to not think about it. I haven't cared a whole hell of a lot for me since then."

The sound of Huston's trumpet came to his ears again and he looked at the man standing on the platform making music, and thought how easy it would be to play out all your soul through an instrument designed for that purpose and not have to live with it or think about it—so easy if only it worked. But *he* had tried that and the soul had come back to him, and now it was always there and there was no instrument, so far as he knew, that would get rid of it.

Huston came over during a break and talked to them in his troubleless Southern voice about nothing at all. His face wore its perpetual sleepless look and he smoked one of his brown cigarettes and smiled, inhaling deeply. When he returned to the platform and the stiff-rod microphone, Sam and Aaron left.

On Sunday he sat around thinking about Matt, and remembered again that his brother had made a mistake like Aaron's two years ago. But Matt was two years younger than Aaron and had been even less capable of handling the time than Aaron—and yet he had exorcised himself right then, with his pulling away into himself, facing himself and working it out somehow to his relief. He had never claimed to be as spiritually tough as Aaron. He had not dragged out his suffering for two years.

He saw Sam again that evening. They drank beer and sat on the back porch of Sam's house, talking softly in the night and reaching no conclusions, finally driven in by mosquitoes, and at home Aaron's mind tumbled and he thought of death and his mother, of Susan and Ann and Marie, lying there stifling, dying it seemed, in the black wet heat.

And in the morning, on the way to Greenville, he almost died.

1.　　　Greenville is in a part of the state not close to large cities, the nearest being Grand Rapids, some thirty miles southwest. It is wood and lake country turned to farms, and the farms often disappear abruptly on the flanks of hills that drop into swampland a few yards into the woods. The area is extremely rural, spotted with summer cottages that crouch in the brush on the wooded lake shores, sometimes isolated, more often clustered like the colonies of old woodsmen during their first push through the Midwest in the days before the forests and lakes began to die. The clusters are served by the sorriest of roads, often not on the county maps, almost impossible to find without knowing the area.

Nobody had a good pole count the first day nor any of the days they worked in Greenville, and Aaron, after his first effort, did not work overtime again (he had shamed everyone with the first day's count). After the night in Saugatuck he was withdrawing again, more than ever. He spent the nights alone in his hot room, reading poetry and sometimes watching television when he needed to keep from thinking. It seemed to him that the whole town was domed and broiling in the

August weather, the single room an oven, the wheat fields dry and parched, the woods steamy. This area was the roughest of all the places he had worked, seemed doubly isolated, removed and lonely after Muskegon. The pole counts dropped as the temperature rose and he drank an incredible amount of water, lemonade, root beer and orange crush to make up for what the heat took every day.

After the first week, Paul did not come back to work. At his parents' home in Royal Oak he had fallen into a coughing spasm and been unable to stop for several minutes. It had been so bad that his parents called an ambulance to take him to the hospital. Paul had tuberculosis, said Steve, with a peculiar coldness in his voice, a detached and businesslike expression on his face, as if the simplicity of it was too much for him to realize.

Aaron had not known where Paul's home was—if his home was with his parents—the very thought of Paul *having* parents seemed ridiculously strange to him. And it seemed to Aaron that something decisive was beginning now, as he found himself slowly crowded in by his fears; death was chipping away at the summer around him, isolating him with his undefined awareness of it, making promises that settled like the heat in his close and darkened room.

Early in the second week Steve followed him home from dinner and invited himself in. The heat was of an intensity now that did not let up much after dark; it merely became a night heat, suffocating rather than burning, closing in like a black-gloved hand so that, lying in it, clad only in shorts on top of the sheet with no blankets, hearing exhausted moths tapping against the screen and cars sliding past, it would have been better to see the sun, to have a greater heat to hide from in shadows. The uniformity of the almost liquid night with no breeze was like drowning in warm steam.

They carried cold wet bottles of Coke from the machine

beside the office and Steve wanted them to come to his room, the double he had shared with Paul, which was air-conditioned and larger. Aaron wanted to go to his own room and was doing that, and Steve followed along behind in an uncharacteristic capitulation. He had tried to get Aaron to go out, had failed, could not arouse Aaron's interest in the guitar, and, as lost now as Aaron without Paul there, seemed even less able to realize that Paul was gone. Aaron had not said ten words to him since dinner, had more or less tolerated him, been more or less oblivious of his presence.

When they got to the room, Aaron sat down on the bed and moved the dripping green bottle over his forehead with his eyes closed. Steve left the inner door open and stood looking out through the screen at the street lights popping on. All the noises in town seemed far away and muffled as if heard through layers of damp cotton. Steve sagged in the doorway, sipping his Coke, a thumb hooked into his back pocket, his eyes hidden and surely half blind behind the green sunglasses he wore all the time now. Aaron watched his back in the light summer shirt, his Negro-dark arms shooting from the white short sleeves like bars of wrought iron.

Steve said quietly, "It's funny how you get attached to somebody." He turned a little, his half profile expressionless, as it had never been, his actor's face now without a pose or a mask. Aaron tipped up the bottle and drank the cold burning liquid until it closed the back of his throat.

"I've known Paul since before he dropped out of college. Four years, off and on. I got to know him better this summer than ever before. In different ways than I knew him. It's as if he picked up new sides to himself, running around the way he does. The funny thing is, I still haven't been able to figure him out. It's like he's playing games with everyone, even with me. As if the whole deal is just some crazy game."

Aaron finished the Coke and set the bottle on the lamp table beside the bed. He took his shoes off and moved back against the headboard, pulling up a pillow to lean his head on. Steve sipped his Coke and mused, looking at the evening. Someone had turned on a television set in the next room, and they heard the rolling sporadic laughter of a situation comedy.

"He wanted you and me to be buddies," said Steve. "Can you beat that? I mean, why should he care? But he did." Steve shook his head, looking down at the Coke in his hand. "The bastard cares about everybody."

"He's a good guy," said Aaron at last, quietly in the room that was so heavy he wondered if the other heard him. Steve was becoming only a silhouette against the screened-out sky and Aaron rolled his head a little, feeling a not unpleasant drowsiness, and at the core of that, a coldness that belied the temperature in the room, an easy floating carelessness directed, he knew, against Steve, who was trying to tell him something, waiting for the opportunity as a schoolchild waits to be noticed by a strange group of potential friends, for the generous given moment which makes all the difference later on, in one sure way or another.

"A very good guy," repeated Aaron, feeling sleepy now, released into a dangerous irresponsiveness, antiresponsiveness, perversely rising from the depths of the summer itself. "There's no one else like him," he said very quietly now. "He's the greatest guy in the world. There's nobody else like him."

Steve half turned, but Aaron was dropping away into the black summer night. "He always told me that you're—"

"Nobody. There's nobody. Not anyone. There's no one like him."

The pause then was extended and deep, long enough and deep enough for Steve to turn all the way around as Aaron's head slipped farther down the pillow, his breathing slow enough and deep enough to permit him not to answer Steve at all.

"Do you think it was my fault?" said Steve. "What happened to him? Do you think I'm responsible?"

2.   The temperature remained in the high eighties and Aaron's car began to overheat. He checked the thermostat and finally removed it after the engine boiled over several times; though he occasionally got water at farmhouses, he still was forced to do as much of his work as possible on foot. One of his maps contained several long sections of road around a cemetery, far out from town, and he ran this map with the car, stopping every hour to come back to the cemetery and replace what water had boiled out of the radiator. He would sit on the grass beside the faucet, letting his engine cool under the trees, and remember the cemetery at the university. During his first term after transferring from the junior college, before he had met Susan, he had taken to walking around the campus alone at night, trying to assimilate himself into the thirty-thousand-student institution. No one in his family had ever attended college before, and he was aware of a vague feeling of responsibility to pull it off with honor and success and all that. Yet the fact was that he was not much happier there than he had been anywhere for the last couple of years: he had few friends and little inclination to make any, with a fatalistic excess he was aware of and did not like but from which he could not shake himself free. So he walked all over the campus several times that fall after dark, and he always noticed the cemetery, a large one with an entrance arch and black iron gates, and a fence surrounding it, directly across the street from a huge complex of dormitories. In his frame of mind he was always struck by the contrast of all those dormitories housing young students ready to grab all

that life offered them, with the dark cemetery across the street. Remembering it now did not help his mood.

While Aaron fussed with his car, the others were running into problems of a different sort. Their area included the town of Big Oak, where the country-western radio station had been built for good reason. Many of the farmers surrounding Big Oak in its dense lowland had come up from the south in that quirk of relocation that causes such pockets of displacement. They were generally independent, quite often poor, and at times extremely unfriendly and suspicious. More than once a crew member found himself explaining his mission to an angry farmer who disliked people walking in his fields. Sometimes his boys would stand around him, long-haired, sassy, not always ill-natured, looking to their father for permission to carry the inventory man out to the road where he belonged, while the farmer scrutinized his identification. Vanneman, caught in such a situation, ordered off the land of an old man, had tried to assert himself, and while mouthing off about right-of-way and cutting electric service, had had a shotgun pulled on him, whereupon he had decided to estimate the pole. Angry misanthropists had turned in many complaints at the Big Oak office.

Steve counseled them on this. "Don't ever try to force it. We have a bought-and-paid-for right-of-way, but some of these characters will shoot first and apologize later. If they throw you out, leave the pole to me—I can usually talk my way in to it. If I can't, we'll let them send a truck from the office." Thus far, Steve had had to check half a dozen poles himself, and the truck had been sent twice.

Later Aaron's maps sent him into the resort areas. He spent half his time trying to find the proper roads, which ran as obscure as cowpaths into the woods toward cottages and lakes that could not even be seen. Then he would leave the car and hike through deep woods until the lakefront came into view. He did not like working this kind of area because of the woods and marshy ground that could quickly become swamp. Several times he was forced to mark a pole "inaccessible" and leave it for Steve to get with his hip boots and mosquito-net hat. He saw a lot of snakes, and no longer cared to go after them.

To the southwest of Greenville, deep in wooded country, there is a small state park with a camping area and a clear stream under pine trees. It is isolated and not much used except on weekends, and it was here that Aaron came to a speculation of what was to happen.

A line of forty-foot poles runs through the park and away on both sides through pine woods on fairly high ground. They are set in some fifty yards from the gravel road, and Aaron was checking them one day, his car running cooler under the tree arch above the road, leaving it to walk out to each pole and then driving on to the next.

He was just leaving the car, having not yet reached the park, when an old wreck of a car turned a curve in the narrow road and approached from the opposite direction. He caught a glimpse of two scruffy men, wearing old clothes, and with unshaven faces, and then the car was past and he was into the trees and heading for the pole. He heard the old engine grumble and then die. He heard, through the breeze stirring the edge of the woods, two voices and the slamming of doors.

Aaron stopped at the pole and felt his pulse skip up. He was aware once more of being alone in rough country, and reminded of all the senseless murders he had read about, committed on people like himself by hitchhikers or teen-agers or various kinds of psychopaths who suddenly found themselves with nothing better to do.

The thought reached him with a slow and ridiculous certainty that he had stumbled into the wrong place at the wrong time, that the two men were probably escapees from

Jackson Prison, and that, his vulnerability being too good to pass up, they were going to kill him, thinking he had money or wanting his car. He called himself a fool and checked off the pole, but there was now a silence from the road and he could not make himself return to the car. He thought of Hickock and Smith in Capote's book. He thought of the still unknown man from Chicago, of the sniper on the Texas tower. He thought of all the people who had killed people for no reason or little reason and how it happened every year a number of times, in situations exactly like this one, where there was really no plausible reason for the victims to be afraid.

He stood beside the pole in scrub weeds for several minutes without thinking at all, simply standing alert and listening with adrenaline pumping, and then he heard someone—the men—coming toward him through the trees from the road, kicking up sticks and old leaves and pine needles as they came. He stood and waited for them with a feeling he did not understand, a cold and calm-as-death seizure that froze him, a feeling of justified finality—almost of anticipation. He heard the engine of his Ford idling, chugging softly.

Then a black bird dog ran out of the trees and one of the men hollered, "Hey, Barney! Barn! *Git* back here, boy!"

The dog stopped, looking back, and the two men came out. One of them spoke to the dog and the other saw Aaron and waved. "Howdy!"

He lifted his arm in a loose wave and watched them go on with the dog, running him, getting him ready for the hunting season in the fall. And it was suddenly summer again and birds were singing in the cool woods and he was alone with himself and alive.

He did not return to the car, but went on to the next two poles, into the park. He got a drink out of the hand pump and sat down beside the stream. He felt a slight sheepishness over the incident, but he was also vaguely certain that justice had been cheated, and he thought: *That's what it all points to, all right—the whole summer has reeked of death, and I am at the center of it. I have been at the center of it all along and it has all been pointed at me.*

He sat, then, by the water, looking up at the pines and hearing the cold swirl of the stream as it flowed over the gravel bed. It was a peaceful scene of knowing for once what lay ahead, and he was in tune with it. Before going on he drank from the pump again because the water was good.

But the next day he went into a hardware store in Greenville and bought a corn knife—a wooden-handled blade of black steel two feet in length—and he put it on the floor in the back of his car, with the mosquito repellent and the heavy shoes. He had bought it, he told himself, so that he could better get through the heavy country where poles ran away from the roads into thickets and brush. He knew without thinking of it the other reason he had bought the knife, having slept little again the night before.

3.   He did not at first get a chance to use the corn knife on anything. Steve gave him a roll of maps and sent him out to Carson City, where he checked in at the motel as its only guest and began to walk the streets. Normally the city crews with their trucks handled urban areas, exceptions being suburbs and small towns such as Carson City. At first he did not use his car at all, though he had had it repaired; he would step outside in the morning and begin with the poles near the motel, strolling around the streets in his sunglasses, checking off poles at a leisurely pace. He began to relax a little and his spirits rose.

When the city maps were finished Rod came in and they

teamed up on the rural areas, working out toward Sheridan and Stanton, overlapping another crew, as far north as Westville, almost the distance between Carson City and Greenville. They alternated cars, and still profited on the mileage.

They worked fast. Rod would hurl his Buick down the highway with Aaron sitting on the fender, come to a shuddering halt, and Aaron would be halfway into a field by the time Rod got out and crossed the road for his own pole. First one back would drive on to the next while the man in the field hoofed it, he getting back to the car before the driver had made it out to his next pole. They barreled into driveways and farmyards as if attacking them, only to be gone again within ten seconds unless someone was outdoors to stop and question them. They pushed hard all morning, Rod as fierce with his job as with his recreation, driven almost, and finally in the afternoon, checking the maps over, he would relax and slow down; they would quit early and go for a beer.

Rod made a practice of driving back to Greenville at night to drink with Steve and the others, but Aaron stayed alone, removed from them. Yet he and Rod ate their meals together and finally got to know each other, finally were around each other enough to talk. There was no tension between them. For all his dissolution (as Aaron saw it) Rod lacked the true dedication in his hedonism that Steve had, seemed more driven, by whatever odd circumstances, than thinking and calculating. It was as if one of them, Rod or Steve, was immoral, the other amoral, and he, Aaron, could not decide which was which. He had noticed a white plastic Madonna on the dash of Rod's Buick and asked him about it.

"Are you religious?"

"Not particularly," said Rod. "Just enough to keep me from saying no." He flicked the statuette. "I picked this up in Kentucky last summer. Got a cousin down there. I just like it."

One evening they were slouched across from each other at

dinner; they had the facility, because of their personalities, of ignoring each other and scorning banal conversation without either of them taking offense, or even noticing. Rod would point his dark blade of a face in some direction and look like a caricature of The Haunted Man, only to pull out abruptly and praise the strawberry shortcake they were eating for dessert. He turned himself off and on with some photoelectric relay unnoticed by anyone else. And, like a radial engine, he was either on or off: if on, he crusaded through whatever he was doing as if trying somehow to convince himself that that was his *job*, it was what he *did*, and he knew there was only one way to get it done and that was to *do* it, with all the professionalism and detachment of an amateur bomb defuser. And if he was off, nothing rattled him and nothing could turn him on except himself, through that secret relay.

He felt terrible about Paul. "I had no idea. There we were, running that poor bastard around every night till he dropped, with him matching us drink for drink, almost. . . ." He shook his head in a little sign of resignation. "Sometimes people are so damn blind. He was coughing his insides out, and I thought it was because he smoked."

"He smoked a lot, didn't he?" said Aaron.

"An awful lot. I never saw him without a cigarette. He shouldn't have smoked so damn much. He should have said something, stayed home and rested, or something. He *must* have had some idea what was happening."

"He pushed himself to keep up, didn't he? I never really understood why. He didn't seem the type. Not like Steve."

"He isn't. He just wanted to, just wanted to be sociable. And he did it for Steve too."

"Steve?"

Rod smiled and nodded again. "That's part of why it's so sad, I think. You know how old Steve leaned on him. Paul was like his big brother, almost. And something else."

"What else?"

"Well, Paul is so—versatile, I guess you'd say. He's the kind of person who cares about everybody. Steve isn't. Steve likes people who are like him; most people do that, I think. Paul, though, he likes everybody. I think Steve needed him as a kind of buffer between himself and other people. The world. Steve is really a pretty vulnerable kind of fellow, you know."

"I hadn't noticed that."

Rod looked at him. "No? How could you *not* notice? That's one reason I live it up with him. I think he's the type who needs somebody around, just to sort of be with him. Paul could do it."

And Aaron knew that it was the truth. He had not allowed himself to recognize it before, but yes, Steve was as about as independent as a baby—that is, he needed a base, a solid base, for his independence. Was that why he valued Paul so highly? Paul, Aaron suddenly remembered, had said that his family was a good one, like Aaron's.

But why, then, had Steve distrusted *him?*

Perhaps because he had not presented a very consistent picture of himself. He had made great and noble mouthings in the Owosso bar, then had stayed out all night with Ann, and Steve had thought— Yes, Aaron reflected, that would seem rather contradictory. And—

Oh, Lord. He had straightened *that* out in Saugatuck, told Steve the truth about that, proved himself consistent—only to run afoul of Marie.

Yes. Well—yes. No wonder Steve did not believe him; Aaron did not believe himself. For whatever obscure reasons, Paul had maneuvered to make them friends, and he had been working not only against Steve's reluctance toward Aaron and Aaron's reluctance toward Steve—but also against Aaron's inconsistency with himself. So where did that leave them now?

"Paul could do it," repeated Aaron. He wondered, though, if anyone else could. There *wasn't* anyone else like Paul.

"Yes," said Rod. "Far as I know, he's never had any hangups of his own. Except for smoking so much. Everybody has something, I guess."

"What about you?" said Aaron suddenly, turning on Rod. "What's the other reason for your—for playing Steve's kind of game?"

"Oh. The Army. The war. I got shot over there last year."

"I didn't even know you'd been in."

"Yeah. Dropped out of college and signed up. I hadn't ever lived much, wanted action—you know. I got a bullet right here in the chest; broke some ribs and messed me up. Didn't you ever notice the scar? When I went swimming?"

"I guess not," said Aaron. "I guess I didn't notice."

"At the time I thought it was all over. I thought I had had *it*. I won't ever forget that feeling, all my life in front of me and facing death. That's why. I don't want to waste another minute. I've got the call."

"I guess that's why you want to win over there."

"Why not? Hell, I got *shot* for it."

"I have a—my brother is over there. Matt. Matthew."

"Really?" Rod looked at him for a moment. "What's he doing?"

"He's with the Fourth Division. He's fighting."

"Oh. Yes. Well, that's clear enough. I guess you want him out."

"I guess I do," said Aaron.

Rod went back to Greenville from dinner, and Aaron walked to the motel in the night. The night smelled of pumpkins though it was summer, the darkness moving quietly around him as he crossed the parking lot, milky in the light of the August night too dim to illuminate him. The pumpkinlike scent was sweet and made him think of autumn. He lay down on the bed, knocking off the book of poems he was reading, and tried to think,

The last time home he had found a letter from Susan that was a direct response to one he had written her after the night in Saugatuck, a letter full of depression and despair, with a single oblique comment about his aborted call to her while she was out with someone on a Thursday night.

Her letter made him sound foolish:

In the first place, I wasn't out with anyone that night. You must have your time zones wrong or something. My mother says you called at five o'clock, which is eight o'clock your time. I hadn't gotten home from work yet. I think you have it backward: your time is ahead of ours, not vice versa.

Oh, Aaron, when are you going to grow up and realize that because I go out with someone it doesn't mean I'm in love with him or am someone's mistress or whatever crazy ideas are in your head. I always date a lot of people, they fascinate me, and you know what I mean by that—and, as usual, this summer most of them have been shallow and money-oriented and uncommitted. Even you come off looking good compared to them, in spite of your childhood/family fantasies and your tendency to cry in your beer at things that should not even be in your mind. Try to be objective enough not to write me off without giving me a chance to measure up—

Of course he had no intention of writing her off, could not have if he had wanted to, and was relieved to discover that she had not writen *him* off, much as he felt he deserved it.

He lay on the bed in the dark, looking out at the sky through a window screen that cross-sectioned all the night into simple identifiable consistencies. He had been fitting things together, willingly and unwillingly, for some time now and trying to make it coherent for himself so that perhaps he could communicate it to Susan—though why he should want to do that he did not ask himself. Thus far he had failed, or had got only part of it, and with the air of impending judgment that clouded his mind, he found himself wishing simply that a thing would happen, a thing that would make thinking unnecessary—happen not to the environment in which he worked, not to birds, not to people and things that did not deserve it. Not the near misses and premonitions and unfulfilled promises, either. Only a simple thing, and only to him.

Otherwise there was thinking, and it seemed simple and at the same time complex, too complex for him. He looked at the volume of poems on the floor by the bed where he had dropped it. A poet was supposed to be able to grasp experience and mold it into meaning through feeling and through thought. But he had not written one poem all summer and he knew that that would not solve it. He would have believed he needed a psychiatrist if he had believed in psychiatry.

He turned on the bed lamp and took some sheets of typewriter paper and a pen from his suitcase and began to write to Susan, in a hand more legible than usual:

DEAR SUSIEGIRL,

The night is all dark around me and I am alone and thinking of you. If that sounds pretentious—and it does—you'll have to take it, as with everything about me, for what it is worth, which admittedly may be very little. I've never claimed otherwise.

I want to tell you the short short story of my life, want to because of the sound the night makes and the way it smells, which reminds me of witches. Maybe I can thrum up some kind of magic—a thing the world is much in need of, or the part of it which I inhabit, anyway. Your interest is psychoanalysis—so you'll be interested in this for the light it may throw on certain types of minds guilty of certain types of crimes. And if not, I endeavor at least to delight if not instruct, which Lord knows should be enough for anyone to expect of his attempt. I digress from myself.

I started out as a child, as the saying goes, with appropriate apologies to Cosby, who has used the line, and not merely a child but a Child (a child's child, I could say, but I won't), and as such a pure jewel of the form, a miracle of rare device—credit to Coleridge. By that I mean simply that for me the child's world was The Compleat Worlde, a self-sufficient, smooth-running machine fueled by fantasy, belief in the goodness of man, and the fantastic love of and for my parents, who kept the machine going. This lasted until I was nineteen.

Wasn't that rather late? you ask, and I answer, That was rather late. It may turn out to have been too late. But I never had any reason to grow up, Susie; life was fine, I had no grouse against my parents (a not allowable feeling these days, since I can't find anyone who believes it possible) and I generally avoided all the hangups: started dating late, got crushes on movie stars, joined unofficially the James Dean cult some years after the fact, thanks to a friend whose mother had a stock of old movie magazines. The sad part about it is the way I shunned reality; I simply made my own reality, the way some of those people who hang out in San Francisco do, without the drugs. And this neurotic self-centeredness allowed me to get along without most people, and hurt others with a callous unawareness that frightens and disgusts me now. I loved my parents very much, so much that I seldom thought about it and so could be as unresponding as only those who take things and people for granted can be. If only I had learned somewhere along the line to take myself for granted—but that was my insulation.

I remember one odd little occurrence that happened once, of the kind that sticks in your mind for no good reason and comes back to haunt you later. We were living in Indianapolis and I must have been about ten years old. We had a television set and I watched it a lot, even though there were few programs on in those days to interest kids (Davy Crockett was just about to hit it big)—quite quite different from now.

Anyway I remember seeing—that is, remember that I saw, for the thing itself is gone from me—a program one night with my parents, one of the many half-hour anthologies that were on then, and there was something on Stephen Foster, dramatizing all the trouble he had and how he was poor and got little or no recognition. I don't even know how I remember that it was Stephen Foster, because I couldn't have known who he was, but it was.

After the program was over, I heard my father say, "He had a tragic life."

And for some reason those words got to me, young as I was, and I wondered what it meant and what it would be like to have a tragic life; I had just seen Stephen Foster have everything that he touched turn to ashes on him, and I knew it was something like that, to be always unhappy.

And I was happy then so I forgot all about it—except I didn't forget; The Tragic Life of Stephen Foster has been a part of me ever since because I wondered what it would be like, knowing it would never happen to me, *my* life wouldn't be like that, but thinking *What if . . . ?*

Then I read books and science fiction magazines and sort of grew up and sort of didn't.

I must have been a weird little guy through high school, getting my science fiction magazine every month (I had a subscription), buying movie magazines in obscure drugstores because I was embarrassed about it, going around with my three friends, with whom I had nothing in common except our oddness, having practically no dates, listening to the radio late into the night, staying in my room like a gnome, writing poems and science fiction stories, drifting away from my father and brother and being impatient and hateful with my mother. I built up enough self-loathing in that period to take care of me for a long time once it started coming out.

It built up to a head, all of this, the spring and summer that my mother was ill, culminating with her death in the fall. I had refused not only to believe that she could die, but even to think about it or face the possibility of her death. My illusions and my fear would not allow it, and I led a double life with my brother then while my father stood up to reality virtually alone. On the day she died I stood with my father and brother in the special room the hospital has for next of kin, and everyone cried but me. I cried later all alone, but even more than the shock and the grief I felt an anger in myself at the world and at God and especially, of course, at me, because now it was too late for anything but that. I played Bogart with the tight jaw all through that period and at the funeral and at the cemetery; people who saw me must have thought I looked awfully angry at someone, and they were right.

I don't know why I've gone into this, Susie, especially with you, who shouldn't have to hear about my problems and failings, but there isn't anyone else I'd care to tell about it now—I've told Sam, my friend, and I've told you. But I have to tell it because I'm caught in something; some holdover from all of that unreality is after me now, and I can't duck it this time. Things are happening out there in the world that I should be paying attention to but am not—and I cannot until I clear this up with myself in some way or other. Yet I don't know how, and I suspect now that it will be cleared up for me and in spite of me before long now.

This summer has promised all sorts of things, as did the early summer of my life—very little of which, looking back on both, has been made good. But I feel now—and this is the point of all this, Susie—I feel that whatever happens will be just, and whatever should happen to me at any time in the future will long since have been bought and paid for, contracted for, and for it I will be the last to complain. Things have stared me in the face and breathed at me, and I understand now that the basis of my reaction has been not so much fear as I had thought.

Write to me, Susie, and be happy.

With love,
AARON

4.   They finished up the Carson City area on Tuesday, the sixteenth, and moved back into Greenville, where the others were cleaning up to the north and west. Steve sent Aaron out halfway to Big Oak. He made fairly good time in the cornfields and beans until, toward noon on Thursday, he ran into trouble.

He had left his car at a crossroad and was walking through

a beanfield on the edge of his map, when he saw a man come out of a barn up ahead. The man saw him and stopped, watching as Aaron checked two more poles and came up in the farmyard for the pole by the house. The man stood with his feet wide apart, hands plunged deep into his Levi pockets and slouched behind his stiffened arms so that he seemed to be leaning backward. He wore an ugly felt hat that had probably been bought in town fifteen years before, bleached out and grease spotted. Aaron smiled and called, "Hi!" and waved at the man, then checked the pole and headed out toward the road. Whenever possible he avoided getting into conversations with people—especially farmers, who were inclined to be talkative—and having to explain what he was doing. It took time and brought down the count.

But the man yelled, "Hey," and when Aaron stopped the man looked at him for a moment and yelled, "Come here." He did not wave, but simply stood waiting with his hands in his pockets.

Here we go, thought Aaron, noticing the dilapidated farmhouse, a high narrow frame house that leaned slightly in a haggish sideways twist. One of the rear windows was broken and patched with newspaper, and the rotten porch was literally falling down. The barn was in similar condition and the yard itself was a mess of chickens and junk; there was a twenty-year-old Chevy in the weeds next to the house.

There was an *air* about the place.

It was the kind of place Aaron liked to get through without pausing, and the man did not look friendly. Nevertheless, Aaron sighed and grinned. "Hiya."

The man spoke in a low and Southern-musical twang: "What're you doin' in them beans? Walkin' on my beans."

"Consolidated Power," said Aaron. "I'm just checking this line of poles through here."

They looked at each other. The man was about fifty years

old, his denim overalls faded and dirty and torn. His face was dark with the accumulation of years of sun and dirt and several days' beard. He did not have much hair in front, where his old wide-brimmed felt hat was pushed back. His eyes were like drilled holes, black and empty and hard.

"I want you young bastards to stay off my farm. Man can shoot somebody for trespassin'. "

Aaron said quietly, "I'm sorry to have to cross your fields a little. I just have to check those six poles, and that'll be it. I'll try not to mess anything up."

"You stay off," said the man.

Aaron noticed faces peering at him from the dirty and broken windows of the house—a woman's face, worn down until there was almost no face at all; and children, three, four, five dirty, string-haired child faces staring from inside that wreck of a house. He felt something, an uneasiness out of proportion to the situation. It was like one of those places he had come upon before, a deserted farm with ghosts in the weeds and no live people any more—and this place seemed like that, as if these people, these *faces*, had not really been alive for years, were not really here at all but only remembered: reflections on the windows, afterimages hoarded by the place itself.

He suppressed all this and tried again. "Look, sir, look, I'm not going to hurt—"

"Yeah, and *you* look," said the man, and turned slightly so his hat shaded the dark face from the sunlight, made it disappear almost—made him a hollow man—and Aaron took an involuntary step backward. It was incredibly hot, waves of heat rising off the ground, off the beanfields; the farm slowly began to revolve around them and they were at the center, on the pivot—they *were* the pivot—or was it only Aaron? Or did everything really come to focus right here, right here—the whole summer?

The man went on with the rising heat, the voice in the shadow under his hat, hands out of his pockets now, dirty stained greasy hands, large powerful hands gesturing. "I heard about the trouble you people cause, you goddamn kids. I seen you myself this morning across the road there, in my corn. I seen you knocking it down when you went through, and it wasn't no accident, neither—swinging your arms—you could of drove a tractor through there and not done no more damage than that."

And this caught Aaron short, this seeming paradox—the border of his map was *this* side of the road—and for a moment it was a problem, a simple case of perplexity which caused the whirling to stop, the focus to blur, the eerieness, the feeling of moment, of event, all to leave or at least lessen, as he remembered it was—it was *Vanneman* who had been working the next section over. Vanneman, Vanneman.

"That wasn't me," he said. "Look, that was another guy—"

"I don't give a damn *who* it was! He was carryin' one of them boards and he knocked down a whole swath of my corn. Now get off of here, and stay off! A man can shoot trespassers."

It should not have mattered to Aaron; it was only a job. It was frustrating—those six poles to get and the map would be finished—but it should not have mattered, did not matter. Vanneman might have argued. Such things might be of importance to Vanneman—but not to Aaron.

"Move," said the man.

Aaron did not move. Aaron said, "All right," but did not move. "But somebody will be back. They'll just send a truck out here—"

"By God." The man's patience was gone. Aaron knew it. The man stepped into the barn and Aaron stood there, and the man emerged with a shotgun, a long-barreled single-shot. He pointed the gun at Aaron's face.

Aaron did not think he would shoot, and started moving away. "Okay," he said, "I'm going," backing up, watched by all those phantoms at the windows.

"And you come back this is gonna be loaded for you!" called the man as Aaron went on out to the road. "Man can shoot people for trespassin'—and don't think I won't. *I done it before!*" he called, and Aaron believed him. He had the feeling, now, in the road, that he had come closer than it seemed.

He could have gone down to the other end of the line and checked a couple of the poles, but he decided to let them go. His pay did not include hazardous duty. Let the truck get them.

He saw Steve at lunch and turned over the map to him, then began on the first of several root beer mugs of lemon crush. The rest of the crew were working farther out and did not come in for lunch.

Aaron nodded at the map. "There's a group for the truck," he said disgustedly.

"Great. What's the matter with this bird?"

"Oh, it seems he saw a guy knocking down his corn in the next section over, across the road. Guy carrying a clipboard."

"Vanneman." Aaron nodded. "It figures. Well, we'll just have to do the best we can. We finish up tomorrow one way or another."

"You think we can cover the area?"

Steve shook his head. "We would have if—if we had a full crew. Erikson is coming up tonight to check on us. We'll probably have to do what we can tomorrow and let him and the trucks handle the rest. They won't extend the job deadline. Tomorrow night we're all done."

Steve gave him a map to finish up south of town. "Paul started this one."

"Guys like him always have the luck, don't they?"

Steve looked at him for a moment. "I guess," he said.

When they were finished and headed for their cars, Aaron said, "Steve—" He hesitated as the other turned. "How long will Erikson be here?"

"An hour maybe; he's going on back. Why?"

"Well, I thought—I wondered if you were planning anything tonight. I mean—we *are* finishing up. I'd like to go along."

Steve waited in the restaurant parking lot, the sunlight falling on them, the gravel so hot they could feel it through their tennis shoes. He shook his head slowly.

"God, Aaron, you're a hell of a case."

"I know. What about it?"

Steve grinned like a satyr and seemed to lose three years and ten pounds of frustration.

"See you later, fella."

5.   Aaron got into the car and unfolded Paul's map as Steve pulled away. The section was nearby. He figured an hour's work; the map had one line of poles left unchecked. Aaron began working at the city limits and got some of them, but they were a half mile back from the highway and he had to walk across rough country. When he had checked most of them he got in too deep and decided to work from the other end.

He drove out highway 57 until he came to Davis Road, and there he turned left and drove over a tractor path of ruts sprinkled lightly with gravel and oil until he spotted the line off to his left. The first pole on the map stood about thirty yards out in a field of stubble and dry grass, parallel to a couple of transmission poles that he was to ignore except as an aid in finding the place. From there the line went straight out perpendicular to the road, three more poles in the stubble field and then—he groaned as he checked the map—seven poles more, and these down in a growth of low woods that looked very thick from where he was, though a small hill was between him and them, so he could not be sure.

It was going to be hell, he thought—and then he noticed what appeared to be ancient covered-wagon tracks heading out through the field, past the three poles and up and over the hill that led down to the other seven and the woods.

He made a sharp left turn down onto the tracks, and began to follow them out toward the first pole. He did not notice at first that the field was sandy, and when he did notice it he was moving so well and was so close to the first pole that it did not disturb him.

The trail ran by about thirty feet from the pole, which, he thought, was considerably better than thirty *yards*. He got out of the car and walked over to and then around the pole, squinting in the sunlight. "Damn," he said quietly, although he would have bet there would be no number on the pole. In this entire line, of the twenty-three poles he had already checked, he had gotten only two clear dates—a '23 and a '24. He marked this one '23E (for "estimate") on his map, and went back to the car.

The car was slow in starting up through the sand, but he went on and checked the second pole, which was also blank, and then the third. That one was branded '24. He changed his estimates of the first two and got back in the car.

He was up over the hill now and coming down the other side, and the tracks petered out in a space of cut lumber and tractor parts and sand. His car began to slow, the wheels spinning. Within a few seconds the rear end was buried almost to the bumper.

Aaron got out and looked at the sand and the rear wheels

and sadly congratulated himself. He got a bundle of rags out of the trunk, gathered all the brush he could find, and, working on the sand in the afternoon sun, managed to move the car three feet ahead and a foot deeper, exhausting himself in the process. This took three-quarters of an hour to accomplish. He sat then in the car's shadow, which lengthened as the sun lowered in the sky, gasping for breath and brushing at the sand that covered him. It was not unusual for someone to need a tow truck on this job, but Aaron had never called one and the circumstances infuriated him. But there was no other choice, and he resigned himself to it and stood up.

It was just four o'clock and he still had some poles to check. The last one he had got was over the hill and the next one stood twenty yards off in a thin cluster of brush. He picked up his clipboard and got the corn knife out of the back and, making saber slashes at the weeds, checked the pole, on which he could find nothing. He estimated it and looked ahead for the next. There were six to go, all of them in the woods that began here and dropped away from the hill into a depression. He could see the next pole, but the ones after that were going to be hard to reach, unless there were clearings around them.

He went back to the car and sprayed himself with mosquito repellent, and put on an old shirt with long sleeves and his jacket, then worked down under and through the trees until, with considerable effort, he reached the pole. It was covered with vines and brush and he cleared away as much of it as he could, but there was no number. He estimated the pole.

The next one was completely obscured by the woods, which were becoming dense with thickets and clouded by mosquitoes. He imagined that he was Johnny Weismuller as Jungle Jim, and hacked furiously at the tangled undergrowth with the corn knife, working his way in toward the crashed airplane or the golden Inca god.

But he could not reach it. The thicket rose over his head until he was in a jungly half light, and the wet vegetation scratched his face and his arms through the heavy shirt and jacket. Already tired from digging at the sand to free his car, he was forced now to stop and rest, but the mosquitoes were beginning to get at him where the repellent had been washed off, so he kept moving and tried to go back. He could no longer see anything but thicket and the trail he had hacked seemed to have grown up behind him. He began to feel an apprehension, and swung again and again at the weeds and vines, working back toward the car.

Abruptly the ground became marshy and he saw the beginnings of a swamp. He was afraid of that, so he turned and tried to work around it, toward higher ground. Then he stumbled forward past a tree, through a bush that raked an arm of thorns across his face, and fell into a creek. He had not seen it because of the bush, and had not heard it because of the noise he had been making.

He went in on his face and cried out from the shock of the cold water, and he sucked in a lungful of water and cried out again, choking, flailing his arms and crying even louder in his head: *I'm drowning! Oh, God, God!* coughing until he retched and trying to get to his feet. He had dropped his clipboard into the weeds and with that hand he grabbed at a branch and hugged himself into it, tasting the muddy green water as his feet began to sink into the bottom. From beneath the quivering branch and weed, a water snake slowly moved out in a V pattern on the surface, and he cried out again in panic, *"Ah!"* and with a mixture of fear and rage he brought down his right hand, which held the black corn knife, sliced down with it as hard as he could and chopped the snake in two. Both ends tried to writhe away, but an incredible anger filled him and he brought it to focus now and chopped down again and again with all his strength, cursing aloud with each

blow: the *snake* and the *water* and the *summer* and *Steve* and
Ann and *Marie* and *Susan* and *Paul* and his *mother* and *him-self*, again and again until all the snake was gone on the flow-ing creek and he was slicing roots and branches and boiling
up the water at his side, crying and cursing. On the last stroke
his blade flew off a root and struck him in the calf and he
began to bleed. He stopped then and looked with horror at
the reddish-brown water and, exhausted, threw the corn knife
up onto the bank and hugged the tree branch with both arms.

For some moments he stood like that, and his feet stopped
sinking but he was still bleeding. He held to the branch and
pulled until one foot came loose with a bubbling sucking
sound, and he placed it on some of the nicked roots and pulled
the other foot free. He made it up onto the bank, but there
was no place to sit down, so he took out his handkerchief and
tied it tightly around the slowly bleeding calf and picked up
his clipboard and looked carefully at the map, shaking vio-lently, his arms and legs weak. He leaned back against the tree
and tried to force the shaking to stop, force strength back into
himself, force his breathing to slow. Then he shoved the corn
knife into his belt and stepped back into the water and, hold-ing to weeds and branches, began to follow the creek toward
the highway.

The water was thigh deep and ten feet across, moving
slowly. The bottom got a little firmer as he walked, and
soon he did not need the branches any more. He walked
without thinking at all, and when he passed a spot where a
piece of the snake had hung up in the weeds, he avoided look-ing at it and went on. With the tight handkerchief and the
water, his leg stopped bleeding, and the mosquitoes, he noticed,
were not so thick over the moving water and away from the
weeds. The water felt good and soothing and his mind began
to drift.

The woods smelled wet and green, a soft and pleasing good-bad smell like oil of citronella, which was used in old mosquito repellents, and he thought of the Tippecanoe River that winds through northeastern Indiana like a dragon's tongue, and the long, few but seemingly unending nights he had sat in darkness on the bank of that old river with Dad and his uncles and cousins at various times. How they had stepped out of the oil lamp-lighted cabin with cane poles and rods and reels and tackle boxes and cans of worms into the river-wet night, to trace with yellow-white flashlight blobs the trail that had been tramped and hacked downstream through weeds and thickets wet with the night and dew, high over his boy's head that followed a father, trailed by an uncle and a cousin and an uncle, along the jungly bank until the thicket became higher and deeper and suddenly disappeared into a bare bank at the edge of The Hole, where the shallow river ran suddenly deep and catfish lay, and bass and crappies in the black still deep quiet water that smelled green though in the dark he could not see it. The flashlights always were out by then, flickering on only to spot the honored and used sitting places: a log that seated two, a rock for one, an old camp stool and a clump of reasonably dry grassy weeds so that all of them could settle in in the narrow confines of the bank beneath the trees with the narrow-laned weeds behind and the river at their feet. Careful to keep their lights off the water, they pulled wet worms from the cans and baited hooks, each man (himself included) baiting his own, for who could not bait his own hook and take off his own fish had no business here but belonged back with the women who came down to fish from the pier for bluegill, which always came off the hook easily, with the lighted cabin there and the boats and each other for company while their men got down to serious business at The Hole.

It was the best spot on this part of the river, and had been found by young Lloyd, Aaron's cousin, and Uncle Ashley, the youngest uncle and the oldest cousin working as a team to ferret out new and untried places that needed to be tried. It was the same Lloyd who had built a tree house with a hatchet and a hammer, high up in the tree beside the dock; the same uncle who had been the first guest willing to climb up the wood-nailed ladder for a look at the Tippecanoe from height, through leaves. These two were respected by the uncles, admired by the cousins, worried over by the mothers and aunts who yet were proud of them, for they showed a trace of the Indian, many times removed, who had lived in these woods and fished this river.

Night fishing is different from the day, and the two young boys sat together learning of it and its differences, lines baited and out in the darkness, down in the darkness, all lights out save for overhead through the dense trees where the Milky Way spilled light across the sky and something of a moon set off the Northern Cross, though they could not see that, nor would have known it if they had.

And the mosquitoes fell on them in happy droves until Uncle Ash reached a black hand into a black pocket and came out with a black bottle.

"Here . . ." (screwing off the lid). "Oil of citronella. Keep them mosquitoes off." And the pungent faint strong smell of it, the slight oily tingle as they rubbed it on their arms and faces, noticing a definite muffling of the droning round their ears and clawing at the back of a neck when one found its way down to skin level.

The sounds of rubbing in the night.

"God *damn* . . ."

"That's better, though," says Dad.

"Dad?"

"Mmm?"

"How can I tell when I've got a bite? I can't see the line."

Dad sets his own rod down, propping the shaft on a forked-weed branch, and shows him how to pull a little slack in the line and curl his finger around it. "You'll feel it tug. Take it easy then. Let him run with it, then you'll know."

"Okay. Thanks." He sits with his finger curled around the line, his right shoulder against Dad's knee, excited and a little bit chilly and just beginning to have to pee, and sure every few seconds that he feels a slight rhythmic tug on the line that seems much farther out, deeper in the river than it actually is. And it is the river itself tugging on his line, singing it, playing with it, drifting all their lines downstream from where they've thrown them out.

"Boy, I'm going to catch a big one, I bet."

"Shhhh."

The night sounds like a thing alive around them, with voices he soon no longer hears, they are so normal and proper and soothing.

Uncle Ash and Dad light cigarettes, and he smells the invisible smoke and thinks: *I'll smoke someday*, watching the yellow flame go out with the *clink* of the lighter cover, and then the red glows that rise and fall like breathing.

And soon he is sleepy.

And soon he has a bite, and he is no longer sleepy.

He feels the slight soft tug at the tip of the pole, on his curled finger where he has the line, and he pictures in the dark the fish on the other end of that line mouthing the drowned worm and gumming it, sucking the juice from it—

"I got a bite!"

—and then it is gone, the line is still and he thinks: *I've lost him—I shouldn't have waited for him to run with it*, and still feels nothing and waits and waits and finally says aloud, "Think I'll check my bait," and pulls on the cane pole and feels the horrible delightful shocking shudder as he lifts, and says without thinking, "I've got one!" and then again, lifting, in a slightly different tone, "*I've* got one." And it comes out into the air and hits him smack in the mouth so that he spits and grabs, but in the dark he doesn't get it and it swings back out over the water and then back in, and he feels it *whap* against his stomach, and then Dad has the light, saying, "You sure have, buddy, and he's a nice one."

The light is on him and he is a nice big channel cat, long and slender, the most beautiful of catfish, with a dark stripe down his side, and he takes him, gripping in the special way that Dad has shown him, with the horns between the fingers to keep from jabbing himself (for he knows the catfish never "horns" you, cannot if he wants to—you horn yourself). *And he has swallowed the hook as catfish often do, and you open his mouth and follow the line down into the throat until you have the end of the hook, and you push and twist at the same time, finally working it free. Dad has the stringer, and you string him yourself, the sharp point through the gill and out the mouth and through the ring and pull it tight, and Dad lowers it into the water and pushes the sharp end deep into the earth to hold it and you've made the first catch of the night and know that more are coming because they are starting to bite.*

He struggled up out of the creek onto the bank, where the woods were thinner now, and said aloud, "But that is all over," said it again with a kind of grieving elation, said it in his father's voice: "That is all over, Aaron, boy; it's all over now and gone."

And now he was calm in a way he had not been all summer.

He began to shake as he had before, his legs got weak and he had to stop and sit down on a dead log, carefully laying the clipboard and map beside him, jabbing the long black corn knife into the dead earth at his feet. He tasted the green water again and suddenly was sick and vomiting on the floor of the woods, on the carpet of leaves. He retched again and again, unable to get his breath, shaking. Finally he stopped and gasped with a choking sound and began to cough. He stopped that with a single clear sob, wiping his mouth on his hand and the hand on his rough denim pants.

I almost died, he thought.

He put his face into his hands, elbows on knees, and tried to quiet his hard and rapid breathing, his banging heart, and he tried to spit out the sour taste in his mouth. After a few moments, when the air came easier, he thought it again: *I almost died.* His breathing quickened a little and he let it go, taking deep gulps of air and trying to let it out slowly without the rattling that had been in his throat. When he could do that he thought again, testing: *I almost died.*

And again: *I almost died*—still with the calmness that had been with him all along, the cool certainty in his head that everything was over now, something had happened a half hour ago—and he tentatively began to touch around the edges of it, afraid yet to grab the thing itself, but feeling it gingerly, and when he thought he could handle it he leaped upon it and saw that he was right, and he had it.

He sat on the log, moving away from where he had been sick, reviewing the summer yet again, the past three months that he had been on this job and aware of a danger in himself, to himself—and on back to what was hiding in a shadow of his mind, there like sharp smoked crystal when he chose or was forced to throw a light upon it, as he had this summer.

But this time, back there in the woods, in the creek, not only had he been afraid to die, but he had come upon three things new to him, one after the other. The first was that he did not want to die. The second, while climbing out of the creek, was that he was not going to die—unless some part of him had died in Saugatuck, the one who went searching into Marie's arms and came out knowing.

The third was that he did not deserve to die. This had come to him slowly as his mind drifted out through the woods like mosquitoes, to the past. He deserved it no more than Paul deserved tuberculosis, who had gone along with the wild excesses of Steve and Rod while befriending Aaron in a different way, with no criticism for anyone. Paul knew. He had said of Steve: *All he knows is that he's going to die one of these days . . . he isn't betting on the come.*

And Rod had been shot in the war, and was not betting on the come.

And Huston had smoked brown cigarettes for years in his dark apartment, and had failed, thus far, to escape.

And his mother had simply died, as people do. And families break up; their parts go on to become other things, other parts of other, different families.

He deserved it no more than they, the involved and uninvolved; his mistakes had crippled him no more than they were crippled, and death was not selective. It would come for him in its own good time. So he had suffered a vain escapism, martyrdom, guilt—whatever—for two years, had been his own ghost haunting himself, held back from Susan and Steve and Ann, until he gave himself to a stranger whose face he could not now recall.

And here he was, with scratches on his face and a throbbing leg, at the end of summer. It reminded him of one of the poems he had read in his book, one by Cummings about summer and wind and people, something like: "what if a much of a which of a wind/gives the truth to summer's lie;/bloodies with dizzying leaves the sun/and yanks immortal stars awry?/ blow . . . (he forgot this part and filled in: blow something to something and something to something—"king to beggar and queen to seem," or something like that—/blow something to something: blow something to something . . .)" Then the last two lines of that stanza he remembered, because they above all made sense to him:

> —when skies are hanged and oceans drowned,
> the single secret will still be man

He got up with an elated little jump, picked up the corn knife and hurled it into the woods. He took his clipboard and walked out through the woods and down a hill to the highway. He drank two cold beers in a roadside tavern, cleaned himself up in the rest room and called into Greenville for a tow truck to come and pull him out.

By the time he got back to the motel it was almost dark. The Triumph was gone and Steve was not in his room. Aaron walked down to the room shared by Rod and Vanneman, and everyone was there except Steve. Mr. Erikson, the supervisor, was there too.

"Hi," said Aaron, stepping into the room and closing the door behind him. The air-conditioning was on, but everyone looked hot. They were all sitting there and he said, "What's going on? Where's Steve?"

Everyone looked at him then and Rod said, "Steve is dead."

6.   He had gone out to check those six poles: confident as always, a smile on his actor's face, no doubt, or whistling. He had gone out across that farmer's field on the farmer's land without asking permission—the permission he would never have gotten—not even Steve could have done that, gold-tongued that Ozark throwback out of a set, unyielding mind. And the man had seen him and had come up behind him just as Steve was looking up at the pole, shielding his eyes with his

hand and squinting behind the hand and the dark glasses in the white sunlight, and the man had shot Steve in the throat with his shotgun, and Steve had died there, that day, right then and there.

The farmer said that he had only intended to frighten Steve, to warn him, to miss. But he had not missed, and the deputy sheriffs arrested him, and his family stood in the windows of the now truly haunted house and watched them take him away.

On Friday the crew worked at a slow pace and quit early. They had checked out of the motel in the morning and loaded their things into the cars. At three o'clock they met uptown in Greenville to turn all the maps in to Rod, who would drop them off with Erikson on the way home.

They sat in a restaurant on Lafayette Street, eating hamburgers and drinking Cokes, none of them saying much, even Vanneman subdued now with Steve gone and Paul gone. It was the same restaurant where Aaron had eaten breakfast on his first day in Greenville, but he knew the place now and so it seemed completely different.

"We ought to send Paul a card or something," said Rod.

"Yeah," agreed Vanneman, chewing. "We oughta."

Aaron swirled the Coke and ice around in his glass, watching the good-looking waitress behind the counter. "Card, hell. I'm going to go see him."

People moved in and out past them, letting in puffs of warm baked air each time the door swung open. Eighty-six degrees outside; a cool sixty-nine in the restaurant.

"Well," said Dooley. "Royal Oak is a pretty long drive from Saginaw. I'll probably send him a card."

"I'd never find the place," added Vanneman.

Rod sighed and twisted around in his chair, piling folded maps on the empty chair beside him. "It's a hell of a thing," he said. "I should go see him, but I've got it all planned to head for Kentucky tomorrow morning. Maybe I can reroute it and stop off. I don't know, though. . . . I don't know how he's going to find out about Steve. I'd hate to be the one to tell him."

"I'll go," said Aaron. "I'll go see him."

They sat for a while and then went outside and stood in a cluster in the middle of the block, sorry to be leaving each other and slightly embarrassed at their sorrow.

"I enjoyed working with you guys," said Rod at last. "It wasn't all fun, but . . ." He shook hands with Aaron and Dooley and Vanneman. "Seems like the job was just long enough to get to know you guys a little. Except for Phil, baby."

"I'll be seeing you around," said Vanneman.

"Yeah. I know."

Aaron wondered where the summer had gone.

Dooley looked morose. "I feel like we're breaking up a team. Two-thirds of a team, anyway. I don't ever want to see this part of the state again."

"Well, a lot of it was fun," said Vanneman. "You got some state heah. I got lost in most of it. . . ."

They laughed quietly, and then, in a movement Aaron could not quite catch, the group disassembled, everyone gone in different directions and he in his car, pulling out into the traffic.

He drove out Lafayette Street to where it becomes highway 91 and on until he turned east at a gravel road to a lake where there were picnic tables and kids swimming. He had checked all the poles around the lake and knew their installation dates and types and heights. He smiled at the thought that he was the only one for miles—maybe the only one in the world right then—who did.

He sat on a picnic table and watched the swimmers, suddenly waking up and wondering what he was doing, by God, *here*, and how he had got there. He thought with an idle detachment about the summer, feeling vaguely sorry about Steve, thinking that if he did not get down to see Paul he might write to him—already the summer and the job and the people fading into a kind of unreality. He would soon be back with Susan, and wouldn't that be good? Wouldn't that be the best of all?

Yes, he thought. Well—yes.

He wondered if the summer had cured him, or was he perhaps lying to himself yet again, one last time, that Susan was the girl for him and he the man for her. Or would Sam say to him in the fall, as he had said before: "You keep waiting for the world to make a move!" Would Sam say to him, as he had before: "I should have your luck: nice car, new apartment, beautiful girl, money in the bank. . . . Why are you so glum?" and he answer, "I don't know." "You must be betting on the come," Sam might say, and would he be right?

But never mind, he thought, the cure at least had begun. And there were people dying in the cities and there was a war going on that someone needed to think about, take a stand on. And knowing this much, he got back into the car and pulled out to where the road ran on in dust motes too small to see, discoloring as the day turned copper and yellow, with voices rising behind him like shouts of lost children from the lake that lay, a blue blanket, on the green and tree-bristled shoulders of the land. The air smelled suddenly with the scent of night, and mosquitoes rose like smoke from the woods where they had waited all day in darkness, for darkness.